# Parallel

# (Magi

# A Novel

# by

# Robert Cubitt

© 2019

Having purchased this eBook from Amazon, it is for your personal use only. It may not be copied, reproduced, printed or used in any way, other than in its intended Kindle format.

Published by Selfishgenie Publishing of, Northamptonshire, England.

This novel is entirely a work of fiction. All the names characters, incidents, dialogue, events portrayed and opinions expressed in it are either purely the product of the author's imagination or they are used entirely fictitiously and not to be construed as real. Any resemblance to actual persons, living or dead, events or localities is entirely coincidental. Nothing is intended or should be interpreted as representing or expressing the views and policies of any department or agency of any government or other body.

All trademarks used are the property of their respective owners. All trademarks are recognised.

The right of Robert Cubitt to be identified as the author of this work has been asserted in accordance with sections 77 and 78 of the Copyright Designs and Patents Act 1988.

# Other titles by the Same Author

**Fiction**
The Deputy Prime Minister
The Inconvenience Store
The Charity Thieves

**Warriors Series**
The Warriors: The Girl I Left Behind Me
The Warriors: Mirror Man

**The Magi Series**
The Magi
Genghis Kant (The Magi Book 2)
New Earth (The Magi Book 3)
Cloning Around (The Magi Book 4)
Timeslip (The Magi Book 5)
The Return Of Su Mali (The Magi Book 6)

**Non-Fiction**
A Commando's Story
I'm So Glad You Asked Me That
I Want That Job

# Contents

Foreword
1. Sun, Sea And Kidnapping
2. A Trail Of Breadcrumbs
3. Logical Deductions
4. Matter
5. Professor Van Golden
6. Another bank Job
7. Memory Lane
8. Dear Diary
9. Return To Aragan
10. A Visit To Barnard's Star
11. The Death Of An Kohli
12. Unparalleled
13. Jaffa The Hut
14. Do Drop In
15. Jetpacks

Appendix
Author's Note
Preview And Now

# Foreword

In writing this series, The Magi, I have described a galaxy in which many strange things exist and many stranger things happen. Some of these things are real and some of them I made up. If you know which is which then you had a good science teacher and you paid attention in school. For the rest I have provided a short glossary at the end of each chapter to help you.
If, after reading the glossary, you still aren't sure which things are real and which are made up, then please can I come and live in your galaxy?

Some of the more common terms are shown below, just to get your started.

c - A constant, the speed of light in a vacuum which is 299,792,458 m/sec. As used in the expression e=mc². In this book speed is measured in comparison to c, i.e. 0.95 c = 284,802,835.1 m/sec. This produces a standard for the measurement of speed to compensate for the many and varied measurements that are used throughout the galaxy. See also 'time'.

Li - A unit of measurement of distance roughly equivalent to 5 Earth metres.

Met - A unit of measurement of distance. Plural Mett. 5 Mett = 1 li.

Nuk - A unit of currency that is exchangeable throughout the galaxy. One nuk is sufficient to buy two Big Macs on any planet except Earth, where they cost 5 nuks each, but that's Earth for you.

Sim - A unit of measurement of distance. Plural Sims. There are 50 sims to a met.

Tea - A generic term referring to all non-alcoholic beverages consumed by public servants across the galaxy. Although they differ greatly from planet to planet in terms of their ingredients, most of these beverages are brown in colour and taste like they need less sweetening in them than they actually have, even if they have no sweetening in them at all. They are never as good as the beverages that are made at home.

Time - With so many variations in the rate at which planets revolve and the duration of their orbits around their stars there was no standard unit for the measurement of time before the Magi took on the governance of the galaxy. Indeed, one of the many wars that had raged was known as the war of the 23 hour day, which had gone on for two years or 933 days, or 1072.95 days if you had a 20 hour day. One of the first acts of the Magi was to introduce a standard unit of time based on the extremely accurate pulses produced by an atomic clock located on the planet Greenwich. Currently no one in the galaxy is aware of the irony of this.

# 1 - Sun, Sea and Kidnapping

As she walked across the vast lobby of the hotel, An Kohli tried not to think of the bill with which she would be presented. A room for the night here must cost the equivalent of what she used to get in bounty for an arsonist, and Gala and Den had been here for nearly three weeks. She was glad Merkaloy and Laurel had decided to remain on board their ship and just visit the planet as day visitors.

She had instructed Gala and Den to find themselves one of the nicer hotels on the resort planet of Canarias, while they took some well-deserved planet leave, but she hadn't expected them to take her quite so literally.

It seemed to take an age to reach the marble and gold fronted reception desk. The receptionist gave her the sort of snooty look that only receptionists in very up market hotels know how to do. It slipped slightly, her eyes widening, as the being recognised her.

"I'm here to see Gala Sur." An Kohli did her best to match snooty look for snooty look.

"One moment please." The receptionist replied, speaking the name into a computer. "I'll just call her room. Who shall I say is here?"

An Kohli gave her name and the receptionist's snooty look slipped a little more as the computer connected her to the room.

"I'm sorry, there's no reply."

Not to worry, An Kohli thought. She may just be lying on the beach.

"In that case, can you get me Den Gau."

This time the receptionist's look gave up the fight as she struggled to keep her face in any way neutral. She spoke into the computer again and waited to be connected.

"Hello. I have an An Kohli here for you."

Why did she say 'an An Kohli'? An Kohli wondered. It was a habit of receptionists across the galaxy. She was the only An Kohli standing at the desk, so why suggest that there may be more than one by inserting the prefix 'an'. It would forever mystify her.

The receptionist handed over the communicator.

"Why are you calling me in the middle of the night?" Den slurred.

"It isn't the middle of the night, it's the middle of the day. Normal beings are out in the sunshine enjoying the sun, the sea and the sand for which this planet is famed."

"Sun, sea and sand is very overrated as far as I'm concerned. I take it you're back."

"Yup, so it's time for you to get back to work. Meet me in the lobby and I'll pour hot black coffee into you until you feel capable of dealing with reality once again."

"That may be a long time."

"By the way, you don't know where Gala is, do you?"

"Not a clue. The last time I saw her was when we had dinner together last night. I told her I was going out to paint the town red and she said she was going to have an early night."

That made plenty of sense. Whatever debauchery Den had planned was something that Gala wouldn't want to be part of.

"OK, be down here in half an hour." She broke the connection and handed the communicator back to the receptionist.

Walking a few met away from the desk, An Kohli pulled out her own communicator to call Gala's. It went straight to voicemail. That was odd. Gala never switched her communicator off. And the voicemail message said the device was unavailable, not that she was busy on another call.

She returned to the desk. "Is it possible to establish if Gala Sur is in her room?" She asked.

"I think so." The receptionist spoke a few words of command into her computer. "Yes, the security log shows her entering her room last evening. It doesn't show her leaving again."

That put a whole new complexion on things. Gala might put her communicator on silent, so that she wasn't disturbed, but she wouldn't switch it off completely. Besides, that didn't account for why she wasn't responding to the hotel's communication system.

"Can you tell me her room number?"

"I'm sorry, that's against hotel policy. We have to protect the privacy of our guests."

An Kohli knew it would be a waste of time arguing with this being. She was the type who stuck rigidly to the rules.

"Very well. I'd like to speak to the manager, please."

The being gave An Kohli the sort of look that suggested that she wished An Kohli was dead, but spoke a number into her communicator anyway. She muttered a few inaudible words as An Kohli paced up and down in front of the desk.

"The Duty Manager will be with you in a moment." The receptionist told her, then immediately tried to pretend that An Kohli no longer existed.

An Kohli didn't want to speak to the Duty Manager. He or she wouldn't have the authority to do as she wanted, but she knew enough about hotels to know that she had to go through this torture-by-minion if she ever wanted to gain access to Gala's room.

It was several minutes before a walking foetus appeared and crossed the vast floor to greet An Kohli. Well, technically it was an adult, but one who appeared so young that An Kohli could scarcely believe that he could hold a title as grand as Duty Manager.

Quickly An Kohli explained her fears and asked for Gala's room number. As she expected, her request was denied.

"OK, I'd like to speak to your superior." She said in a voice that had icicles hanging off the words.

"I'm afraid she's very busy ..."

"Look, if I don't get to speak to her, I'm going to start opening doors my way." She let her hand fall to the grip of the large pulsar sitting in a hand tooled holster on her hip. The being gulped.

"Perhaps I can make an exception." He crossed to the desk and exchanged some whispered words with the receptionist. Returning to An Kohli he said, "If you would like to follow me."

He strode across the lobby floor like a being who knew what he was doing, but An Kohli's long stride was more than capable of keeping up with him. They took the elevator to the ninety second floor and then stood before the door of room ninety-two zero one.

"One of our penthouse suites." The Duty manager explained.

It was An Kohli's turn to gulp. She bit back a complaint. It wasn't the Duty Manager's fault that Gala had been so extravagant.

"Open the door, please." She managed to say through gritted teeth.

Instead the Duty Manager pressed the bell push that was mounted on the wall next to the door. They waited for what seemed, to An Kohli, to be an eternity. He pressed the bell push again, for longer this time, then they waited some more. With a deep sigh of resignation
the Duty Manager pressed his palm against the door's reader and the door swished open.

"Hello? Is there anyone here?" he asked. There was no reply.

Impatiently, An Kohli pushed past him into the suite, ignoring his protests. She was greeted by a scene of devastation. Furniture was overturned, the entertainment centre smashed. An Kohli hurried through the large, well-appointed room, heading towards another door. It led to the bedroom, where there were more signs of some sort of disturbance. The air-mattress lay half off the bed, jetting its streams of air diagonally and fluttering the flowers arranged in a vase. The bedclothes were scattered around as though thrown by a toddler having a tantrum.

The Duty Manager held his hand to his mouth in dismay. "Who's going to pay for this damage?" he blurted.

"Idiot." An Kohli snapped. "Don't you recognise a crime scene when you see one?"

"Crime? I don't understand …"

"There has been some sort of fight in this room, that's why everything is smashed up. You don't think one female is capable of doing all this damage?"

"Well, we have seen damage like this before, but …"

"But it involved a rock and roll band, several bottles of hard liquor and large quantities of drugs."

She spotted something lying on the bedroom floor. She bent down to pick it up, several bits becoming detached in the process. She showed it to the Duty Manager.

"My friend's communicator. Looks like it's been deliberately smashed."

"Who would have done such a thing?"

"I don't know. But I aim to find out. More to the point, where is Gala?"

"I'll call the police."

"You do that. Then I want to see your security camera footage."

"I'm not sure …"

"Don't mess with me, sonny. I think it's time you spoke to your Manager, don't you?"

The Duty Manager did another of his audible gulps. "Perhaps you're right."

As they returned to the corridor they bumped into Den Gau, emerging from his own suite, looking very much the worse for wear.

"Who told you, you could book a penthouse?" An Kohli snarled, making Den recoil with fright.

"We didn't. When we checked in we asked for budget rooms. We were just on our way to the elevators when the Duty Manager spotted us and recognised us. We have been in the media quite a lot recently, so he must have seen us. Anyway, he offered us a free upgrade. Why would we refuse?"

"This Duty Manager?" An Kohli pointed at the quivering wreck standing next to her.

"No, a different one."

An Kohli's antenna twitched. An upgrade wasn't unusual; she had been upgraded herself in hotels on more than one occasion, but an upgrade to a penthouse was a bit over the top.

"Is this usual?" She snapped at the Duty Manager.

"Not unheard of, but if it had been me and I had recognised them, I would have upgraded them to a Premier room. Bigger and better appointed than a standard room, but not so expensive. You'd have to be a rock star or a President to get an upgrade to a penthouse suite."

"That's what I thought. Den, you're going to have to talk to the police."

Den went visibly pale. "Why? I haven't …"

"Gala seems to have been kidnapped. Did you hear anything last night?"

If it was possible, Den went even paler. "No. I didn't get in until about … oh, I don't know, but it was very late, or maybe very early. Then I pretty much lost consciousness. I'd had a bit to drink, and then there was the …."

"I'd rather not know. Go and get yourself some coffee and something to eat. I'll find you later." She turned her attention to the Duty Manager. "Come on you. I want to meet your boss."

\* \* \*

An Kohli warmed to the hotel manager as soon as they met. She was the no-nonsense type of being that didn't ask stupid questions and knew instinctively the right thing to do.

As the Duty Manager stuttered through his explanation of what seemed to have happened, An Kohli cut across him to explain the situation in fewer words. The manager at once dispatched the Duty Manager to contact the police and await their arrival, while she escorted An Kohli along a short corridor to the security suite, where they could trawl through the security camera images.

"We'll start with the cameras on the ninety second floor." She announced, passing her hands across controls and bringing images up on multiple screens.

She fast forwarded through the earlier part of the evening, though with the corridors empty it wasn't possible to gauge the speed of playback, other than with the rapidly advancing time code at the bottom of each screen. A uniformed figure appeared in the corridor and the manager froze the images.

"That's our night security patrol. He sweeps through the whole building every hour, starting on the roof terrace and working his way down to the basement, then he takes a turn around the pool area and gardens. Once we've checked all the security coverage I'll contact him and ask him to come in, in case he saw something that the cameras didn't pick up."

An Kohli nodded her approval and the manager unfroze the images again. The timecodes continued to advance at speed, confirming the hourly frequency of the security patrol, until the images went blank.

"Odd." The manager declared, checking all three feeds to make sure nothing had become disconnected. "Nope, they've managed to block the signals in some way. They're wireless, so if they blocked the radio feeds, the system wouldn't be able to record anything." She frowned. "That's a weakness we hadn't considered before. Still, that's my problem, not yours."

Her hands began to fly over the controls again. "All is not lost. If they managed to get to the ninety second floor, it must mean that they got in and out of the building somehow and they won't have spotted all of the cameras."

The elevator cameras had also been blocked for the same, crucial period, as had those in the basement and the delivery dock.

"They seem to know what they're doing." The manager commented, as she called up a plan of the outside of the building to check which cameras might have captured something without the intruders seeing them.

"Could they have blocked the WiFi for the whole system?" An Kohli asked.

"In theory, no. Each camera works independently and has its own frequency. They'd have to use such a broad-spectrum jammer that they'd interfere with other parts of the WiFi system, such as the computers and the customer service terminals. You know, the ones that customers use to order drinks without leaving their sun loungers."

She selected a camera that had an exterior view and fast forwarded to the time when the other cameras had ceased to send their messages for recording.

"There we are. That's them." She announced, freezing the image

A plain coloured hover van was driving past the camera, on its side the words "Boulder & Boulder, Suppliers of Synthmeat to The Hotel Industry."

"Where's that camera?"

"It's concealed in one of the gate posts. We don't want guests to see it as they arrive. It sends out the wrong message."

"It isn't just a routine synthmeat delivery?"

"It could be, but we only use that company in an emergency. Besides, the chef doesn't work that late and he's very conscientious. He likes to check all food deliveries himself. I'll check with Chef, but I'd stake my reputation on it being the intruders. Anyway, the time matches exactly." She moved the images forward a few minutes and they watched the van depart again.

"See, almost exactly when the other cameras came back on line once again."

"Well, it isn't much, but it gives us a starting point. I'm guessing the van was stolen."

"That's for the police to establish." The manager leant back in her chair and offered up a small smile. "Or you, of course."

"Can we check the ninety second floor again. I didn't see the occupant of the neighbouring room arrive back. He is one of my associates as well and he was out for most of the evening. He didn't appear back before the cameras went blank."

The Manager was happy to oblige and they fast forwarded the footage until they saw Den returning, about an hour after the cameras stopped working. They watched as he bounced off the wall, slumped against the door and managed, eventually, to enter his room. An Kohli chewed on the inside of her cheek, wondering if Den had been under observation.

* * *

When An Kohli tracked down Den he was in the dining room working his way through a giant breakfast. It was worth asking him a few questions before she let the police do the same. He had a keen nose for danger and if he had spotted anything it would be lodged somewhere in his brain.

"What have you been doing since you arrived here, apart from spending my money?"

Den had the decency to look a little abashed by the question. "Well, just the usual holiday stuff, really. Lounging around by the pool or on the beach, a bit of sightseeing. Gala did some shopping and I went along to carry the bags, that sort of thing. In the evening, we ate in the hotel and then went out clubbing or to see a show. They have some really good shows here."

"I'm sure they do. Why didn't Gala go with you last night?"

"Well, we had stopped going out together at night a few days back. Beings would see us together and they'd think she and I were an item. It cramped my style a bit."

More like it cramped Gala's style, An Kohli thought, but she let it slide.

"She did go out by herself a couple of times, but she said she wasn't going to do that anymore."

An Kohli's antenna twitched again. "Oh? Why?"

"She was in this nightclub and some guy started coming on a bit strong, you know, getting really persistent. Anyway, she said she was going to the bathroom, then snuck out and grabbed a cab back to the hotel."

That was interesting. Was there going to be an attempt to grab her that night? Or was it just a guy who couldn't take 'no' for an answer? A grab in the street would have been far easier than getting in and out of the hotel unseen. Or maybe drug Gala's drink and get her that way. An Kohli knew all about the ease with which that could be done, after her own recent experiences *(see Robinson Kohli)*.

"Did you ever get the feeling you were being watched?"

"Actually, I did get a bit of a tingling in the back of my neck from time to time. Then there was the afternoon we went up the mountain."

"What happened then?"

"Well, we booked onto a bus tour up that big mountain in the middle of the island. It wasn't really my thing but we were getting a bit bored of lounging around by then. Anyway, I kept seeing the same being every time the bus stopped anywhere. He wasn't on our tour, but you know how it is, all the tour buses follow each other around, stopping at the same places, but he didn't seem to fit."

"Why not?"

"For a start, he was on his own. Most people were in either in couples or groups of friends. The other thing was, that he always seemed to be trying to stay out of sight. I'd spot him behind a rack of sun hats, or maybe a souvenir stand. It wasn't obvious he was watching us, I never caught him actually looking at us, but he always seemed to be where Gala and I were."

"OK, could just be coincidence, but you don't think so, right?"

"No, I don't. I saw him near the pool in this hotel as well, but I'm pretty sure he isn't staying here."

"OK, maybe the security cameras caught him. If you can remember the day and time it would help." An Kohli spotted the Duty Manager, standing by the door still waiting for the police.

"I'll be back later." She said, getting up from the table and leaving Den to finish his gargantuan meal.

She approached the Duty Manager, who seemed to shrink in size when he spotted her.

"I need you to show me the route that the kidnappers would have taken to get from the ninety second floor to the loading dock."

"I have to wait here to wait for the police."

"Get the concierge to do it. I need you now."

The Duty Manager was sufficiently cowed to comply. They rode the elevator up to the ninety second floor and then got out. They knew which elevator to use, because the security cameras in the rest of the twelve elevator bank hadn't been disabled. The Duty Manager used his pass key to override the controls and reserve it for themselves.

An Kohli studied the penthouse suite again, then the corridor. There was nothing out of place between the door of the suite and the elevator. They got back in and rode it down to the basement. Here they found a rabbit warren of passages flanked by storerooms, the laundry, plant rooms and the other places that visitors to hotels never get to see.

The Duty Manager led her through the maze to the loading docks.

They must have been able to access the floor plans, An Kohli surmised. They couldn't have found their way to the elevators just by chance. She remembered the other Duty Manager, the one who had upgraded Den and Gala. Maybe they'd had a guide, she thought. As they walked, An Kohli scanned the walls and floors for any sign that anyone had passed that way the previous night.

"Are there many people down here at night?"

"None. Well sometimes there are some, but there are no staff working down here permanently. Some of the kitchen staff may come down to get stuff from the storerooms, but the laundry is fully automated. If there's a problem with any of the equipment the duty maintenance operative might be down here. And of course, the security patrol comes through once an hour."

So, not much chance of bumping into anyone, and the presence of a member of staff, such as the Duty Manager, would be enough to provide bona fides for the intruders.

Automatic doors slid open to reveal a loading dock set underneath the overhang of the hotel. Stacks of containers stood there, that day's deliveries waiting to be moved into the storerooms. An Kohli walked out into the sunshine and looked along the service road. Nothing but grey concrete walls could be seen as far as the rising curve that would join it to the hotel entrance road.

She turned and went to go back inside the basement. Something small and brightly coloured caught her eye, half hidden beneath a stack of boxes containing guest soaps. She bent down and picked it up, examining it closely. A smile crossed her lips. This answered a lot of questions. Making sure that the Duty Manager hadn't seen her, she slipped the object into a pouch on her belt.

"Thanks." She said to the Duty Manager. "I've seen enough. I'll go and talk to the police now."

*  *  *

The absence of Gala was only accentuated by the presence of the others in the Sunray's large lounge. Merkaloy and Laurel had come across from their ship and Den had checked out of the hotel to come back on board.

The Sunray was a fine ship, despite its age, and An Kohli was grateful to the Grand Master of the Guild for its loan while her own ship was being rid of its infestation of vikes *(see Robinson Kohli)*. But fine as it was, the four of them being crammed into the small lounge on the Adastra would have helped disguise Gala's absence.

An Kohli briefed Merkaloy and Laurel in as few words as possible. When she had finished recounting the apparent events of the previous night, she summarised her views on Gala's disappearance.

"The way I see it, there are three possible reasons why Gala has been snatched. One is a straightforward kidnap for ransom. But I don't think that applies. There are far richer targets on Canarias. But it's still possible that we'll get a ransom demand, just because it provides a smoke screen for the real reason.

Reason two is that Gala is being held to intimidate me into ending my search for the last Magus egg. If I don't, Gala gets killed, probably slowly and painfully." She paused, not wishing to contemplate what Gala's death might entail.

"And the third reason is that it's a trap set for you." Merkaloy provided.

"Yes. I'm supposed to go running to Gala's aid and in doing so I spring the trap."

"They've tried that before and it didn't work." Den commented.

"Yes, but that was because they were using Jackon or pirates to do the dirty work. All the signs I saw from last night are that these kidnappers were highly professional. They got in and out of the hotel almost unseen. They got into Gala's room without battering down the door and they did it at a time they knew you wouldn't be in the suite next door, which suggests they were watching you at the time, just to make sure."

"That still doesn't make it a trap." Den continued. "It could still be ransom or intimidation."

"This makes it a trap." An Kohli reached into the pouch on her belt and removed the object she had found on the floor of the loading dock. She placed it on the coffee table where it could be seen for what it was.

"It was hidden just enough for it to avoid casual observation, but was just visible enough to be seen by someone looking for clues. Someone like the police, or me."

"I still don't see why it means that they've set a trap." Den said, picking up the brightly coloured poker chip from the coffee table and turning it over in his fingers.

"If it had been in Gala's room I might agree with you. It was clear that Gala put up a fight and in the struggle it might just have fallen out of a pocket. But once they had subdued Gala, no way. There's no reason for it to fall, so it must have been placed. It's the first crumb in a trail of breadcrumbs that I'm supposed to follow. It was supposed to be found and it was supposed to be understood. Call it a message, if you like. I'm guessing that if we go to Towie and start asking questions we'll find someone who 'remembers' seeing something or 'overheard' a conversation that will take us further along the trail until we find ourselves in a place with no witnesses and a whole lot of firepower. Then it's goodbye An Kohli and whoever is with me at the time."

Den read the inscription "Gladstone's Casino, Towie. Fifty Nuks." He replaced the chip on the table. "I've been there, I think. Whoever dropped it isn't exactly a high roller."

"No, just a large enough denomination to suggest that the kidnapper knows their way around a casino. We're now supposed to rush off to Towie and start asking questions."

"You've escaped from those sorts of traps before." Merkaloy seemed to be taking the same blasé sort of view as Den.

"Which is why, this time, I won't be allowed to escape. I'll be dead before I even know it and so will anyone with me. I'm guessing Gala will join us."

"So, what are we going to do?" Merkaloy asked.

"We're going to do what they want us to do. We're going to rush off to Towie to follow the trail of breadcrumbs to Gala. What else would I do?" A broad grin settled on An Kohli's face.

## Glossary

Gau - A shape shifting species from the Flage star system. They have a telepathic bond with each other which means they can sense the presence of another Gau in the vicinity and they can identify each other by sight.

Pulsar - A weapon that uses high energy pulses to destroy its target. Smaller versions are hand held and larger versions can be fitted to mounts for use on vehicles and space craft. Has an advantage over projectile weapons because it can be used under water with only minor loss of efficiency.

Synthmeat - Synthesised meat products. Many star systems, such as Vega, have prohibited the rearing of animals for food, resulting in a new industry dedicated to synthesising meat products to cater for those who enjoy the taste of dead animal flesh, which is most people. Most synthmeat products taste like cardboard and have a similar consistency, but the top-quality products can recreate a passable shepherd's pie. Unfortunately, Canarias, one of the most popular resort planets, happens to be in the Vega system. Stick to the fish.

# 2 - A Trail Of Breadcrumbs

The basement was dark and smelt of damp. Just audible was the steady drip, drip of water. There was no reason for any of it. There was adequate lighting available at the flick of a switch and the smell of damp was being synthesised and pumped into the room. The drip of water was a recording being played through hidden speakers. It all added atmosphere, Tiny Blur thought, and set a tone that he hoped would intimidate visitors.

The basement was where he met people he would rather the rest of the galaxy didn't know he was meeting. The entrance was some distance away and access was gained through a building protected by a trusted aid. If you weren't expected, you didn't get in.

Tiny Blur's unwilling guest on this occasion was a Prathian by the name of Professor Horst Van Golden.

"But are you sure it will work?" Tiny Blur asked for the fifth time.

Van Golden stifled the impatient sigh he had been about to expel. This human was trying his patience more than any of his first-year students ever could. However, it would be a bad thing for him to upset the President of the Galaxy. Not simply because he was the President, but also because his family were currently enjoying the President's 'hospitality' in an unknown location, in exchange for his, Van Golden's, co-operation.

"As I have tried to explain, Mr President, it is a prototype. It is untested, so I can't guarantee anything. The maths is sound, as is the science. The engineering, however, is untried. Each component has been tested and they work. However, the system as a whole is untested and it isn't possible to state with any certainty how the functioning of one component, or combination of components, will affect the workings of another component or combination. The computer simulations show that it should work, but simulations have been wrong in the past."

Tiny Blur started pacing up and down the room, just outside the pool of dim light that illuminated the Professor. Hidden microphones picked up the sound of his footsteps and relayed them back with added echo.

"You wouldn't be trying to cheat me, would you?" he asked at last, his growing paranoia making him see enemies everywhere, even in the inoffensive scientist sitting in front of him.

"There is no reason for me to try to cheat you, Mr President, and plenty of reasons for me not to do so. I love my family and all I want is to be able to return to them."

"Could we carry out a test?"

"Of course, but a test by itself will not prove very much. If it works the target will no longer be visible. On the other hand, the same result may be achieved if the equipment doesn't work. In fact, I would go so far as to say that we will never know if the equipment works unless we experience it for ourselves."

A thought crawled across Tiny Blur's mind. Perhaps he should make the Professor test the equipment on himself. But he dismissed the idea. If, as he said, success and failure could result in the same visible effects, then he would still be none the wiser. And he needed the professor for the first real use of the equipment.

"If it fails, but the target is no longer visible, what will happen to the target? Will it no longer exist at all? If so then that is an acceptable outcome."

"No. While I can't say for certain, it may be that the target has been transported to another set of co-ordinates within the universe. They could be just a few thousand li away, a few light years away or perhaps a million light years away. But if they exist in this universe they can return to their start point."

That was a chance that Tiny Blur did not wish to take. To meet his aims the target had to disappear permanently.

"You haven't told me what the target is to be, Mr President. As I explained when we first met, we have the little matter of conservation of matter to consider." Van Golden allowed himself a small smile at his own pun.

"We'll cross that bridge when we come to it." Tiny Blur snapped. He had no interest in the conservation of matter, or conversation for that matter. He only had an interest in the removal of An Kohli from interference in his affairs.

"Very well. Prepare your equipment. I will have you and it transported to the chosen location."

"And my family" Van Golden asked hopefully.

"Will remain where they are until you have reported the success of the experiment."

* * *

The planet of Towie, is the sort of planet that every galaxy needs. It is somewhere for the sort of people you really don't want to be in your own neighbourhood to go and annoy some other neighbourhood. Towie is the starting point for many lucrative businesses, the owners of which move to other planets as soon as they can afford it. Den loved Towie.

Right at that moment he was in Gladstone's Casino, disguised as a Durantine and playing some small stakes blackjack. An Kohli had been very strict on that subject and any attempt to play for higher stakes on her credit card would probably result in the card bursting into flames. Or at least, that was what she had implied.

The croupier was a typical Towian female, orange skinned, impossibly white teeth and making no effort to conceal the fact that she'd rather be somewhere else, having people admiring her good looks and discussing shoes or sex.

"Player has twenty." She intoned, disinterest dripping from very word.

"Actually, it's nineteen." Den corrected her. Education wasn't highly valued on Towie and it wasn't the first time that night he'd had to correct her arithmetic. It wouldn't be his fault if his hand was declared the winner on the basis of her mistake, but the casino security staff might not see it that way and they had a very direct approach when it came to dealing with people they considered to be cheats.

"Oh yeah. Silly me." The female giggled. She dealt herself two cards. "House has ten." She announced, displaying a four and a five.

"The house has nine." Den said through gritted teeth.

She giggled again. "What am I like?"

Den declined to answer, as the casino also had very strict rules about verbally abusing their staff.

"House takes a card." The croupier announced, turning over a seven. Den could almost hear the cogs grinding as she frowned over the difficult sum. Well, Den assumed that she was frowning, even though not a wrinkle could form on her chemically treated brow.

"House has sixteen." She finally declared in a loud voice, even though Den was the only player at her table. "Pay out on seventeen and over."

Den pushed his cards forward and the croupier went through the painfully slow process of counting once again. Satisfied that Den had the required total, she slid a small pile of chips across the table to him.

Den decided to give up on blackjack. There was no fun to be had in teaching croupiers simple arithmetic. He had a job to get on with and having played enough to justify his presence in the casino, he decided he had a little bit of leeway to get on with what he was supposed to be doing, which was trying to find the next breadcrumb in the trail.

An attractive Sutran sidled over to him, in the guise of a Sabik. "Need a lucky charm?" she cooed at him. As a Sutran, a sub species of the Gau, Den was able to sense her thoughts, if not to actually read them and she had the same ability to detect him, so their disguises weren't fooling each other.

"Don't mind if I do." He said.

"Would you like me to change into a Durantine, so we're a matched pair." She offered.

"No need. We won't be doing any of that tonight."

The female pouted. "Why, what's wrong with me?"

"Nothing, but I'm here on business and it isn't your sort of business."

Female Sutrans had a very high sex drive, which was a great pity for them as male Sutrans were more interested in beer and football. This left a lot of frustrated female Sutrans to find an outlet for their energies. In doing so they found that there was a ready market for their shape shifting talents, so they saw nothing wrong with charging clients for a service that they would have been just as happy to perform for free. A female has to eat, after all.

"My name is Alia." She offered her hand and Den solemnly shook it. "What sort of business are you in?"

"Bounty hunting." Den replied. "I'm looking for someone."

"A criminal? Well, there will be no shortage of them in here." She chuckled.

"Actually, the person I'm looking for isn't a criminal. She's a very close friend and she's gone missing. My colleagues and I are trying to find her."

"When you say 'gone missing', do you mean kidnapped?"

The unsubtlety of the question made Den want to laugh, but he had to play along. If he was right, the next breadcrumb was just about to be dropped in his path.

"Yes. She was taken from Canarias. We were on holiday there."

"Are you and she …"

"No, nothing like that. We're just friends."

"Look, I have a room here." Alia informed him. "Why don't we get a bottle of something fizzy from the bar and go there and you can tell me all about it."

Den was tempted. Sutrans were good at what they did. But An Kohli would not to be too happy for him to pay on her credit card. On the other hand, he did have a pocket full of poker chips that, while technically An Kohli's property, she had no idea existed. They were a negotiable currency in a place like this.

But he had no idea what was waiting for him on the other side of the door. Maybe she wasn't here to lay another breadcrumb. Maybe she was here to entice him into a place where he could be taken and used in the same way as Gala was already being used. Two hostages must be better than one, right?

But if Alia was there to give him the next breadcrumb, she didn't seem to want to do it in public. Perhaps it wasn't something she would tell him. Perhaps it would come in some other form, something that was in her room and which he was supposed to see by accident.

It suggested pre-planning, however. Could they guess that he would be the one sent to the casino? Well, it made sense. If An Kohli was the target for the trap, it would be stupid for her to risk herself by doing the investigating. That left him, Merkaloy and Laurel. Laurel didn't have the experience necessary for the job and Merkaloy stood out in a crowd. Most Arthurids stood out in a crowd, of course, but Merkaloy had become well known over recent weeks, thanks to media coverage of the Battle of Osiris (*see Robinson Kohli*).

So, yes, they might have been able to anticipate him being given the mission, which would allow them to pre-plan it in a way that was most attractive to him. They might even have several plans prepared, of which this was just the one that was aimed at him. As he thought the options through, his brain began to hurt, so he gave up.

"OK, why not?"

Alia made a hand gesture to the barman and as they crossed to a doorway at the back of the room, a waiter droid followed them, bearing two glasses and an ice bucket, in which sat a bottle of overpriced fizzy wine. The bottle, Den knew, would be automatically charged to the credit card that had been provided when he bought his gambling chips.

The door opened without them having to touch it and they made their way along a corridor. It was smartly decorated, in keeping with the overall ambience of the casino. Customers were supposed to venture down this way, which eased Den's fears a little. They reached an elevator and it took them up two stories. The corridor into which they emerged was similar to that in any hotel, flanked along both sides by plain doors with numbers on.

They passed one door and a high-pitched moaning crept out. Den refrained from commenting, but was comforted by the fact that there were other beings close by. Would they come to his rescue if needed? No, that was unlikely. They'd be more likely to grab their trousers and run for the fire escape.

Alia pressed her hand against a keypad and the adjacent door slid open. She stood back to let Den enter first. He braced himself for the bang on the head from a concealed thug, but all that happened was that some subdued lighting came on and mood music started to ooze from hidden speakers.

The room was unremarkable for its purpose. It had the obligatory 'art work' displaying semi-clad males and females of various species and a few who were a bit more androgynous. There was an expensive looking entertainment system, which Den assumed would provide a wide range of erotica. A large four poster bed stood to one side. Den couldn't see from where he stood, but he guessed that the canopy housed a mirror. To one side stood another door, almost certainly giving access to a bathroom adapted to cater for the needs of a wide range of species.

Against another wall, positioned for a good view of the entertainment system, was a long, well padded couch.

Alia lifted the ice bucket and the glasses from the droid and it hummed out of the room, the door swishing closed behind it.

"Would you do the honours?" Alia passed Den the dripping bottle, before taking a glass in each hand, ready for him to pour the wine.

He struggled with the stopper before it came free. There was a fraction of a second's delay as the built-in sound system simulated a popping noise. Den poured some wine into each glass then replaced the bottle in the ice bucket.

"Nice place you have here." Den said, more for something to say than for any other reason.

"I don't live here. I just rent it each evening. It pays for itself, though."

"Ah, yes. Erm how…"

"Let's leave that for the moment, shall we." She lowered herself onto the couch and patted the place next to her meaningfully.

Den wasn't taken in. Sutrans never deferred payment until afterwards. It was a strict rule throughout the galaxy and Den had never heard of it being broken. On the other hand, a Sutran would never cheat a client by taking the money and not giving up the goods. Which meant that he wasn't here for the traditional reasons.

The entertainment system sprung into life as Alia operated a hidden control. A menu appeared on screen.

"What would you like? We have old school, we have gay and lesbian, we have orgies and we have the more exotic, such as S&M and bondage."

"Tell you what, why don't you choose."

This was it, Den felt sure. The entertainment system would be the way the next breadcrumb would be delivered. There was no other way.

"Oh, well, I like the live feeds. You know, beings at home streaming what they're doing for our entertainment."

"If you say so."

She used the hidden controls again and a series of thumbnail images appeared on the screen. She scrolled through them until she appeared to pick one at random. Den's Gau senses could feel that Alia was tense. She was doing something she didn't really want to. Given the function of the room it had to be pretty bad for her not to want to do it.

The thumbnail expanded to a full sized picture. Den stifled a shocked gasp. Alia put her hand up to her mouth. Like him, she hadn't been expecting the image that they were now seeing.

Sitting in the centre of the image was Gala, dressed in a bath robe. Across her eyes was a sleep mask of the sort that come free in some hotels. The logo of the hotel from which Gala had been snatched was visible on both items. Gala's arms were stretched behind her, evidence that she was being restrained.

The room could have been anywhere in the galaxy. It was an empty cube; its sole furnishing was the chair on which Gala was seated and its sole occupant was Gala herself. In the background there was music playing. The sound was at once intrusive and familiar to Den, though he couldn't quite place it.

He pulled his communicator from his pocket and started filming the image on the screen of the entertainment system.

"I'm sorry, I didn't expect this." Alia tried to explain. "You know her, don't you?"

"I do, but I was half expecting to see something. I just didn't know what. What instructions were you given?

"Just to find you and tempt you to come along with me, then to make sure that thumbnail was activated. They said you wouldn't be difficult to convince, but I thought that meant …"

"I know what you were supposed to think, but they knew that I'd guess you'd been sent to find me. I'm guessing that if a different member of my team had been in the casino, they had a plan to get them in front of an entertainment system as well."

"Den, is that you?" Gala's voice sounded across the ether to them. The feed was two way, but that didn't surprise Den. That sort of entertainment had to be interactive for the punter to be kept paying for the maximum amount of time.

"Yes, it's me Gala. You hang in there. We're coming to get you."

Den wished he had as much confidence as he made it sound.

The question Den couldn't yet answer, was whether or not the kidnappers were still working on the basis that An Kohli hadn't worked out that Gala was the bait in a trap, or whether this was a double bluff, a sort of 'We know that you know' situation.

A figure appeared on the screen to stand next to Gala, probably summoned from another room when Alia selected the thumbnail.

"Who am I addressing?" The figure asked. It was a tall male, but a hooded suit and a face mask concealed all but the being's general outline.

"I am Den Gau, a colleague of An Kohli."

"Very well, Den Gau. You recognise this female."

"I do. It's Gala Sur."

"Very good. I have a very simple message for your boss. She is to cease and desist all efforts to recover the final two Magi eggs. Do I make myself clear?"

Two eggs? They couldn't have received news that the eighth egg had been found. Which meant that they were operating at arm's length from whoever had commissioned this. It didn't matter. Without the ninth egg the Magi couldn't be brought back to life. It could cause war, driving star systems into the arms of the phoney galactic government. Already there were star systems wavering, thinking of stating their allegiance to the government, believing that it was better to be inside the tent pissing out.

"Tell An Kohli not to stop, Den. She must carry on." Gala shouted.

"Silence!" The masked figure shouted, delivering a stinging back hand slap across Gala's face. She let out a cry of pain.

Someone would pay for that slap, Den swore. He gritted his teeth. "I will convey that message." Den replied. At once the screen went blank.

Den stood to go, but Alia placed a hand on his.

"I'm sorry about this. I didn't know anything about that. I was just doing what I was paid for." She let the thin strap of her figure hugging dress slip off of her shoulder and ran her tongue across her lips, making them shine. "Perhaps I can make it up to you."

Den was torn between his duty and his lust. Duty won. Damn An Kohli, damn the Guild and damn the Guild's code of ethics. Just a few months ago he would have had no qualms about hooking up with this very attractive and willing female, but now he couldn't. It would be wrong. He wasn't quite sure why it would be wrong, but he was sure that An Kohli, Gala and Laurel would be happy to tell him why it was wrong.

"I'm sorry. Tempting as your offer is, I have to get back to my ship. My friend is in danger and my other friends have to hear that message."

Den left the room before his lust could get the better of him. As he headed back towards elevators he hummed the tune he had heard on the entertainments system. Why did it sound so familiar? And why had it been playing in the background?

As a bell dinged to announce the arrival of the elevator, he pushed it from his mind.

* * *

The atmosphere in the lounge of the Sunray was subdued. The image of Gala being ill-treated was one that had had made them all feel helpless. An Kohli clenched and unclenched her fists in mute frustration.

"Where's that music coming from?" Laurel asked.

"There must be an entertainment system in the room, or maybe in the room next door." Merkaloy suggested

"I was wondering about that. It didn't seem to fit." Den replied. "Also it seemed very familiar. I've heard it before, but I can't quite remember where or why."

"Do you think it's significant?"

An Kohli leaned forward. "We were expecting another breadcrumb. Maybe that's it."

"Music. A bit odd for a breadcrumb." Merkaloy observed.

"Think about it. There's absolutely no other clue in that recording as to where Gala might be. A bare, empty room and a male figure in an outfit that you can buy from any workwear outlet in the galaxy. So, if they were delivering another breadcrumb, it has to be the music. It appears to be accidental, that they were trying to deprive us of clues and made a mistake by leaving a door open, but I think you could bet your last victel on it being deliberate, just like the poker chip."

"Why not run it through the computer and see if it can identify it for us." Laurel suggested.

A few minutes later they were looking at the results.

"That's an Earth TV station." Den said.

"Are you sure? Remember, TV stations swap content with each other." Merkaloy wasn't so sure.

"I knew I recognised. It's played at the beginning and end of all Earth TV news broadcasts, at least the ones on that specific channel. Another TV channel might share the content, but they wouldn't use the same music ident." Den declared.

"I remember it now." An Kohli agreed. "We heard it a lot when we were on New Earth."

"Which means …" Merkaloy continued.

"That they want us to go to Earth next." An Kohli finished.

"That's Tiny Blur's old stomping ground." Den reminded them.

"Yes, more than just coincidence, I think. He had a lot of clout there before he became President of the Galaxy. He'll have even more now."

"But it's a heavily populated star system. Surely, he wouldn't risk trying anything there. There would be far too many witnesses."

"But that wouldn't be an issue if he only wants to drop another breadcrumb."

"We're assuming that Blur is involved." Laurel tried to give them a reality check.

"Oh, he's involved alright. He won't get his hands dirty, but I'll take any odds that he was the one that gave the orders." An Kohli stood up. "Well, we may as well get going then. I'm on watch. Merkaloy, do you want to come with us or will you take your own ship?"

"There's no way I'm leaving my ship in orbit around Towie. It would be up on bricks by the time we got back. No, I'll follow along behind if you don't mind."

"As you wish. Let's go then."

* * *

As required by galactic space traffic control law, the Sunray dropped out of its artificially created wormhole at the outer edge of the star system, just beyond the orbit of the planetoid the humans called Pluto. Even at their sub-hyper speed rate, it would take them several more hours before they would approach Earth orbit.

"Why do they need so many damn planets?" An Kohli muttered. Den did his best to suppress a smile at her impatience.

"Are you with us, Merkaloy?" She called into the communications system.

"Right on your tail." Came the reply, his face appearing on the communications screen at the same time. "What's the plan?"

"We go to New Earth and try to get permits to descend to the planet."

"They won't let us anywhere near." Den commented. "At least they won't let you anywhere near. I can adopt a different form and use a fake ID. Merkaloy and Laurel won't have any bother. They're not wanted for questioning in relation to blowing up a bank." *(see New Earth)*

"I didn't blow up a bank." An Kohli said, sniffing huffily.

"No, but you did rob one and even the dimmest police officer on Earth must have worked out how you did it by now. I'm telling you, if you go down there, the Fell won't need to lure you into a trap because you'll be banged up in one of those hell holes they call prisons. The way they treat prisoners they don't deserve to have any.* They give prison a bad name, if you ask me."

"Well, I wasn't asking you."

"Children, children." Chided Merkaloy from the safety of his own ship. "I think we can assume that An Kohli can't descend to the planet and she can't even set foot on New Earth. That leaves it down to me and Laurel to try to find the next breadcrumb. In the meantime, An Kohli, I suggest you stay well out of sight, somewhere in amongst the rings of the epsilon planet will probably be best, the one they call Saturn. It will be hard to pick you out amongst all that space dust."

"OK, we'll head there first, then you can come aboard and we'll have a chat about how you proceed. Earth is a very crowded planet. I'm not sure where we even start looking."

"I think that they'll probably do what they did on Towie and come looking …."

Den was cut off by a violent shaking, as though the ship had just run over a cattle grid in space.

"What the... Did you feel that Merkaloy? ... Merkaloy, can you hear me? ... Merkaloy?" But as often as An Kohli might say the name, there was no reply and the communications screen was blank.

"Computer, check the location of the ship Laurel."

"No ship of that name in this star system." The computer replied.

"That doesn't make any sense. We were talking to the captain just seconds ago. Check again."

"You were communicating with the ship Laurel up until one minute and fourteen seconds ago, however, there is now no evidence of the ship's presence in this star system." The computer confirmed its earlier verdict with a pedantry that only computers and authors are capable of.

"Are we still in the Sol star system?"

There was a long pause as the computer checked its star maps and other location data.

"The star map data confirms your current location as being the Sol star system. However, there does not appear to be a galacticnet node present here." The computer informed her. The presence of a galacticnet node made it much easier to plot a ship's positions than the three-dimensional geometry involved in plotting a position against the star maps.

"That makes no sense. Every planet that has been explored has a galacticnet node, even those with no inhabited planets."

"I can only confirm that node number 810924721, which is the galacticnet node for the Sol system, is absent. It isn't possible to connect to the galacticnet." The computer stated flatly.

"That isn't possible." Den declared, though he wasn't sounding quite so certain as he should. "Galacticnet nodes don't just disappear."

"Nor do Meteor Class ships, but it seems that both have." An Kohli paused to think for a moment. "Computer, scan the Sol star system. Identify any other anomalies between your data and the scan results."

They waited for several minutes. There were several scans that had to be carried out and compared to the data: visual, infra-red, ultra-violet, X-Ray, gamma ray, electro-magnetic and more.

"I have identified over a thousand anomalies. Do you want me to list them?" The computer eventually stated.

"No. Just show the three most significant."

A list appeared on a viewing screen.

1. The space station New Earth is absent from its orbit.

2. There is a colony on the Saturn moon known as Titan which is not recorded.

3. There is no space traffic in the star system other than that native to the planet Earth.

"OK, I can accept there not being a galacticnet node." Den said. "That could be explained. The same applies to the Laurel disappearing, well, almost. But you can't lose a space station the size of New Earth. There's something seriously wrong, An Kohli."

"No shit, Sherlock. Computer, what is the most likely explanation for the anomalies that you have identified."

"I am not allowed to speculate."

"I am allowing you to do so. Speculate."

There was a long pause, almost as if the computer was having some sort of inner debate. Eventually it spoke.

"There are two possible explanations. One is that we have travelled back in time to a period before Earth made intra-galactic contact with other civilisations and also before the space station New Earth was built."

An Kohli considered that possibility. She was well aware of the possibilities of time travel, having experienced it twice before *(see Timeslip and The Return of Su Mali,)* but in both of those cases she'd used a time machine. Nothing of that sort had happened here, unless the Sunray had inadvertently entered some vast machine and she hadn't noticed it. No, that possibility didn't seem very likely.

"OK, computer, what is the second possibility."

"The Sunray has crossed into a parallel universe."

\* Oscar Wilde, his comment after being released from Reading Jail.

## Glossary

Galacticnet - A vast network of data connections that means that, for a price, just about any source of information can be connected to any other source of information and can be accessed by anyone with the means to do so, legally or illegally, across the galaxy (broadband speeds may be limited on planet Earth, please consult your broadband supplier if you can get them to answer the phone). It can also be used as a form of communication, including use as a virtual meeting room. Popular amongst teenagers as a medium for socialising as, let's face it, anything is better than actually talking to your mates. No one owns the galacticnet, though several major corporations own individual components of it which gives them the right, they feel, to spy on your e-mails. Warning: 99.9% of all information stored on the galacticnet is inaccurate and I know that because I found that statistic on the galacticnet.

Sutra - A planet in the Flage system that is purported to be the home of the most beautiful women in the galaxy. Like the Gau they have the ability to shape shift to appeal to the different subjective opinions of what constitutes beauty. Male Sutrans are addicted to beer and football, leaving female Sutrans with a lot of time on their hands, which they use to earn extra money doing what they would otherwise do for free.

Victel - A unit of currency worth $1/100^{th}$ of a nuk. A one victel coin is effectively valueless.

Wormholes - Physicists had long theorised that wormholes in space could be used as short cuts that would provide travel in excess of the speed of light without all that dangerous $e=mc^2$ business. It is akin to running round the outside of your house to get from the front door to the back, or taking a leisurely walk along the hall to get to the same place. However, turning theory into practice was something of a challenge. It was solved one day when a research assistant accidentally dropped his pencil and when he bent over to pick it up found himself in the changing rooms of a women's basketball team several light years from his lab. Hardly had the screams started when he dropped his pencil again and when he picked it up he found he was back once more in his lab. At least that was the defence he relied on in court. After that it was only a matter of reverse engineering the moves the lab assistant had made to be able to find one's way back to the changing rooms… sorry to solve the riddle of travelling through wormholes. Wormholes are also used to achieve speedy communication through space and are the foundations on which the galacticnet was built. Broadband speeds may vary according to your location, especially on Earth. For further information contact your galacticnet supplier if he can be bothered answering his phone.

# 3 - Logical Deductions

"I think that they'll probably do what they did on Towie and come looking …."

"I'm sorry Den, I didn't get the end of that." Merkaloy said.

Silence was the only reply.

"Den? An Kohli? Can you hear me?"

"Look." Laurel grabbed Merkaloy's arm. "The Sunray isn't there anymore."

"Don't be daft. We were just talking to them."

"If you don't believe me, take a look at the viewing screen. And the comms screen. Nothing on both."

"It's just some sort of glitch. Computer, reconnect the communications with the Sunray."

"Unable to comply. The Sunray is no longer responding to communications."

"This is stupid. Several thousand ziku of spaceship can't just disappear. Computer, replay the last three minutes of images showing the Sunray."

They watched in silence as the Sunray proceeded normally a thousand Li ahead of them, then just winked out of existence.

"Maybe they went into a wormhole." Laurel suggested.

"Not possible at that speed. No, something else must have happened. Computer, zoom in and enhance images."

The computer did as it was instructed and zoomed the image size until the Sunray filled most of the screen. The digital enhancement was almost perfect; so good they could make out individual components such as surveillance cameras and radio antennae.

"Slow the image down to quarter speed." Merkaloy said.

As they watched, a pale grey patch of space appeared against the backdrop of stars in front of the Sunray, shading them out. It was as though someone had opened a door. The Sunray entered the grey area and as it did so it started to disappear, from the front and moving rearwards, the ship just no longer existed, until it had all gone. The grey patch at once melted away, leaving nothing to be seen but the vista of the stars.

Merkaloy and Laurel sat there looking at the screen, dumbfounded.

"I know that this is going to be a stupid question, but what did we just see happening?" Laurel asked.

"I have no idea. In all my years piloting spacecraft, I've never seen anything like that. It certainly wasn't a wormhole."

"I don't want to seem too melodramatic, but we did set out thinking that someone had set a trap for An Kohli."

"You mean, you think that was it?"

"We don't know what happened, but let's face it, we knew there was going to be a trap. We didn't think it would be here, because this is a heavily populated star system and any attempt to grab An Kohli ran the risk of being witnessed. But that? What would witnesses say? One minute a spaceship was there, the next it wasn't. No one would believe us, even with the video evidence. They'd say we faked it, the way everyone was faking stuff three or four centuries back.

"Yes, before they changed the law to make it illegal to fake video and stills images, except by licensed businesses. You're right, of course, no one will believe us. No one except the Grand Master. Computer, set up a comms link to the Grand Master of the Guild, then transmit a copy of the enhanced images to his e-mail address."

A few moments later the Grand Master's face appeared on the comms screen. He didn't look too happy. "I haven't had a decent night's sleep in weeks, Merkaloy, so this had better be good."

"I'm not sure 'good' is the word I would use, Grand Master. We've lost An Kohli."

"What do you mean, lost her? Do you mean you've mislaid her, or … oh no, she isn't dead, is she?"

"We don't know what, or where, she is, Grand Master. Look, it's easier if you watch the video images we've sent you. They were taken just a few minutes ago."

They watched the Grand Master's expression change from annoyed, to mystified, to horrified in a few seconds as he watched the images on a different screen.

"OK, Merkaloy. I understand what you're getting at. Now, which star system are you currently in?"

"The Sol system, Grand Master. We were on our way to Earth when … well, when whatever it was happened."

"Earth? What were you doing going there?"

Merkaloy quickly updated the Grand Master on all that had happened with Gala, right up until the point where the Sunray had disappeared.

The Grand Master let out a theatrical sigh. "Well, there was never any chance that An Kohli would abandon Gala, but really, that female is the limit. One day she'll learn to focus on the task in hand."

"To be fair, Grand Master, it was a collective decision. None of us considered any other course of action than saving Gala, even if it meant walking into a trap."

"Which, it seems, is exactly what you did. OK, I don't want you barging round the Sol system asking questions and breaking heads till you get the answers. Tiny Blur would have a field day and we can't afford to provoke him. You get back here as quickly as you can. While you're in transit I'll get a few big brains to look at these images of yours to see what they can make of them."

Before Merkaloy could answer, the communications channel was closed.

"That's it? We're just going to leave An Kohli to fend for herself?" Laurel protested.

"Wherever An Kohli is, I think she is beyond our help right now. I think the Grand Master is right. We have to find out what happened before we can find a way to rescue her."

\* \* \*

"OK, I think we need to eliminate the time travel thing first. While it isn't impossible, it's quite improbable. Computer, can you access this star system's communications networks?"

It took a few seconds for the computer to respond. "I have accessed what the humans call the 'internet'. It is laughably insecure. It is also quite primitive. Its communications speed is incredibly slow and it seems to be mainly used for sharing pictures of females' breasts and cute kittens."

"A strange combination." Den said, a smile forming on his lips. "Computer, display some of those images."

"Computer, don't do that." An Kohli countermanded, giving Den a disapproving look. "Computer, analyse the date information and compare it with our own calendar."

"The human calendar gives a date of $13^{th}$ November 2436. That is contemporary with our own calendar." The computer informed them.

"So, we haven't time travelled. That's reassuring anyway." An Kohli chewed the inside of her cheek. "Computer, assuming that we have crossed into a parallel universe, why would the one we have shifted to be this one, and not one of the billions of others that must exist?"

"That would require too much speculation and would invalidate my manufacturer's warranty."

The computer seemed adamant on the subject, so An Kohli tried another tack. "Computer, I will speculate and I require you to analyse the consistency of the logic in my speculation."

The computer remained silent for a moment before replying. "I can find nothing in my operating system that prevents that course of action." It finally conceded.

An Kohli allowed herself a small victory smile. "Computer, multiverse theory allows that for every action that occurs in one universe, a parallel universe is created where that action hasn't occurred. This makes the number of possible parallel universes infinite. Is this correct?"

"That is a lay-beings' interpretation of multiverse theory, but it is one of the generally accepted versions."

"So, in our universe Gala was kidnapped, but in this version, it is possible that she hasn't been."

"That is correct, but not provable."

"I'm not worried about proof at this stage. However, it is possible that this version of the universe is the one we arrived in, because we were already in the Sol system and the actions that created this version of the universe occurred here. We therefore moved to the closest version of the universe to our own."

There was another long pause before the computer replied. "That is a logical deduction, but again, not provable at this time."

An Kohli chewed the inside of her cheek some more, as she worked her logic through another iteration. "Computer, if the change that differentiates our universe from this one occurred in this star system, it should be possible to trace the nature of that change by comparing the data in your databanks with the data available in this universe's databanks."

"That is a possibility within the limited capabilities of this star system's databanks, which are far from exhaustive. We would get more reliable data if we were to find a star system where we could access the galacticnet."

"I don't want to leave this location until the theory has been tested so, computer, carry out the analysis based on whatever data you can access."

"It will take some time." The computer replied.

"Well, we haven't got anything else to do right now, so go ahead."

Den had been following the exchange with keen interest. "So, what's your thinking?"

"If the change that occurred only occurred in this star system, it could mean that all the other star systems in our galaxy are unaffected. Out there, beyond the limits of the Sol system, the galaxy is exactly the same as the one we left behind. The same beings, the same technology, the same politics, the same everything."

"Which means …"

"The person in our galaxy that created the technology to shift us to this universe, can also create it to shift us back; if he hasn't already done so. But he will also exist in this universe. All we have to do is find him."

"But we need to find out what caused this universe to be created in the first place, just to prove your theory, to make sure it didn't also make changes to the rest of the galaxy."

"Exactly."

It took the computer over an hour, but at last it was able to report. "The change can be traced back to Earth year 2016 and the precise date of 8$^{th}$ November. Do you want the time as well?"

"Not at the moment. Tell us what happened on that date in our universe."

"In our universe Donald John Trump was elected President of the Earth nation known as the United States of America."

"That seems to be a pretty specific event. OK, what happened in this universe?"

"His opponent in the election, Hilary Diane Rodham Clinton, was elected."

"I take it that these election results significantly changed events on Earth."

"They did. President Trump made several changes to national policy that had adverse effects on the planet as a whole. This necessitated an acceleration in the development of space technology that created one of the more obvious anomalies between our universe and this one, the existence of New Earth."

"What was the most significant change he made?"

"He withdrew his nation from an international agreement on climate control. It made the industries of his nation cheaper to run and therefore more competitive. It also allowed the Americans, as they are called, to increase their use of fossil fuels, which had been declining. Over time other nations' economies were damaged by this competition and they, too, withdrew from the climate control agreement and increased their use of fossil fuels. The result saw a massive change in the climate of Earth which forced them to look for new ways to grow food. This led, ultimately, to the building of New Earth to house the kelp farms which provided the raw material for the synthesising of food."

"He sounds like a pretty bad President if he didn't see that coming." Den observed.

"Our history records him as the third worst President of all time. The other two came after him and compounded his mistakes." The computer added.

"So, what did President Clinton do that was different?" An Kohli asked.

"Her principle act was to adhere to the climate control agreement. This ensured that economic competition was fairer and that the use of fossil fuels continued to decline, keeping the Earth's climate in a state of status quo. While she made many poor decisions, none of them were as detrimental to the planet as the ones made by President Trump."

"So, without massive climate change, the pace of technological growth and space exploration has been slower. But that wouldn't affect the other species of the galaxy making contact and transferring technology to Earth, as has happened elsewhere in the galaxy."

"Our history records that the first contact between species alien to Earth was made on 21$^{st}$ January 2110. Alarmed at the rapidly rising temperatures that were being observed on Earth, the Magi sent a mission to try help the planet. The mission was secret and contact wasn't revealed until much later, when New Earth had almost been completed."

"But in this universe that intercession hasn't been deemed necessary, so the galaxy is waiting for Earth to develop at its own speed." An Kohli said.

"That is speculation." The computer replied. "But the logic is sound. This Earth's climate is still under control and their technology is still quite primitive, so there is nothing to be gained by making contact at this stage in its development."

"Computer, is it safe for me to assume that the rest of this universe, and our galaxy in particular, is unchanged compared to the one we left."

The computer paused, testing the logic of An Kohli's statement. "Because of the galaxy's lack of contact with Earth there will be differences. President Tiny Blur is from Earth, therefore he can't be the President of the Galaxy. Similarly, George Bush the One Hundred and Twenty Fifth cannot be a member of the Magi and Lloyd Merkel will never have been a Deputy Grand Master of the Guild of Bounty Hunters. There will be other differences where humans have impacted on the galaxy, but those serve as examples."

"Computer, who in our universe is the galaxy's most highly regarded scientist in terms of multiverse theory?"

"That is Professor Horst Van Golden of the University of Zygor."

"Is he human?"

"No. He is Prathian."

"Den, set course for Zygor."

## Glossary

Calendar - As with time there was no common system for calendars prior to the start of the rule of the Magi. They used their new time system to set up a calendar of 10 months, of four weeks in each month, each week being 10 standard days in duration. The governments of the planets and star systems of the galaxy were invited to submit names for the months and a competition was held to select the most suitable. It came as no surprise to anyone when the names that were selected turned out to be those of some of the leaders of governments of the planets and star systems. The numbering of years was agreed to begin from the date of the birth of the Dully Farmer, the wise man who had first suggested that the governance of the galaxy should be placed in the hands of the nine wisest beings in the galaxy, who became the Magi. It would take two and a half millennia, based on the new calendar, for his dream to come true.

Ziku - A unit of weight equivalent to about one Earth kilogram.

# 4 - Matter

In the star system of Seginus there are only two planets, Zygor and Xantos. Each houses a major university and each university claims to be the greatest university in the galaxy. In the past, there has been open warfare between the two universities as each tried to prove its superiority. More recently these rivalries have been fought out on the rigby field, on the rivers, and in the debating chambers.

Consequently, An Kohli had to take it on trust that Horst Van Golden of the University of Zygor was indeed the greatest authority on multiverse theory and that no one from the University of Xantos was actually better qualified.

They found Professor Van Golden in his laboratory, feeding nuts to a monkey.

"Good day, Professor. My name is An Kohli and this is my associate, Den Gau." She introduced them.

The Professor stood and gave An Kohli an appreciative look, almost ignoring Den. He shook their hands. "How can an old physicist help you?"

"Have you ever heard of me?" An Kohli asked.

"That is a rather egocentric question, if I may say, but no, I haven't heard of you."

"I'm sorry, Professor, but there was a need for me to ask, other than to massage my own ego. Are you aware of the Guild of Bounty Hunters?"

The professor shrugged. "I have heard of them, but I have never needed their services. Is there a reason for you interrogating me in my own laboratory? I am a busy man."

"Experiments to run on the monkey, eh?" Den said with a knowing smile.

"No bastard runs experiments on me." The monkey said, before loping along to the end of the laboratory bench and turning its back on them. It wrapped its tail protectively around its genitals.

"You must forgive Hector. He is a little touchy this morning, but he is also right. We don't conduct experiments on living beings at this university. Unlike the other place." The professor gave a contemptuous nod towards the window, as though the University of Xantos was just across the street. "Hector is a friend. But you haven't answered my question and I think I have more right to ask it in my own laboratory."

"Of course, Professor. Something has happened and I think that you are the only person in this galaxy that can help me. I am a member of the Guild of Bounty Hunters, but I'm … er, I'm not sure how to phrase this without freaking you out. I'm not from this universe. I'm from a parallel one."

The Professor seemed un-phased by this declaration. He raised a hand and stroked his chin, contemplating what An Kohli had said.

"I am a noted scientist in the field of multiverse theory, but I am sometimes derided for my theories. You haven't come to make jokes at my expense, have you?"

"I have never been more serious. A few days ago, I was on my way to Earth. Are you familiar with the planet?"

"I am, but no contact has so far been made with Earth. It is a strict edict from the Magi. They aren't ready for us yet."

"That is how it is in this version of the universe. But in my universe Earth is a fully-fledged member of the galaxy. One of its inhabitants is a member of the Magi and another is a usurper who is attempting to overthrow the legal government."

"Now I know you are toying with me. It is unthinkable that this planet could have developed to that level." He stopped and thought for a moment. "Of course, there is currently a struggle between the old order and the new. A new galactic government has been elected. Here at the University of Zygor we intend remaining neutral."

"Believe me, Professor, where I come from the humans of Earth may still be technologically backwards, but when it comes to playing political games there is no species that can master them. They know every dirty trick in the book and they aren't afraid to use them." A thought struck her. "Who is the leader of this new government?"

"Her name is Kronar."

Of course, with no Tiny Blur, the Fell would have had to find another stooge to front their phoney government.

"In my version of the Universe the President is a human by the name of Tiny Blur. Sorry, professor. I digress. Please continue."

"If it wasn't for my own research I would find it very hard to believe what you are saying, but I suppose I must until I can prove that you are either lying or deranged. Tell me about how this happened."

An Kohli recounted their experiences of a few days earlier and the work they had done to establish the differences between the universe they were in and the one they had come from.

"I have to say, for non-scientists you have taken a very methodical approach, however, nothing you have done proves that you are from a parallel universe. You could have just made it all up. Even if I were to interrogate your ship's computer it would prove nothing; computers can be reprogrammed."

"I know it all sounds far-fetched, professor, but all I can do is assure you that we aren't lying."

"Let me run a few checks of my own. If you are right and it is only changes to Earth that differentiate between this galaxy and the one you allege you come from, then I should be able to find a trail that provides some substance to your story."

"That's all we can ask, Professor." An Kohli breathed a sigh of relief.

"Hector, please take our visitors to the Professors' dining room and get them something to eat. Bring them back in one hour."

"You'll be able to establish our bona fides that quickly?" Den asked with some amazement.

"We have the finest computers in the galaxy. Better by far than anything they have." He did his nod towards the window again. "If they can't tell me what I need to know then there is no possible way of establishing the truth of your story."

They followed the monkey through the empty corridors.

"Where are all the students?" Den asked.

The monkey looked at him as though he had just farted. "Universities no longer have students. At least not ones that come in every day. All study is now conducted over the galacticnet. It is easier and cheaper and it means that we academics don't have to come into contact with the illiterate morons that the schools churn out these days."

"Are you also an academic then?"

The monkey drew itself up to its full height, which was barely a met tall. "I am Professor Hector Mannville. I am the foremost authority on primate evolution."

"If you don't mind me saying so, you don't appear to have evolved much." Den sniggered.

Hector took Den's hand and bit it, causing him to cry out in pain and snatch his hand away.

"That was an extremely rude and a rather crass remark from a being that doesn't seem to have evolved to do any more than to have sex and drink itself into oblivion every night."

An Kohli hid her laughter by disguising it as a cough and dropped back a pace or so behind the squabbling pair, so that they couldn't see her.

"That is unfair. You don't know me well enough to make such a judgment."

"Rubbish. The Gau evolved their shape shifting ability purely to enhance their sex games."

"That is an unproven theory."

"It is proven enough for me, but I have to admit it isn't actually my field of study." The monkey conceded.

"And what about the drinking. How do you judge that?"

"That is a simple matter of primate evolution. To my sensitive nose you stink like a brewery."

This time An Kohli couldn't stifle her laughter. "He's got you there Den." She gasped between howls.

They had an uncomfortably silent lunch in a deserted dining room, before returning to the Professor's laboratory at the appointed time.

"Well, I have established that there are bounty hunters by the name of An Kohli, Gala Sur and Den Gau. They are currently located in orbit around a planet by the name of Stavros. It is in the Hellenic star system. But I have also searched for images of these beings. I can disregard the image of the Gau, for obvious reasons, but I have to admit that your similarity to image of An Kohli is remarkable."

An Kohli was just about to tell him that Stavros was the presumed location for the last of the Magus eggs, but thought better of it. She needn't have held back.

"According to my research, that is thought to be the location of the last of the missing Magus eggs. Am I correct?"

"You are Professor. But that information is not supposed to be in the public domain."

"And nor is it. But nothing can hide from the University of Zygor's computers. I have also been able to extract An Kohli's DNA code from the Guild of Bounty Hunters' database. If you would do me the service of providing me with a small sample I will do a comparison." He offered An Kohli a swab. "Just run that around the inside of your cheek please."

An Kohli did as she was asked. The professor inserted the swab into a portable DNA analyser and in a few seconds it provided a read out.

"There is no doubt that there is a one hundred percent DNA match. That leaves three possibilities. You are An Kohli, you are her twin sister, or you are a clone. The database shows that An Kohli doesn't have a twin sister, but that doesn't rule out you being her clone."

"Well …"

"Relax. Just my little joke. I am satisfied that you are who you say you are. But that still doesn't satisfy me that you are from a parallel universe. The fact that your ship is in orbit around Stavros doesn't mean that you are on board it. On the other hand, I have also checked the bona fides of your ship, which is in orbit around this planet. It appears to be an exact duplicate of the ship in orbit around

Stavros. However, that is an artefact and as such it could be another Quasar Class disguised as the Sunray. Do you agree?"

"You are a scientist. You develop hypotheses and then find the evidence to support them. What evidence do you have that our ship is a duplicate?"

"None, which is why we are still talking. But there is one other discovery that I was able to make. Through the monitoring of Earth's media channels, I was able to establish that there is indeed a human politician by the name of Tiny Blur, who is widely held in contempt. In itself that proves nothing. You could have access to those same channels. However, it all seems rather too elaborate for it to be a lie."

The Professor seemed to make a decision. "Come, let's find somewhere more comfortable to talk."

He led them along a short corridor to a room that was some sort of study. There was a large desk littered with papers, as well as some comfortable chairs for visitors. With the exception of the windows and the door, every vertical space was lined with books. An Kohli reached to touch one. Physical books were almost unknown in the galaxy, as were physical libraries. She found that they were also unknown in the Professor's study. The books were fake spines glued to the wall.

The Professor laughed. "It catches everyone out. I like the look of them so I had the replica spines made up as a decoration. I have to tell you that I have read every one of the real ones, as well as writing several of them."

The Professor settled himself into a large chair behind his desk. "Please, take a seat." He indicated the guest chairs. "You were right to come to me. We have a very big problem."

"I know." An Kohli replied. "We really need to get back to our own universe."

The professor waved his hand dismissively. "That is not the problem to which I am alluding. Have you heard of the 'preservation of matter', also known as the 'law of conservation of mass'?"

"I sort of remember something about it from my science lessons." An Kohli admitted.

"Don't look at me." Den shuffled in his seat. "The only science I remember is the lesson where we learnt how to distil our own booze."

"No matter. I'll explain it as simply as I can. Basically, at the time of the Big Bang, all the matter in the universe was created. Everything you can see, touch, smell, taste or hear was essentially made at that time. The only difference is that it has changed its form. Atoms have combined with other atoms to form molecules, and those molecules have joined together to make rocks and trees and water and so on. It is not possible to create new matter, it is only possible to change the form of matter from what it is, to something else. We do this when we combine atoms of copper with atoms of zinc to create molecules of brass."

"Thanks for the lesson, Professor." Den grunted. "But what has this to do with us getting back to our own universe?"

"Everything. You, Den Gau, have a mass of what? One hundred and twenty ziku, give or take a few. While you, An Kohli, have a mass of maybe ninety ziku."

"Eighty." An Kohli bridled.

"OK, Eighty. Then there is your ship and everything in it. Perhaps that has a mass of one hundred and forty thousand ziku. So, your presence here has removed a mass of matter from your universe of approximately one hundred and forty thousand and two hundred ziku. Not only that, but it has added that same mass to this universe, creating a net imbalance in mass of over two hundred and eighty thousand ziku."

"Is that important?"

"The general consensus is that it is. Think of it as a heavy object applying pressure on a lighter object. The heavier object will eventually crush the lighter one. In other words, our universe will now be applying pressure to your universe and attempting to crush it."

An Kohli gave a soft chuckle. "I'm sorry, professor, but universes are huge and filled with trillions of ziku of matter. Surely, the transfer of a few thousand ziku can't be significant."

"I wish that were so, An Kohli. I really do. The problem is that your absence from your own universe doesn't just create an absence of you and your ship, it causes matter to start moving of its own accord. Just as nature abhors a vacuum, it also abhors an absence of matter. Matter will be attracted to the space left by your ship. In turn, matter will be attracted to the space left by the matter that is now moving towards where your ship last was. It is a chain reaction that will end up with a black hole forming; one that might swallow your whole universe. Matter and energy are interchangeable, so the movement of matter is going to result in the conversion of energy from one form to another. What form that conservation takes is difficult to say, but there is the real risk that something will go bang and in a very big way.

Conversely, your presence here is sending waves of matter away from your ship, as the matter that exists in this universe attempts to find fresh space in which to exist. Again, this universe will have that conversion of energy from one state to another. Matter will smash together creating new molecules and possibly even whole new elements and, with it, huge amounts of energy. That movement will grow like a tidal wave until it hits something, and when it does it will be devastating."

An Kohli sat with her mouth hanging open, hardly able to deal with what she was hearing. "W … W … erm," She struggled to get control of her tongue.

"I think you are trying to ask what we might do about that. Fortunately, that is where your objective and my objective overlaps. We have to send you back to your own universe before the effects of your presence here, and your absence there, can be felt."

## Glossary

Rigby - An extremely violent ball game in which each team tries to rip the heads off of members of the opposing team. Occasionally one or other of the teams will remember that a ball is involved and will attempt to score a goal. This is called an "attempt" and grants the scoring team the right to take a kick at goal. For some reason "attempts" are more highly regarded than actual goals and earn more points. Not to be confused with the Earth game of rugby which was a ruffians game played by gentlemen until it turned professional and they let just anyone play it. And don't get me started on Rugby League!

Zygor U - The University of Zygor. Zygor is a planet that has been turned over almost totally to academic and scientific study. If the academics at Zygor U don't know how something works then no one else in the galaxy will understand it. Most of the great scientific and technological breakthroughs in the galaxy have been made at Zygor. As with all such institutions, the academics that work there are horrific intellectual snobs. Zygor U has enjoyed a rivalry that has endured over twenty centuries with another academic institution, the University of Xantos, which is located on a neighbouring planet. On a number of occasions in the past this rivalry has escalated to open warfare, with scientists attacking each other with mathematical equations and academics launching attacks with unsupported theses. The carnage was horrific

# 5 - Professor Van Golden

Horst Van Golden was a very worried man. He was no longer worried about his family though. They had been returned to him, no worse for their experiences than some mild mental trauma that would keep some counsellors in profitable employment for several years.

No, Horst Van Golden was worried about what would happen to the universe that he lived in now that he had successfully moved a couple of hundred thousands of ziku of matter from this universe to a parallel one.

It was what he had tried to explain to Tiny Blur while ensconced in his cellar, but the President of the Galaxy didn't seem inclined to listen. If ever there was someone who wasn't inclined to listen to the views of experts, it was Tiny Blur.

Part of Van Golden's problem was that he couldn't really talk to anyone about what he had done. He could hardly go to the university authorities and say "Er, excuse me, Vice Chancellor, but I seem to have put the whole universe at risk in order to save the lives of my family." They might be understanding, but they wouldn't be forgiving. They might sack him and he might have to ... no it was unthinkable. He might have to go and work for the University of Xantos.

On the other hand, he couldn't just stay silent, hoping that the problem would just resolve itself. One day there would be a reckoning. How long it might be in coming he had no idea. He also had only theoretical ideas about what form the reckoning might take.

There could be no doubt about culpability in this matter. He apologised to himself for the pun. It was he that had developed the prototype device that allowed him to open a door between this universe and another. He had even used university grant funding to do it. It was that which had caused Tiny Blur to have his family kidnapped so that he would comply with the President's wishes. If he had never built the device to test his theories, he could have told

Blur that it would take several years to develop it, just as it had actually taken that long.

Unfortunately, however, Blur had found out about the prototype, so he couldn't deny its existence. He had even written the academic paper in which the working of the prototype was described, so he could hardly have denied its existence when Blur had interrogated him.

There was, perhaps, one way out of the problem which might let him emerge from the whole debacle with some credit. He might be able to use the device to re-open the door between the two universes and bring the two hundred thousand ziku of matter back or, failing that, bring back the same quantity of matter in another form; an asteroid perhaps.

He had tried very hard to forget that inside the spacecraft that he had moved from this universe to another, were actually two real live beings. He realised that he didn't even know their names. That was something that his conscience found hard to deal with. Wherever they were they were almost certainly alive. Confused, maybe, but alive. If they played by the rules of the new universe in which they were living there was every chance that they would have long and happy lives, at least for a while.

No, the problems that would emerge would affect the trillions of beings in this universe. Oh yes, and the other one, of course, his conscience reminded him. Whatever the consequences were of having too little matter in this universe, they would be similar for the other universe now having too much matter.

That was something that he could do nothing about. That universe was ignorant of its fate; probably. Eventually some scientist as clever as himself might spot the emerging problem, but they wouldn't know that he had caused it. If he succeeded in bringing back two hundred thousand of ziku of matter, they would suffer no harm and his conscience would be clear once again. But you can't just open a door and hope to lasso an asteroid and bring it back.

There was a loud knocking on his study door. He was in no mood to entertain visitors and he was very tempted just to ignore the sound, but it came again, very insistent. So insistent, in fact, that he worried that the door might collapse under the assault to which it was being subjected.

"Come in." He said in a resigned sort of way.

The door slid open and two figures entered. One was rather pretty, Van Golden had to conceded. The other was large, in much the same way as giant sequoia are large.

"Professor Van Golden, my name is Merkaloy Van Troy." The large one said. "We need your help."

\* \* \*

"If someone in our universe had developed a way to open a doorway between this universe and ours," An Kohli mused, "Who would be most likely to be capable of doing such a thing in this universe?"

The professor looked uncomfortable, shifting in his seat and suddenly taking an unusual interest in his shoes. An Kohli knew she had scored an unintentional hit.

"Have you ever been approached by the government to work for them? Recently, perhaps." She persisted.

"You see right through me, don't you, An Kohli."

"I'm a bounty hunter. The ability to read body language has kept me alive. Your body language says you shouldn't play poker. Was your family threatened?"

"They were. Fortunately, I was able to move them to a place of safety. I assume it was the government that was making the threats, but I can't prove it. The being that contacted me didn't specify. But after that, all they could do was threaten me. Which they did, making the most severe threats. When they saw that I wasn't going to help them, they gave up. They could have carried out their threats and had me killed, but I think it might have attracted too much attention, so they left me alone instead. I assume that they have laid some new trap."

"You knew that An Kohli, the one that belongs in this universe, was in the Hellenic system before I arrived, didn't you?" She guessed.

"I did. It was she that I was supposed to send to another universe, just as you have arrived here. At the time I refused, not just because it was unethical, but because of the problems it would create with matter. With you now present, it would actually help to send her somewhere else, or to send you somewhere else."

"Well, we can help you with your ethical conundrum, can't we? You can send us back where we came from. Ethical problem solved; matter problem solved."

"Unfortunately that isn't as simple as it sounds. Although it is now clear that my device will work, your presence here confirms that, it can't be guaranteed that the universe I send you to will be your own. The device isn't advanced enough to pick and choose universes. I may be creating another problem in another universe, and you may be further from home than before. Is that what you want?"

"This isn't scientific in any way, but when we arrived it was in the same star system as we had left, because it was the point of difference between your universe and ours. Whatever change had spawned this new universe took place in that location. We got our ship's computer to check the historical databases and we found the causal event."

"No, you found *A* causal event. It isn't necessarily the one that created your universe. You are assuming that this universe was created from yours. Not an unnatural assumption; most beings believe themselves to be more significant than they are. That may be the case. But it is also possible that it's the other way around. Your universe may have been created from ours. In which case, this universe may have been created by a different causal event in a third universe. If we try to send you back to your own universe, we may just end up sending you to the universe that created this one, not the one that this one created. Are you following me?"

"I think so. If I understood you correctly, I think I'm looking forward at a chain of new universes, but in fact I may actually be looking backwards at previous universes."

"A fair analogy. Consequently, if I try to send you forwards I may actually end up sending you backwards instead. We need more proof before we can risk doing anything." He gave a heavy sigh. "Not only that, this universe, or your universe, may have created others and we can't be sure which one we will be sending you to. It is only a theory that parallel universes run in straight lines, starting with the Big Bang then proceeding in a linear series. It could be that any causal event can create more than one new universe, so there may be clusters of them, like bunches of grapes. In which case, which is the correct universe for me to send you to?"

Den had been silent for so long that Van Golden almost jumped with surprise when he spoke. "What sort of proof do you need to show which way these parallel universes are flowing?"

"If we can analyse the data a little bit more, perhaps we can draw some conclusions. Does your ship's computer have an exhaustive databank, covering the entire history of your universe?"

It was An Kohli who replied. "I wouldn't say it is exhaustive. It's more like a library. Not all libraries contain all books. The computer has many sources of reference, but if any are missing then there may be gaps in the computer's data."

"Well, we can identify any gaps in the data and allow for them. I think that if you will allow me to download the data from your computer, we can run a comparison and see if there are any conclusions that can be drawn."

"There is some data that I can't let you access, I'm afraid. Even in this universe there is some information that I can't let you have. Call it my own ethical issue, if you will. But Once I have locked that off I see no reason why you shouldn't have access to the rest."

"Very well. I think that it is too late for us to start anything today. I insist that you stay as my guest for tonight and we can start work early tomorrow."

\* \* \*

Dismantling the cairn took An Kohli some time. It was a big cairn and she had no idea under which level of stones the egg might be concealed. At the same time, if one of the rocks slipped, it could easily crush the egg. She straightened her aching back and checked her surroundings once again.

"Any sign of any company?" She called up to the Sunray, orbiting high above her.

"No." Gala's voice came back. "The nearest life forms are at least a thousand mett away. The shuttle seems to have scared them off, so none of them seem to be taking any interest in you."

"OK, well, keep a close eye on them. I may be some time. This is a big pile of rocks Su Mali put together."

The silence spoke volumes. Gala was no doubt gritting her teeth in annoyance at An Kohli telling her the obvious. She shook her head. She really should be more careful how she phrased things. It was a wonder that Gala hadn't quit on her years ago. Overhearing the conversation from where he was standing, a few met from the cairn, Den stifled a smile.

She returned to the cairn and removed another head sized rock and threw it to one side. Reaching for the next rock she saw a sliver of black poking between the ones below. She took it between her thumb and forefinger and rubbed it gently. Polyviol; the sort of material used in the bags that Su Mali put the eggs in.

Quickly she moved the two rocks, impatiently throwing them to one side rather than placing them on the ground as she had the rest of them. She gave the bag a tug but it was still partially pinned by another rock. She identified which one it was and lifted it slightly, freeing the trapped material. As she rolled the offending rock off of the top of the cairn she felt the ground shake under her feet.

\* \* \*

It was a long and boring day for An Kohli and Den. While Horst Van Golden ran the Sunray's computer data through the university's computers there was little they could do except wander around the university campus looking for some suitable distraction. The only places where such distractions might exist, such as the high energy physics labs, were off limits to all but the scientists working in them.

Out of curiosity they wandered into a lecture theatre in the Arts faculty, to watch a virtual lecture on the history of some artist or other, but they didn't find it very stimulating. The lecturer stood in front of a camera while her students watched from distant points of the galaxy. Images of the artist's work were flashed onto the screen as the lecturer referred to them.

Their intrusion seemed to upset the lecturer, causing her to stumble over her words. It was as though the presence of real live beings in the lecture theatre was in some way off putting. After a few minutes of dark looks from the podium, An Kohli and Den left to seek other diversions.

After what seemed like weeks rather than hours, Professor Van Golden summoned them back to his study.

"I think I have made progress with regards to whether your universe created this one or vice versa. I examined the causal act that you referred to, but I'm afraid your computer was wrong. It wasn't the election result that was the causal event, it was a previous act.

At this point, I have to make it clear that not all decisions will result in the creation of a new universe. It is clear that there would be far too many variables for that to be plausible. For example, if you were to take the pretty route to your mother's house rather than the shortest route, that wouldn't cause a new universe to be created in which you took the shortest route. No, what is important is the significance of the action. If, by making your choice of route, you created a significant action, such as a road accident in which a President died, then that may create the new universe, but not otherwise.

An Kohli bit her tongue, willing the Professor to get to the point, but he seemed to be in no hurry.

"We are also unsure how these universes co-exist. For example, does this universe occupy the same space as your universe, but utilising different dimensions, or does it exist alongside your universe, in a different physical space. This makes decision making very difficult. We may accidentally create another universe in which we don't try to send you back to your own and the problem with matter in this universe remains exactly the same.

"One question, Professor." Den interrupted. "How can a new universe come into existence without having to be recreated from scratch, right from the Big Bang?"

"A very good question, and one to which we don't know the answer. This is the argument in favour of the different universes occupying different dimensions. If that is the case, then you don't require fresh matter to be created, because it already exists in all possible dimensions. It just has to be given form. That form is given by the decisions that are made. This means that in whatever dimension the new universe is created, its history already exists and the only difference between it and the original universe is that one causal event."

"And what is the causal event for this one, or for our universe?" An Kohli tried to drag the Professor back to the point.

"Ah, yes, I was just coming to that. It was the decision by the Presidential candidate Hilary Diane Rodham Clinton to use her personal email account for official emails. Had she not taken that decision none of the following events would have been possible. The emails from her personal account would have been insignificant in terms of the election; official emails couldn't have been leaked; there would have been no investigation by the FBI and all the other factors that influenced the voters in Earth year 2016."

"I'm not sure how …"

"I'm just getting to that as well. According to multiverse theory it is only an action that can create a new universe, not inaction. The action, the improper use of the private email account, took place in your universe, not in this one, which means that your universe created this one, and not the other way around."

"Does that mean you can now send us back to our own universe?"

"I don't see why not. As you have assumed, because the causal event took place in the Sol system, all we have to do is take you back to the exact same co-ordinates in space and we can open up a new doorway for you to pass through. The balance of matter between the two universes will be restored and all that has happened is that you have been delayed in your mission for a few days."

"Is there still any chance that we might go through to a different parallel universe?" Den asked.

"Erm ..."

"I'll take that as a 'yes' then. What it will mean is that your universe will be back in balance, so you can relax."

"Erm ..."

"Another yes." Den started pacing the room, worry furrowing his oversized brow.

"Calm down, Den." An Kohli soothed him. "We always knew there would be risks. It's like time travel all over again."

"You've time travelled?" The Professor asked, excitement ringing in his voice.

"I didn't say that." An Kohli dissembled. Knowledge that time travel was feasible didn't exist in her galaxy, so hinting at it to a Professor of astrophysics was a risk in itself. She might just have changed the course of this universe, and in doing so created yet another one.

"I'll take that as a 'yes' then." He smiled. "How did it work?"

"I have no idea. We just walked through a door and whoosh, back we went. How the machine worked is as much a mystery to me as how your machine works."

"I will trade you information on that." The Professor suggested slyly. "I'll tell you how my device works. Even better, I'll give you a copy of the schematics."

"We don't need to trade. The Professor Van Golden in our universe also has the device."

"But if you arrive in a new universe, where the version of me hasn't got that far yet, there will be no way for you to get out of it again."

An Kohli realised that his argument was persuasive. If this transfer between universes didn't take them home, then they might never be able to return to their own universe.

"I'm really sorry, Professor, but I can't tell you what I don't know. I'm a bounty hunter, not a scientist. My co-pilot, Gala, might have some clue, but she is a prisoner back where we came from."

"In your universe, she is a prisoner. But not in this one. In this universe, she seems to be still aboard the Sunray. Not your Sunray, of course, but the one that already existed here."

"Are you suggesting …."

"A small subterfuge, perhaps. An introduction to Gala, that's all. I'll take it from there."

"But what about the An Kohli that belongs here. She won't take kindly to me just barging in and talking to her co-pilot. Besides, that would be a causal event and we know what problems that might create."

"That is my risk to manage. All I need is your co-operation. You do want to get home, don't you?" He smiled sweetly. "Eventually."

An Kohli realised that he had her over a barrel. He controlled the device that could open doors between dimensions, so without him they were stranded. He was also right about them needing to know how the device worked, just in case they landed in the wrong universe. This was getting messy.

"OK, I'll see what I can do. But I mustn't come face to face with An Kohli and Den mustn't come face to face with his alter ego. We have no idea what the consequences of such a meeting might be."

The Professor tried hard not to show his delight, but failed completely. "Very well. Let's see if we can establish An Kohli's current whereabouts, shall we?"

## Glossary

Polyviol - A material similar to plastic but which is wholly biodegradable. Not normally used as a container for beer except on those planets where high levels of beer consumption are guaranteed to be produce a high turnover of containers, e.g. The Hideaway, New Klondike, Towie, Earth, etc.

# 6 - Another Bank Job

The Sunray slowly made its way through the orbits of the outer planets. While Earth technology was still quite primitive, it had advanced enough to detect objects within its own star system, so a bright shiny spaceship would be bound to attract attention. By keeping to the opposite side of the star it would prevent any direct observation from the planet and its moon, but there was a possibility that observation stations had been built on other planets within the system, or on their moons, which were generally far more hospitable than the planets themselves.

"What's your plan when we get there?" Den asked.

An Kohli adopted a thoughtful expression. "I have no idea. Getting there is going to be a major part of the problem. We can probably sneak in and hide behind their moon, but there is a real possibility that they'll spot a shuttle approaching."

"I was thinking more about when you actually get down there. Compared to humans, you do rather stand out. Would you prefer me to go? At least for the initial reconnaissance."

"That might be an idea. You've been here before, haven't you?"

"Yes, years ago. A little bit of investment business, you might call it."

"Gambling, in other words."

Den gave a smug smile. "Not the way these humans do it. They've got more tells than a speaking clock."

"So why did you leave?"

"Turns out that human casinos don't like losing any more than the ones on Towie. Word got around about me and no matter how often I changed my disguise, they always seemed to spot me. Or maybe they just got more suspicious of strangers. Anyway, I got away one step ahead of a beating and decided not to bother coming back. It was good while it lasted though. I lived on Canarias for a year on the proceeds."

"How did you convert Earth money to nuks?"

"There's a market for everything. Seems there's a bit of illegal trading going on for certain minerals only found down there, so someone was prepared to buy Earth currencies. How they got the minerals off planet without being spotted I can't imagine, but that wasn't my business."

"Probably one of those very rare radioactive isotopes. A little of them goes a long way and they're hard to come by legally elsewhere in the galaxy."

"OK, I've got a sort of a plan. You get me behind their moon and we'll look out for one of their space craft returning to Earth, probably from that colony on the moon they call Europa. We may have to wait a couple of days or so, until one passes, but that's not a big deal. I'll get in behind it and follow it through into their atmosphere. I doubt their detection systems can pick up two objects close together. Once I'm through I'll head for … where am I heading for?"

"According to Su Mali's data she spent her time in the city called London. I've got the co-ordinates. But you won't be able to land a shuttle there without being spotted, so you'll have to find a landing site in a remote area and then travel into the city. I have no idea how you're going to do that."

"I'll need something negotiable that I can convert to cash. If I can do that then there's a number of travel options available. I'll also need to pay for accommodation and food."

"What's negotiable down there?"

"Got anything gold, or the sorts of stones they regard as being precious? Diamonds, rubies, sapphires, that sort of junk."

"I've a few trinkets you can have."

"OK. In that case we just have to find a landing site and I can get going."

"You can probably use the same landing site as Su Mali, but we'll take a few images as we pass and see what we can see. I intend crossing their orbit in the middle of the day, so that the star overloads any sensors they might have."

"Tradition has it that we aliens land at a remote location in the middle of the night, causing electrical systems in vehicles to fail, before exposing ourselves to drunks who spend the rest of their lives trying to convince the rest of the humans that they've encountered aliens."

"Do you want to be traditional?"

"No. It used to be fun but the novelty's worn off. We'll do it as though we were going after a bounty."

"Sounds good to me."

"What are you and Gala going to be doing while I'm wandering around down there?"

"Tapping into their internet system and seeing if we can unearth any clues as to where Su Mali hid the egg. If we can identify the location you can case the joint for us."

Den's grin broadened. "Your starting to sound like a professional criminal, An Kohli."

"It's hanging around with you! It rubs off after a while."

* * *

As the Sunray crept into the edge of the Sol system, An Kohli summoned Horst Van Golden to the command deck.

"Nearly there, Professor."

"Can you see the other ship?"

"No, but I'm getting its electronic signature. It's tapping into the intranet system. That's Earth's equivalent to the galacticnet. Very primitive and so slow you can get yourself a cup of coffee while a page is downloading."

"Will they find what they're looking for?"

"They are me. They're persistent, so they'll find it eventually. I can't give them any help though, in case I change things in this universe. Besides, there's no proof that Su Mali used the same hiding place. This is a very different Earth to the one in our universe. For a start, you can breathe the air in this version."

"I've got her." Den announced, pointing to a viewing screen. There was the alternative version of the Sunray, slipping around behind the Earth's moon.

"She's doing what I would do." An Kohli said, so quietly that the Professor had to strain to hear.

"When will Gala be alone?"

"Not until the location of the egg has been established. Then she and, probably, Den will go down and try to get it."

"You say 'probably Den'. Can't you be sure?"

"No. An Kohli usually works alone, but it may be helpful to have Den with her. It depends on where the egg is and how hard it will be to extract. It may need Den's specific talents."

"You mean shape shifting." The Professor interpreted.

"Yes, but I was also thinking of burglary. Our Den has had a chequered career."

The Gau threw her a dirty look but refrained from commenting in case An Kohli started to elaborate in front of the Professor.

"Den, take us in behind Phobos, then position us so we can monitor the Sunray."

"Will do. There doesn't seem to be any attempt to go down to the planet yet though, from the other Sunray."

"No, they'll be waiting to get something to cover their approach. Probably one of the shuttles from Saturn. I assume that you will be staying aboard the other Sunray once you've made your way over there. After all, you can't come with us."

"That's right. I'll take my device over there when you take me across and introduce me. Once you're back here, I can use it. I'll get Gala to help me wire it up to the communications system and use their antennae to send the particle beam that opens the door."

"You know, Gala might not co-operate. After all, we're going to be telling her a pretty tall tale."

"Well, it's your job to convince her. If you can't do it, I certainly won't be able to."

\* \* \*

A gentle beep notified the ship that the sensors had picked something up. Den had the watch. "There's a transport coming in from Saturn." He told An Kohli over the intercom.

She appeared on the bridge so quickly it was as if she had been hovering outside the door. "Any activity from the Sunray?"

"No. She's probably still too far away. No, there goes a shuttle now." They watched as a tiny dot appeared from behind the moon and headed on a course to intercept the much larger ship.

Professor Van Golden joined them on the command deck. "Won't the captain of the transport spot them?"

"I doubt it. They think they're alone in the galaxy, so they won't bother with detection systems on their spacecraft." An Kohli replied.

"Sensors say just one being on board the shuttle." Den informed them. His face broke into a smile. "Two heartbeats detected, one slightly arrhythmic. I'm guessing that's me."

"Don't scan them anymore. I don't want to trigger any alarms in the shuttle, or on board the Sunray. It looks like they're sending their Den to take a look, while the other two stay on board."

* * *

The shuttle landed in the centre of a wooded area of countryside. Observations over several days suggested it was sufficiently remote for people not to visit. At least, they hadn't seen anyone visiting. The shuttle had displayed no lights and its impulse drive would have attracted little attention. They had also taken the precaution of arriving in the hours before dawn, when the fewest people were likely to be up and about. Most of the detection systems capable of spotting the shuttle were pointing outwards, over the sea, so Den wasn't worried about them picking up a tiny craft that was entering their airspace from almost directly above.

Den had already changed into his disguise of a middle-aged human, but he needed to obtain some clothing to match. What he was wearing would attract too much attention. According to the images they had studied, there should be a house about a half hour's walk from his landing site. If he was quiet then he should be able to get in and out without being noticed. An Kohli hadn't liked the idea of him committing a crime, but as Gala had pointed out, he could hardly walk into a gentleman's outfitters dressed as he was.

Dawn was breaking as Den quietly opened a gate and let himself into what appeared to be an area for growing vegetables. A large four-legged shape bounded across the planted area. A guard animal was to be expected, Den thought as he sent a shot of brain waves towards the animal. At once the animal stopped in its tracks, unsure of what was happening to it. The brain waves wouldn't have been felt by a human, but animals were more receptive and telepathically attuned to beings such as the Gau. It was a trick that Den had played several times before on other planets. The dog lay down, panting slightly, watching Den approach the house. It felt no need to bark, not anymore.

Den tried a door handle and it gave under his hand. He pushed gently and the door opened, making no noise. It was heavy wood and had the feeling of being very old. He stepped through and found himself in a room filled with equipment of varying sizes and shapes. None of it looked familiar to him, but standing on a table was what he had hoped to find. A pile of neatly stacked clothes stood ready, almost waiting for his arrival.

He picked the items up and measured them against himself. After very little consideration he selected a shirt and a pair of trousers in some heavy, dark blue material, with ridged seams and studs dotted around various parts. The studs seemed to have no purpose other than as decoration.

From a pouch in his belt Den drew one of the smaller items of jewellery that An Kohli had given him. She had been most insistent that he pay for anything he took. He placed the diamond ring on the table next to the disturbed pile of clothes and hoped it would be enough.

Idly he looked around the room, wondering what the various bits of equipment did. It occurred to him that one of them might contain food. He was getting a little hungry and the walk had made him thirsty.

He opened various doors and panels one by one until one lit up when the door was swung wide. A cold blast of air hit him. Within it Den found food of various types. He recognised a cooked chicken, so he took that, along with a couple of cans. He didn't speak much English, but he did recognise the word for beer when he saw it. In fact Den could recognise the word 'beer' in more languages than there were actual languages.

He was about to leave when his conscience pricked him about taking the food. He fished in the pouch once again and found a pair of earrings, each with a small ruby set into it. He laid those beside the diamond ring.

Leaving the house, he found the dog waiting obediently next to the door. Its tail thumped rhythmically on the ground in greeting, but it made no other sound. He left as silently as he had arrived and the dog eventually gave up on seeing his new friend again and returned to its kennel to sleep until someone fed him.

The next bit of the journey would be the longest Den would have to walk. They had estimated at least three hours. Den found a secluded spot in a field and ate the chicken and drank the beer, before putting the shirt and trousers on over his own Superskin™ outfit. He put his boots back on then started his journey. He was in no hurry. From what they had found on the internet the local businesses wouldn't be open for several hours and Den's next order of business was to convert the rest of the jewellery into cash.

They had no idea of the value of what they had. The descriptions they had found on the internet meant nothing. The gems were all described in terms of their weight in something called carats and they had no idea how to convert those into a system of weighing things that they could relate to. The precious metals were no easier to work out. They were valued in accordance with their purity and weight and they couldn't work out how pure their samples were in comparison to the Earth measuring systems.

There was also, it seemed, a value placed on the workmanship that went into the jewellery and that was the hardest of all to place a value on. The stuff that An Kohli had was made in so many different places in the galaxy and in so many different styles that they couldn't find anything comparable on the internet. Den worried that what he had would be seen as junk by the trader they had picked out.

The traffic on the roads became more frequent as the morning wore on. It was a measure of how old their technology was in comparison with the rest of the galaxy that the vehicles all still used wheels. They approached silently with their electric drives. The occupants dozed or worked away on communications devices of varying types, content to let the computerised guidance systems take them to where they needed to go.

Den noticed that the density of housing was starting to increase. Small villages gave way to larger ones, which merged to form what the humans called 'suburbs'. Higher rise buildings started to dominate the sky lines, homes to the majority who couldn't afford their own plot of land. Factories, warehouses and retail outlets mingled with the domestic accommodation, jostling for space. He began to encounter people walking to work or riding on small personalised two wheeled transports. The crowds thickened as the morning wore on.

At last Den found himself at his destination. There was a large retail outlet, what the humans called a 'mall', surrounded by streets with more specialised businesses taking up less fashionable space. It was in one of these streets that Den stopped, examining the exterior of a building, trying to ascertain if it would meet his needs. It had sounded promising when they had read about it on the internet, but now he was less sure. What faced him was a blank wall, slightly recessed in places to suggest windows that had been bricked up. Above the door a flaking painted sign said that it was the premises of Frederick Darwin, Bespoke Jeweller. The door itself was solid and metal. There was no handle on the outside, not even a place where a key might be inserted. He pressed a button that seemed to be there for the purpose. He waited, but nothing happened. He pressed the button again.

"What do you want?" A tinny voice demanded.

"I have some jewellery to sell." Den announced, using his personal translator. They had spent hours of their waiting time programming the device with several of the more common Earth languages.

"Wait there."

It seemed to take an age but eventually a small panel, set into the door, was opened at face height. There was still a thick layer of glass between him and the occupant of the premises.

"Are you on your own?" The face demanded. It was old, but completely unsullied by wrinkles. The hair, what Den could see of it, was a jet-black colour that didn't look natural. The figure's teeth glowed an eerie white. He still couldn't make out whether the person was male or female, because the intercom was distorting the voice so much.

"Yes, completely alone."

"Show me your hands." Den did as instructed. "Now turn right around."

Realisation dawned. Den was being checked out for weapons. This suggested that the figure behind the door had reason to feel under threat. Perhaps this was the right place, after all.

"OK. You can come in, but no funny business. You'll be inside a secure cage and if you try anything funny I'll lock you in and you'll be trapped until the police arrive."

The face disappeared and the door swung open, allowing Den to step inside. The door immediately slammed shut again. Den found himself in an empty room. Not a thing adorned the walls or the floor. A small section of one wall was given over to a window made from glass thick enough to stop a charging rhinosacow. Below it was a narrow ledge on which goods might be placed. Behind the glass a man was watching Den with some suspicion.

"OK, let's see watcha got." He said without any preamble.

Den fished the items from the various pouches on his belt, laying them on the ledge. The man's eyes opened wide, telling Den all he needed to know. Across the galaxy Den had seen looks of avarice on the faces of many beings. Nothing matched the pure, naked greed he saw in the man's eyes.

Seeing Den watching him, the man tried to rearrange his face into some sort of disinterested look, but it was already too late. Den had seen what he needed to see. The collection he had brought was more valuable than they had realised.

"OK. I need to check each piece to see what the gems are and what sort of metal has been used. Most of it looks like gold, but I can't be sure. There is a hatch in the wall to your left. Place one bit inside and I'll check it. I'll return that to you and you can pass through the next bit."

Den picked up a necklace, a rather gaudy affair as far as he was concerned, but An Kohli had liked it. He located the hatch, which was no more than a sliding panel with another ledge inside. He placed the necklace onto it and it disappeared. Returning to the window Den watched as the man opened up a door in the front of a small machine. He placed the necklace inside and closed the door, before pressing a button.

"It's a mass spectrometer." The man explained, his back still turned to Den, so that his voice was slightly muffled. "It analyses the makeup of the stones and the fittings to tell me what it's all made of."

Den suppressed a smile at the primitive nature of the technology. Hand scanners were used throughout the galaxy to do such simple analysis.

Numbers started to glow on a screen, changing rapidly as the device carried out tests and calculations. The numbers were too small for Den to make out, which he guessed was deliberate. Mustn't let the punter know what they have.

The procedure was repeated until each piece lay before Den once again. The man placed his hands on the counter on his side of the glass and leaned heavily on them. His face was a frown, but behind the man's eyes Den could see cunning. The man was calculating how low he could go in making his offer without it being obvious that he was trying to cheat Den.

"Where did you get this stuff?" He asked, an implication behind the question that Den might not have come by it honestly.

"It's been in my family for centuries." He replied, using the words that An Kohli had made him learn. Something called 'antiques' seemed to be prized on this planet, which Den worked out to mean old, second hand stuff. "My family went to Russia in the nineteenth century and they bought most of it there. Goodness knows how old it was when they bought it, but it has been in the family since the days of the Tsar." Den was posing as a Russian to explain the need to use the translator. They hoped that the supposed age of the items would explain the unfamiliar styles.

"You're lying. This stuff isn't Russian. I have no idea where it was made, but I've never seen anything like it before. It's jewellery, of course, the usual gems and gold, a bit of platinum and silver, but that bit," he pointed at a pendant on a long, slender chain supporting a green stone, "I've never seen metal like that before. My equipment doesn't recognise it. The stone is right, that's supposed to be an emerald, but the metal, well …"

He gave Den a speculative look. "You haven't been working on Europa, have you?"

Den understood the question. If the metal didn't come from Earth, then it must come from off of Earth and the most likely place, as far as the old man was concerned, was the Earth colony on Europa. That would make it rare and therefore more valuable.

"You've got me." Den said, giving a rueful grin. "I picked up a chunk of ore there, just a sample, but I'm not supposed to have taken it. Anyway, when I got it back here I had it worked into that chain and setting, to take the stone. The stone has been in my family for years."

Cunning lit up the man's eyes once again. He had just heard something that increased the value of the hoard and that excited him.

"Look, it's not bad for costume jewellery." He said, sweeping his hand across the collection on the other side of the glass in a dismissive gesture. "But it isn't worth a huge amount. I'll give you a hundred thousand Bits for the lot."

Even if it was as poor quality as he made it sound, it didn't sound a lot. Bits, Den knew, was the internationally negotiable digital currency of Earth now, having replaced a lot of the paper currencies of earlier centuries. An Earth Bit, as far as they had been able to work it out, was about the same as a nuk, based on the price of a popular brand of burger.

"No. It's more valuable than that. If you aren't interested then I'll take it somewhere else." He started to collect the pieces together.

"Hang on, hang on. Let's not be too hasty." The man held up his hands in protest. "Look, the settings are fine. The gold is worth something, but the gems? No, they're mainly paste. A few of the smaller ones are real, but not worth that much."

Den knew that wasn't true. No one anywhere else in the galaxy made jewellery out of anything other than genuine gem stones. They didn't have to. Gem stones were found on so many planets that they cost less than their artificial forms. But not on Earth. On Earth, most gem stones were still rare. Or at least the markets were manipulated to make them appear rare, and therefore expensive. They should have done more research for comparison purposes, but it was too late now.

"If you can't recognise diamonds when you see them," Den said pointing at several the size of a peas, set into a necklace, "then I know I'm in the wrong place."

He placed the first item back in one of his pouches and picked up the second.

"OK. You've got me. They're diamonds, and that's a ruby," He pointed at another pendant, "and emeralds. A couple of sapphires and more diamonds. You should have told me you'd had them appraised already."

"So you wouldn't try to cheat me from the start?" Den cocked an eyebrow.

"A bit harsh. Look, it's just part of the game, the negotiations." He shrugged off the accusation. His face looked thoughtful, doing the proper calculations to establish the collection's value, instead of plucking numbers out of the air.

"Look, I need to photograph them, so I can check the internet to make sure they aren't stolen. If that comes up blank then I'll give you, oh, let me see …"

Den picked up another piece and ostentatiously put it into his pouch.

"OK, fifteen million Bits."

Den was pretty sure that he was still being cheated, but not by as much as before. A thousand Bits would get him a hotel for the night, he knew, and another five hundred would get him a meal. Working that through it meant he and An Kohli would be able to fund their visit for several weeks.

"OK, but same as before, you only get the pieces one item at a time and you don't get the next one until the first is safely back with me."

"You aren't very trusting, Sir."

"Can you blame me after your first offer was less than one percent of what you have just agreed to pay me?"

The man looked uncomfortable and shuffled over to the hatch to collect the first piece.

An hour later Den walked out of the shabby premises with a cash card loaded with one hundred thousand Bits, after checking that the balance had arrived in the bank account An Kohli had opened for them. The security of the bank's internet site was so poor that they had been able to open the account without any supporting ID. Gala and he had worked at it for a day and a half, but had managed to hack into the bank's files and create the whole account and make it appear that it had been open for several years, including fake transactions and fingerprint and retina data scans that would allow him and An Kohli to access the money through the credit transaction systems. If he needed to reload his card with cash then it was available from automated machines that scanned the retina and paid out when it had identified him.

Den had pointed out that they didn't actually need the jewellery. They could just have typed in the amount of money they wanted in the account and the bank system would have recognised it, but An Kohli refused.

"It's about bending the law, not breaking it. We need a bank account, so we need to hack into the bank's systems to create one because we can't just walk in and do it. But if we take money out of the account that isn't ours, that's theft. That isn't bending the law to meet an urgent need, that's a criminal act."

An Kohli could be so sanctimonious at times.

After leaving the jewellers, Den headed into the mall, where he purchased a small back pack and filled it with new clothes and a pair of soft canvass shoes of the style that most humans seemed to favour. He then treated himself to lunch in a chain coffee store that sold execrable coffee and even worse food. The humans seemed to be enjoying it.

At last he was ready to head for London. The railway seemed to be the preferred mode of transport for someone without a car and the departure point was directly below the mall.

\* \* \*

Den checked into a modestly priced but comfortable hotel. It was centrally located, not far from where they had concluded that Su Mali had hidden the Magus egg.

Having found it easy to hack into one bank account they had discovered that none of the other banks presented more of a challenge. They searched the records of each bank in turn until they found that Su Mali had rented a safe deposit box in Smooge and Harley's Bank. The rent was paid each month from an account that had been set up seemingly for that sole purpose. The balance was now quite low, suggesting that Su Mali had expected to collect the egg before this. An Kohli's arrest of the master criminal had prevented that.

An Kohli had wondered what would happen when the money ran out. There was no way that the bankers on Earth could contact Su Mali, even if she hadn't been in prison. But An Kohli hoped to solve that problem for the bank by removing the egg. They had everything they needed to access the box: the retina scan, the fingerprint scan and the identification numbers for the safe deposit box that would also be used to open the various security doors. What they didn't have was the key and a female Gau.

The key would be no problem. An Kohli knew where it would be and would call in a favour to get someone to collect it and convert it into data that could be used to produce a 3D print down on Earth. A female Gau was much harder to get hold of.

Den could appear like a female, and the female human form that Su Mali had used, as shown on her account data, wouldn't present him with any physical problems in terms of visible appearance. But he wouldn't have the necessary biological add ons that were needed to fool a full body scanner. A pair of socks stuffed into a bra just wouldn't cut it. And then there were the surplus bits of his own anatomy that he couldn't disguise!

But that was crossing a bridge that they hadn't yet come to. Den's purpose on this visit was merely to locate Smooge and Harley's Bank and carry out a reconnaissance. There might be ways of entering that would negate the need for a female Gau to disguise themselves as Su Mali.

* * *

An Kohli slammed her way onto the command deck and slumped into the captain's chair. "This is taking forever. Maybe I need to go down and give him a hand."

"You know you can't do that, An Kohli." Den did his best to soothe her jangling nerves. "If they discover we're here, who knows what damage we might do."

"But we know how to get into the bank. We pull the same trick as last time, but instead of doing it with two An Kohli's, we do it with two Dens. It will be the same trick, but with a twist."

"And how might that change the course of history here? It could be devastating. If the humans find out that there are beings from other star systems walking amongst them, they'll go bonkers. If they catch one of those same beings, then it could mean … oh, I don't know, but I bet it wouldn't be pleasant. You see how humans treat each other. Just think how they might treat us. You've seen the images of those places where they keep the animals! Zoos, circuses, marine parks. It's unthinkable that we might end up in a place like that just so people can gawp at us."

"You're right, of course. It's strange to think that they already have beings from off planet living amongst them and they don't know it."

"Oh, yeah. The Surchifs. I don't know how they get away with it."

"They get away with it because they blend into the background. They're like the cleaners in office blocks. In fact that's what most of them do to earn a living. You see one and you've forgotten them almost immediately. It's something in their pheromones, I think. Hang on. I think I've got something. Let me think…"

An Kohli got up and left the command deck. Den could hear her pacing up and down the corridor as she worked her idea through, then she reappeared as abruptly as she had left.

"See if you can raise a Surchif community in that Britain place. They rarely send messages out, but I'd be surprised if they weren't listening for incoming signals."

Den did as he was instructed or, rather, he got the ships' computer to do it for him. He had met Surchifs many times over the years. They had even helped An Kohli escape from the Fell, though they had later paid a heavy price for it *(see The Magi* and *Genghis Kant)*. They were a strange species, totally unassuming in their appearance and behaviour. They had an ability to blend into the background of a planet, going about their business without anyone noticing them. They weren't like Gau, able to change their appearance to fit in. They just didn't seem to be noticed. It really was uncanny.

"I've got a channel here." He announced eventually. "Voice only, I'm afraid."

"Who am I addressing?" She asked.

"I am Glom, leader of the Surchif colony on Earth. Who am I talking to?"

"I am An Kohli from the Guild of Bounty Hunters. Have you heard of me?"

"Your reputation goes before you, An Kohli. How can a humble Surchif assist you?"

\* \* \*

Den had spent many days sitting in the pub across the road from Smooge and Harley's Bank. He knew he was in the right place, because Su Mali had left a rather distinctive marker.

The pub was old, very old. Perhaps as old as the city itself. It must have been under some sort of protection, because the modern city had been built around and above the black and white exterior. Inside it had dark beams discoloured with centuries of smoke. The ceilings were low, as were the tops of the doorways. Den wasn't particularly tall, but even he had bruises on his forehead where he had failed to remember to duck as he passed from one part of the pub to another. But however old the pub was, its name was only a few years old. It was now called O'Mali's Irish Pub.

He had observed people looking up at the sign and chuckling, but they didn't see the real joke. But then again, he wasn't British or, more appropriately, Irish.

He felt, rather than saw, a being sit down next to him. He turned, hoping to discourage any attempt to engage him in conversation by delivering a frown. Instead his jaw dropped open. Sitting next to him was a Surchif female.

"I've been told you need our help." She whispered in Common Tongue.

Den looked around, trying to see if anyone had spotted this clearly alien being in their midst, but the small crowd of early evening drinkers seemed to be unaware of the presence of a being from another star system.

"How do you do that? How do you just disappear into the background?"

"It's a knack we have. We don't think about it much."

"I'm assuming that you are looking for me specifically?"

"Oh yes. I recognised you straight away, even in your disguise. By the way, who dressed you? A blind person?" The Surchif chuckled.

"What's wrong with my clothes?" Den looked down to see if he could find any flaws, but he couldn't.

"Never mind. Your choice helps people to ignore me even more easily than normal. By the way, my name is Gleam. You will find that all our names begin with G, so don't be surprised when you meet the rest of the crew."

"Oh, yeah, that's a thing of yours, isn't it?"

"It is part of our clan identity, if that's what you mean." The Surchiff sniffed. "Now, I'm afraid I am under strict instructions not to tell you who sent me. So strict, in fact, that I haven't been told myself, so don't bother asking. However, I know you need help to get in and out of that bank unnoticed and with the contents of a certain safe deposit box. Am I right?"

"You are right. Is that why you're here."

"It is. Now, if you don't mind me using a well-worn Earth cliché, take me to your leader."

\* \* \*

"That's it. There's three of them on board the shuttle this time. It can only be An Kohli, Den and the Surchif." Den announced, delighted to put an end to the interminable waiting.

"OK, I'll get the professor and we'll head across to the other Sunray. Hmmm, it may be an idea to give Gala some sort of warning that we're coming."

"I'll send her a message saying that the shuttle has developed a technical problem and has had to turn back. That should do it."

"Good thinking. Right, we'll be on our way. Be ready to move as soon as I return. If I'm not on my own, then it means we've failed and we'll have to find a new plan."

With that An Kohli left the command deck and headed for the shuttle bay, collecting the Professor and his luggage on the way.

The shuttle journey was uneventful and they were soon docking with the Sunray. An Kohli had worried that the ship's computer might recognise a difference between their shuttle and the one that had departed a short while earlier, but it seemed to accept them, probably as a visiting craft.

An Kohli and the Professor made their way along the corridor to the command deck. She took a deep breath and entered.

"Hi, didn't expect you back so soon. So, what's wrong with... "Who's he? And where's Den and that Surchif? Er, what's going on?"

"Gala, what I'm going to tell you now is really weird, but I swear that every word I'm about to say is true."

"OK, but you're freaking me out already."

"First of all, let me introduce you to Professor Horst Van Golden, of the University of Zygor. He is from your universe."

"Meaning…"

"Meaning I'm not. If you let me tell you the story from the beginning, it might help."

As quickly as possible, An Kohli told Gala the story of how they had ended up where they were. "So that's it." She concluded. "Now we just need the Professor to get us back where we came from, then, if you will do us the favour, you can take him home."

"Are you the reason that the Surchifs have suddenly shown up?"

"Yes. We needed your An Kohli down on the planet breaking into the bank. The Surchifs can help you with that. They can do what we did when we had the same problem back in our galaxy a couple of years ago."

"So, everything we've done here, you've already done?"

"Pretty much. The egg on Earth was the third we went looking for, rather than the last, but otherwise we've done everything you've done."

"OK, I can't pretend to believe you. It's all too farfetched, but I guess that I have no choice but to go along with it."

"Professor Van Golden is the greatest expert in multiverse theory in the galaxy. You can look him up if you doubt me. He'll be in the data banks. He'll explain it all to you after we've gone. And I'm sure he has questions of his own, for you." She added, with heavy emphasis.

"OK. Well, what do I have to do?"

"Nothing for the moment. I'll go back to my own Sunray, while you help the Professor wire his device up to the communications antenna. When the Professor see's our Sunray approaching an agreed set of co-ordinates, he'll activate the device, we'll go back to our own universe and that will be that."

"And you say there's another Gala and she's been kidnapped."

"That's right. She needs me to rescue her."

"That will make a change. In this universe I'm usually the one getting An Kohli's arse out of a sling." Gala chuckled

"Just as my Gala does in my universe." An Kohli smiled.

"OK, well you'd better get back to your ship, just in case An Kohli decides to come back up here. I'm going to have a pretty complicated story to tell her when she does get here."

"Well, at least you'll have the Professor to help with the technical stuff." An Kohli leant forward and gave Gala a hug. It felt good, even if it wasn't the right Gala.

\* \* \*

"I think the portal has just opened." Den announced, pointing at a viewing screen where a grey blob was masking the stars behind it.

"Well, we haven't got much choice about going through it, no matter where we end up." An Kohli said in a resigned sort of tone.

The ship nosed into the void and started to shake like a dog climbing out of a pond. Then they were through.

"There's New Earth." Den pointed triumphantly.

"Don't get too excited. We could have just gone into another parallel universe that also has a version of New Earth. We're going to have to check everything to make sure that there isn't another version of the Sunray here, complete with alternative versions of you and me."

# Glossary

Common Tongue - A language that evolved gradually as the various species of the galaxy started to encounter each other and discovered that communication worked better if both parties understood each other. The most extreme example of what happens when both sides fail to communicate was when the Andromeda system went to war with the Antaries system after an Antarian said "Good morning, that's a nice hat" but was interpreted by the Andromedan as having said "Your mother is a twenty toed agravarg who has sex with donkeys". 95% of all known species now use the common tongue to communicate. The remaining 5% don't have the necessary vocal equipment to actually speak the language but are able to use universal translation programmes to interpret, though occasional failures resulting from incorrect use of context still leads to misunderstandings similar to the one described above (users of Moogle Translate will be familiar with this problem). Planet Earth is one of the few in the galaxy where different languages are spoken in different parts of the planet and Common Tongue has been used to overcome this shortcoming with varying degrees of success. The people of some countries, such as The Netherlands and Denmark, are so fluent that they often use Common Tongue in preference to their own languages. The French are fluent but refuse to speak it and the British rarely get past "Two pints of beer and a packet of crisps please, Tonto".

Moogle - A galacticnet search engine that occasionally finds the source of accurate and/or useful information, but more often directs the user to the sites that pay Moogle the most.

Rhinosacow - Domesticated animal used to produce milk, meat and leather. It has an extremely thick hide and a single horn mounted on its nose. In fact the horn is made of tightly compacted hair, but that is something that most people don't remember when an angry rhinosacow charges at them, head down.

# 7 - Memory Lane

When it came to keeping beings waiting, it was usually Tiny Blur who did the keeping and the other beings who did the waiting, so the situation that he found himself in was an unusual one. But, he had to admit to himself, there were some beings worth waiting for.

In his cellar, deep beneath his Presidential Palace, Tiny Blur had installed a bed. A very big bed. It was screened from the rest of the cellar by thick walls that kept out the noise of beings undergoing torture, and the hidden speakers that usually relayed the sound of dripping water had not been installed. Access was controlled by just two retina scans; his own and that of the being that he was waiting for. The décor was what he imagined a high-class female's boudoir might look like, had he ever seen one. He was wrong, though a high-class hooker might have recognised the style. A bottle of fizz sat chilling in an ice bucket. If she was hungry there was a selection of cold snacks being kept fresh in a refrigerator. Soft mellow jazz dribbled through the speaker system and the lighting was so subdued that it was difficult to see across the room.

A discreet tapping came on the door.

"Come in." he said, his voice sounding, he hoped, warm, welcoming and seductive. The door slid open.

"Your guest has arrived." A trusted aide, wearing a military style uniform, announced before stepping to one side to allow a tall, slender female to enter.

"Thank you. I'll call if I need anything." Tiny Blur dismissed the aide without a further thought, before turning his attention to his guest.

She was dressed head to toe in Superskin, but not the normal opaque material. This was gauzier, giving tempting glimpses of lilac coloured flesh as she walked. She wore thigh length boots and Blur wondered idly how he might get the Superskin suit off while keeping the boots on. Her purple hair cascaded down either side of her face, framing it perfectly. She wore little make-up; she didn't need it. Her face was slender, as was her nose, but her mouth was full and generous.

Around her waist was her belt, hanging from which was the holster that normally held her pulsar but which was now empty. Not even An Kohli was trusted near the President with a weapon. A polyviol bag hung from the belt on the other side.

"An Kohli, my love. I have waited a long time for you." Blur gushed.

"Not too long I hope, my love." she replied, a twinkle in her eye and a soft smile on her lips. "I got here as soon as I could." She crossed the room in two long strides and took him in her arms, kissing him passionately on the lips. His knees turned to jelly and he had trouble staying on his feet even after she released him.

"You managed to get away OK?" He asked as he picked the bottle of fizzy wine out of the ice bucket and began opening it.

"Yes, no trouble. They're in orbit around Sabik, or more likely in the Three Moons Bar, getting pissed, while they assume that I'm on my way to deliver the egg to the GCIE."

"And have you delivered the egg?"

"I have delivered *an* egg." She grinned, "But not *the* egg. That is for you." She undid the fastening that secured the polyviol bag to her belt and offered it to him. He reached to take it and she snatched it back out of range. He tried again and she snatched it away again, taking a step backwards towards the bed. He advanced on her, enjoying the game. She took another step backwards, felt the edge of the bed hard against the back of her calf and allowed herself to fall backwards, landing in a licentious sprawl. Tiny Blur launched himself forward, landing on top of her. He let the bottle of fizz go and it fell to the floor with a heavy thump.

"I'll swap you." An Kohli whispered in his ear.

"For what?" He whispered back.

When she whispered her answer into his ear he let out a long, earthy chuckle. "It's a deal" He said, as he started to unfasten his shirt.

\* \* \*

"This is not the correct universe." The computer intoned, as it completed its checks against the data held on the galacticnet.

An Kohli let out a sigh of resignation. It had taken the computer too long to come up with the answer. That meant that there were anomalies, which meant that the computer was re-running some of its data comparisons, just to be sure.

"What are the anomalies?" An Kohli asked.

"There is only one that means anything." The computer replied. "There is another ship called the Sunray. It is in orbit around the beta planet of Barnard's Star."

"But that's where the Government is based." Den broke in. "What in the name of the galaxy would we be doing there?"

"We're going to have to find that out in due course. Computer, what is the causal incident that split this universe from the previous one, or from ours if that is where this universe originated?"

The computer stayed silent, forcing An Kohli to ask the question again. The computer seemed reluctant to answer, which computers shouldn't be.

"You met President Tiny Blur and seem to have fallen in love with him." It said at last.

\* \* \*

Tears slid down An Kohli's face as she viewed the images of the incident that had created this new universe. She remembered the day very well. Only in her universe she had refused the invitation. The images only covered the parade and the ceremony, but her own memory provided the rest.

"I can't believe I would do that." She whispered, not for the first time.

"You didn't do that, An Kohli." Den reminded her. "Our universe was created because that An Kohli did something. In our universe you didn't do it."

"But ... Tiny Blur ... I didn't trust him back then any more than I would trust him now. So what would make me accept the invitation?"

"Inside every one of us is the capability to do good ... or to do bad. In this universe it is the capability to do bad that has come out of you. Be thankful that you are you in our universe." *If we ever get back there,* he didn't add.

She watched the recording again. It was the day of George Bush the One Hundred and Twenty Fifth's induction into the Magi. The galaxy was stunned that such a ... well, George Bush, could have won the election, but that was what had happened. The Guild had been given a quantity of tickets to the celebration and An Kohli's name had been drawn out as one of the lucky attendees. Even if no one really liked the candidate, the ceremony was still a big deal and, despite being a very new member, An Kohli would be an official representative of the Guild, which meant lots of free meals and even freer bars. Not to mention the fact that there would be quite an after-party and her ticket included admission to that.

So An Kohli took her place in the stands and stood to cheer as the eight existing Magi paraded down the broad avenue to greet their new colleague. The bands played and the Space Cadets marched, as did group after group of other worthies. There was even a contingent from the Guild of Bounty Hunters, resplendent in their ceremonial robes and led by the previous Grand Master. The present Grand Master was only a Deputy at the time but he, too, was marching. An Kohli was relieved that she wasn't required to do that. It was a hot day and the Guild's ceremonial robes were heavy and not very well cooled.

The ceremony went on for hours and An Kohli soon got bored, but she couldn't leave without disturbing everyone else, so she sat it out, waiting for the end. Once free, she and the other Guild ticket holders headed for the nearest free bar to work up a good head of steam ahead of the after-party.

By the time the evening event came around, An Kohli was feeling no pain. If a waiter droid had dropped a tray she would have got up and danced. Later in the evening, after the formal banquet, George Bush the One Hundred and Twenty Fifth arrived, in company with Tiny Blur and a host of other hangers on. They glad handed their way around the throng and a sudden impulse came over An Kohli. Breaking through the security detail she managed to fling her arms around George Bush the One Hundred and Twenty Fifth and plant a big kiss on his cheek. Security guards hurriedly disentangled her and returned her behind the barriers, but she had caught the eye of someone else.

A short while later An Kohli was approached by a human; not one she recognised.

"Tiny Blur would like to buy you a drink." The human said. He pointed to the roped off VIP area, where Tiny Blur raised an arm and waved at her.

"The drinks are all free." She slurred, draping an arm over the human's shoulder, more for support than anything else.

"Yes, but the good stuff is in the VIP area, and you're invited."

"What about my friends?"

"Sorry, it's a solo gig. Are you coming?"

An Kohli considered the question, her alcohol befuddled mind taking its own sweet time to process the idea. On the one hand, she had never been in a VIP area in a club before. On the other hand, she didn't trust politicians in general and Tiny Blur in particular. When it came to dodgy dealings, Blur never seemed to be far away. His hands never got dirty, of course. He was too important to ever have his hand on the smoking gun, but he was there, in the background, the smug grin on his face and his nose in the air, as though sniffing out the sources of money and power.

She made her decision. "No thanksh. I'll shtick with my pals if you don't mind." She turned her back on the human and was surprised to find that he was back in front of her once again, blocking her path.

"Mr Blur is a very important person." The human said, his voice developing a hard edge. "It wouldn't be a good idea to upset him."

"Mr Blur can kiss my lilac arse." An Kohli giggled. "I'm not interested."

The human went to grab An Kohli by the arm and was surprised to find his wrist in the iron grip of a very large Arthurid.

"She said 'no'." The Arthurid growled, his grip tightening to the point where the human feared that the bones in his wrist might snap. "I suggest that you go back to your boss, kiss his arse and tell him the answer. If you come back, I won't be so gentle."

With that the Arthurid released the human's hand. The human grabbed it with his own hand, supporting its weight and hoping that there was no permanent damage. He scuttled off and took the Arthurid's advice not to return.

"Thanks, but I could have handled him." An Kohli looked up into the face of the Arthurid.

"I'm sure you could have, but it was more fun my way." He chuckled as he extended a meaty hand for An Kohli to shake. "I'm Merkaloy Van Troy." He announced.

"My name is An Kohli."

"Pleased to meet you, An Kohli. Shall we dance?"

"Not here. They're playing all that Earth junk in honour of Bush. Let's go somewhere where we can get some decent music."

"A victel for them." Den broke into An Kohli's reverie.

"Overpriced." She replied. "Just remembering that day. I guess the other An Kohli accepted the invitation." She told him the story.

"Sounds like an areshole." Den concluded.

"Well, we know that now. Back then we weren't quite so sure. He was wined and dined by the most reputable beings in the galaxy, including the rest of the Magi."

"Shows you what poor judges of character they were then. If they're that easily fooled I'm not sure that restoring them is such a good idea."

"That's not our call to make. We're just bounty hunters. We're doing it for the money."

"That may be true of me, An Kohli, but you're not just doing it for the money. Anyway, this trip down memory lane isn't getting us anywhere. What we have to do now is decide what to do to get ourselves back to our own universe, before this one comes crashing down around our ears because there's too much matter in it."

"So what are we waiting for? Set course for the University of Zygor."

## Glossary

GCIE - Galactic Counsel In Exile. When the Magi were forced to flee, power was transferred to the GCIE pending the restoration of law and order. This is a group of senior civil servants who are the permanent heads of the departments of the galactic government. They immediately took action and set up a series of committees through which to administer the galaxy. Each committee had the same members though each one had a different Chair and a different title. By coincidence each member of the GCIE chaired one committee. Because all decisions are reached by consensus it takes a long time to get anything done and then it's usually the wrong thing. For example, because of disputes over which budget would pay, it took six months to agree to have biscuits served at committee meetings and then garibaldi's were chosen when the members all wanted either chocolate digestives or Hobnobs.

Space Pioneers and Space Cadets - An Intra-galactic youth organisation dedicated to tying knots and helping old ladies across busy roads. The two activities are not mutually exclusive.

Superskin material - Many advances have been made in the manufacture of synthetic fibres that are warm, waterproof and breathable. The Superskin Company (a subsidiary of the Gragantua Corporation) produce some particularly attractive skin tight clothing that is thermally insulated and also water repellent, while being the thickness of a hair. Their clothes are also very hard wearing, which is why bounty hunters like them.

# 8 - Dear Diary

An Kohli pulled the shiny black sheet across her and tucked it under her arm to prevent it sliding off again. Why did Tiny have to have such slippery sheets, she asked herself once again? Twice during their recent exertions, she had nearly gone flying off the bed due to lack of friction.

She picked up her glass of fizz and took a sip. With the bottle lying on the floor, it had become a little warmer than she liked, but it would take too long to get another bottle sent down, and this one would do for now.

Tiny Blur snuggled into her shoulder and nuzzled at her neck. The delivery of the latest egg was her visible reason for coming here, but she had another purpose and it was time to broach the subject.

"So, just one more egg to find. What happens after that?" She asked, keeping her tone light.

"You know the plan, beloved. The GCIE gathers the galaxy's media together for a fanfare uploading of the intelligences in the eggs into nine volunteers, then they suffer the embarrassment of discovering that the nine eggs they have are totally useless. I'm still not sure how you convinced them not to check the eggs more thoroughly."

"I didn't need to. They're bureaucrats; they believe whatever you tell them. How else do you think you end up with fifty nuk hammers for the janitors and two nuks worth of aspirin being charged at a hundred nuks per prescription? All I had to do was transfer all the data to new eggs and then wipe the originals before handing them over, and that was not a difficult task. The rest they did for themselves by not checking anything other than the serial numbers." She smiled a smile that none of her friends in other universes would recognise. "Then I have the pleasure of acting all innocent. After all, those were the eggs I found, just where Su Mali hid them. How could I know they're fakes?" She let out a chuckle that would send chills down the spine of most beings, but which Tiny Blur found arousing. "But that wasn't what I meant. I meant, what happens to you and me after the last egg has been found?"

"We carry on as before. I see no reason to change our little arrangement."

"You may not, but I rather had a hankering to become the First Wife of the Galaxy."

"Sorry, darling, but my wife rather likes that job."

"You could divorce her."

"You have to be kidding me. With all she knows, she would bring me down in a second. Being the President's lover may not be what you were hoping for, but being the ex-President's lover would be far worse."

"There are other alternatives to divorce." An Kohli whispered, letting her free hand slide down over the President's stomach. He was putting on weight, she noticed. Too many ceremonial dinners. She would have to do something about that when she became First Wife.

"You don't mean …. No, I couldn't have her killed."

"You've had plenty of other beings killed in your scramble up the greasy poll. But no, I didn't mean that. Killing is so old school and totally unnecessary in most cases. I know a little planet where there is plenty for her to eat and nothing that will eat her. I'm sure that she would be quite happy there, living out the rest of her natural life."

The silence that followed told An Kohli that the President was giving her idea some serious consideration. It was true that his wife's presence did rather cramp his style. While she was happy to ignore his side interests, such as An Kohli, she demanded recompense and she had extremely expensive tastes. Not that money was a problem these days, but it was the principle of the thing. The idea of ridding himself of his wife's presence was attractive. And An Kohli was far better in the sack than she ever had been.

"This planet; tell me a little bit more about it."

\* \* \*

Professor Van Golden steepled his fingers and looked over their tips at An Kohli. "Actually, I doubt that it was your decision that was the causal link between your universe and this one. When you think about it, in terms of decisions, yours was neutral. Philosophically speaking, anyway. Was your decision not to go with that human a positive decision or a negative one? Similarly, in this universe, was the decision of our An Kohli to go with him an actual decision, or just a passive action caused by our An Kohli being under the influence of alcohol? I think the causal link was actually your friend Merkaloy's decision to intervene. That was undoubtedly a positive action. In this universe he didn't take that action, so this universe was created from yours and not the other way around. In terms of which universe created which, however, it doesn't matter. But in your mind, it does seem to."

This Professor Van Golden wasn't one bowed by having to make difficult decisions, worried about his family or the threats that had been made against him. In this universe his family had never been kidnapped and neither had he been threatened with death if he didn't co-operate with Tiny Blur, because in this universe Tiny Blur didn't want rid of An Kohli; far from it. Professor Van Golden seemed more cheery and genial than his other incarnations and An Kohli had warmed to him.

"But I have to stop your An Kohli, before Blur completes his takeover of the galaxy. If she is working for him, or with him, then that will prevent the restoration of the Magi."

"There is nothing you can do about that. If you intervene you will simple cause another universe to be created where you didn't intervene. That is the nature of the multiverse. You could end up chasing your other An Kohli through the infinite number of universes, always stopping her from completing her purpose, but at the same time never stopping her."

He paused before speaking again. "Are you familiar with the concept created by the human meteorologist, Karl Lorenz?"

"Let's assume I'm not." An Kohli snapped, not happy at being told she couldn't do something.

"He is the one who first used the analogy of the 'butterfly effect'; the idea that a butterfly might flutter its wings in one place and it might cause a hurricane to happen in another. It is often incorrectly quoted as an analogy for Chaos Theory; seemingly unconnected events that grow bigger and more significant over time because of their actions one upon another. That, essentially, is what we have to deal with when we think in terms of the multiverse. Something insignificant in one universe causes a new universe to be created where the same event becomes much more significant. That is what happened in that club that night. It was seemingly insignificant in your universe, but highly significant in this one."

An Kohli's shoulders slumped. Of course, whatever she did would only change this universe. It wouldn't change anything else. And if she did end up chasing herself across multiple universes trying to put things right, it would prevent her from doing the most important thing in her own, which was rescuing Gala and then recovering the final egg. She owed those other universes nothing, but she owed her own a lot.

"Well, it does explain Tiny Blur's personal animosity towards me. I doubt that he took my rejection well."

The Professor gave a wry chuckle. "That may be true in your universe, but we have to accept the fate that is in store for us in this universe." Van Golden, too, seemed suddenly despondent. "If this An Kohli is to be stopped, then it can't be you that stops her. Fate must be allowed to take its course."

"You said the butterfly effect is incorrectly used as an analogy for Chaos Theory. Why is it incorrect?" Den asked, anxious to lighten the mood.

"Because it is impossible to create a causal link between the butterfly and the hurricane. There are so many other factors that may also have an impact. Yes, the butterfly may cause the hurricane, but at the same time it may have nothing to do with it. But it does provide a simple straw that the lay being can grasp in order to try to make sense of science. Real scientists would never take such a simplistic view. Even Lorenz didn't actually believe what he said. He was only offering an illustration of cause and effect."

An Kohli had tired of the philosophical turn that their meeting had taken. At first professor Van Golden had refused to believe that they had arrived from another universe, but the weight of evidence that they had presented, in terms of their ship's computer records, had persuaded him, so he had listened to their story.

"Back to more practical matters, Professor. Can you help us get back to our universe, or, more accurately perhaps, to leave this one?"

"Ah, sadly, no. In this universe I have yet to develop the device you spoke of. I have done the calculations that demonstrate the theory, but I'm afraid in this universe, the university has yet to grant me funding to take the project forward."

"Is it possible that the influence of the Fell hasn't been applied to hurry the University Grants Committee along?" Den asked. "After all, if everything is going the Fell's way here, they haven't any need for a device that would get rid of inconvenient beings like An Kohli."

"That is possible. There are a number of other projects that might help the Fell that haven't received funding because of ethical concerns."

"Ethical concerns that the Fell might have persuaded the University to ignore in our universe." An Kohli concluded.

"That is not possible to determine." At the suggestion that his university colleagues might be corruptible, the Professor became defensive. "All I know for certain is that I have to answer some questions about the ethics of my experiment and if my answers are satisfactory I will be given a grant to allow me to proceed."

"We could provide you with a considerable shortcut." An Kohli removed a small PMD from her belt and held it aloft.

"What is that?"

"A copy of the plans of another Professor Van Golden's device." An Kohli replied, a smile on her lips."

The professor eyed the device hungrily. It had the potential to win him a No Bell prize, one of the most coveted accolades in the galaxy. "I would still need funding to build the device."

An Kohli took Gib Dander's credit card *(see Genghis Kant)* from her belt and held it aloft alongside the PMD. "I think I can help with that as well. How long will it take to build?"

"I would need to see the plans. Can I take a look?" He indicated the computer terminal on his desk.

"You can, but the files are 'read only'. You can't copy them unless I give you the password."

The Professor gave her a thin smile. "You aren't very trusting, An Kohli."

"I have learnt to be very careful who I trust, Professor." An Kohli inserted the PMD into a free port on the computer and opened the master schematic.

The Professor studied the plan, muttering to himself occasionally and letting out the odd exclamation, cutting himself off as he realised that An Kohli was listening. "Ah, so that's how to …" and "Oh, that's clever …" At last he looked up from his studies, a beatific smile on his face.

"So, Professor, how long?"

He sighed contentedly. "Oh, no more than a couple of years, I should think."

"A couple of years! We can't wait that long. Our galaxy is about to go to war and we're needed there. We have to get back now!"

"OK, I can shorten the test programme because we know that the device already works. I can also subcontract some of the manufacturing work out, seeing as you're paying, But it can't be done in less than six standard months.

"Six months? That's still too long."

"It will have to be. Some of those components just don't exist. They're going to have to be manufactured from scratch. I don't even have access to some of the raw materials that are needed. Others are strictly controlled, because of their potential use in weapons. It all takes time, An Kohli. I'll also have to work in secret, because if the

Fell get to hear of this they will either want to take control of the device for their own purposes, or they'll try to stop me."

An Kohli's shoulders slumped once again as she realised that the Professor wasn't exaggerating. She had expected too much of him and that was her fault, not his. "Very well, Professor. It is what it is. When can you start?"

He brightened up considerably. "Is tomorrow too soon?"

"Why not today?"

"Today I'm playing glof with the Dean. But while I'm with him, I can request an immediate sabbatical to take on this work. It will mean I won't be interrupted. You will cover my salary during that period, won't you?"

"Assuming this credit card works in this galaxy, then yes."

\* \* \*

An Kohli's communicator buzzed and she struggled into wakefulness to answer it. It was her 'burner', the disposable communicator that was destroyed after it had been used so that it couldn't be traced back to her - or the being to whom she had been speaking. That could only mean that the caller was Tiny Blur. For him to be calling at this time of night it must be urgent. She rubbed the sleep from her eyes and tried to focus her mind.

"What is it Tiny?"

"Sorry to wake you, Babe, but I think you need to see this." He put a video image on the screen. The quality wasn't the highest, but she could make out the figures that had been captured walking into a building. It was her and Den.

"So what? I don't see the significance … oh." Her eye caught the date and time stamp running along the bottom of the image. "That isn't me." She announced, firmly.

"That's what I thought. According to the reports I get, you arrived on Sabik this morning, which means you couldn't have been on Zygor two days ago. That's the entrance to the University of Zygor, by the way."

"You have me followed?" An Kohli was taken aback by the revelation.

"In case you have forgotten, my love, we are supposed to be on opposite sides. You are the law-abiding bounty hunter trying to recover the Magi, while I am the President of the Galaxy, trying to stop you. My agents would find it odd if I didn't ask for reports of every sighting of you. That's how this came into my hands. Your transit time from here to Sabik meant that you couldn't have made a diversion to Zygor."

"I'm sorry, it's late. I wasn't thinking. You're right, we have to keep up appearances." She paused before adding "For the time being."

"As for Den, a paid informant told one of my agents that she was in bed with your compadre at the time this video was being taken, also on Sabik."

"So, who are these two, and what are they doing on Zygor?"

"According to my source, they gave your name and Den Gau's name, but who they really are isn't known. What they were doing on Zygor, however, is known. They were visiting Professor Horst Van Golden. He is the foremost expert, in this galaxy, on the subject of multiverse theory."

"Multiverse Theory? Isn't that all hogwash?"

"Some scientists believe so but others, with some well-respected figures amongst them, believe that it is theoretically possible that there is more than one universe. Proving it is another matter, which is why the discipline is not held in high regard even among experts."

"I'm not sure ... OK, so we have two beings that look like Den and I, visiting an expert in multiverse theory. What of it?"

"I don't know why, but I think it's significant. But we do know that the very next day the good professor started a six-month sabbatical to pursue a private project. He hasn't told anyone what it is. I think it might be a good idea if you were to find out."

"But I was just about to drag Den out of whatever bar he's in, get Gala to stop tinkering with the Sunray and go and find that final egg. Isn't that what you want?"

"That was what I wanted up until a short while ago. Now I suspect that this may be more important. Oh, and mentioning the Sunray, GSTC shows a Quasar class ship identical to the Sunray, in orbit around Zygor. Its name isn't recorded, but if you are being impersonated, then whoever it is has also gone to a lot of trouble to get hold of a ship similar to yours. This isn't just some sort of weird coincidence, An Kohli. I have a bad feeling about this."

"They could be Gau. Well, Den is a Gau, but I mean the female. I've been impersonated before, remember."

"That thought had crossed my mind. But it just begs the question, who are they and why are they impersonating you? I think you should go and find out why."

"What do I tell Den and Gala?"

"Tell them whatever you like. Show them this video if you like, just don't tell them how you got hold of it."

He cut the connection before An Kohli could ask any more questions or raise further objections. She broke the communicator into tiny pieces and flushed them down the toilet. Opening up her travel bag she accessed the secret compartment in the base and activated a new burner. Tiny Blur already had its number so that they could maintain contact. She realised that it was her last spare communicator and made a mental note to buy some more.

Checking the time, she decided it wasn't worth returning to bed. Instead she used the hotel entertainment system to access all the information she could find on Professor Horst Van Golden and the university at which he worked.

* * *

"I've been thinking." Den mused aloud.

"I've told you not to do that. You know how it overheats your brain." An Kohli smirked.

"Oh ha ha. No, seriously. It's that causal effect thingy. How would the computer know that you met and fell in love with Tiny Blur? In this universe, I mean. After all, it's hardly the sort of thing that would appear in the data archives. It's too insignificant."

"Actually, that's not a bad question. I don't keep a diary or journal, so it couldn't be traced that way. Of course, in this universe maybe An Kohli does. Or Tiny Blur."

"Tiny Blur's diary would be held in secure files. I'm guessing that it would be harder to hack than ... well, than just about anything."

"Let's ask the computer then. Computer, have you been monitoring this conversation?"

"I have. The answer to your question is that in this universe Tiny Blur does keep a diary and that diary records your first meeting and all the subsequent meetings." The computer paused for effect. "In graphic detail. The diary is held in secure files and it was beyond my capability to hack them without it being noticed. However, the same cannot be said for the files of Tiny Blur's wife. They are considerably less secure. In her files I found complete downloads of Tiny Blur's diaries, which suggests that she is spying on him and is also able to access his files at will."

An Kohli laughed. "That means she knows all about his affairs. I love it. One day she's going to use that information and he's going to crash and burn. I wonder what the trigger will be?"

"This is speculation, which I am not supposed to do." The computer paused, giving An Kohli the chance to instruct it not to speculate. An Kohli stayed silent. "I suspect the trigger will be Tiny Blur and An Kohli's plan to maroon the First Wife on an uninhabited planet."

An Kohli chuckled again. "At least I'm consistent. OK, computer, as I don't keep a diary, how can you be sure that the causal effect that created this universe was this. In our universe I could also have met and fallen in love with Tiny Blur. You can't possibly have access to his wife's files from our universe."

"Correct. However, I do have access to all of the Adastra's and the Pradua's navigation data and that of this ship. That data is also stored on the computer of the Sunray in this universe, which I was able to hack, because it is me and I am it, so I know the way in. I compared all the navigation data and it is very different. It shows you visiting locations in this universe that you didn't visit in ours. I then compared those locations with Tiny Blur's known whereabouts at the relevant times and in many cases they coincide. The only conclusion I could draw was that in this universe you are having an affair with Tiny Blur, but not in our universe."

"Very clever." Den said.

"I know." The computer replied.

"But incorrect." An Kohli chuckled. "You were unaware of the intervention made by Merkaloy that was the actual causal effect. However, given the lack of data on that, your conclusion is logical."

An Kohli frowned. "If you can hack into the computers on the other Sunray, can its computer hack into you?"

"It can, once the crew know of our existence and give it instructions to do so. However, I can re-programme myself to make it harder. I can't however, make it impossible. In the end, we operate using the same software systems with the same vulnerabilities."

"Do that. I don't want An Kohli getting access to the sort of data that you have stored on you. It would give her too much of an edge."

"So, what do you intend doing?" Den asked her.

"We do nothing?"

"Isn't that a bit risky? Tiny Blur has agents everywhere, at least in our universe he has, so there's no reason to think he doesn't also have them here. It's only a matter of time before our presence here is detected. We're going to be stuck here for six months."

An Kohli gave Den's opinion serious thought. "You're right. At the very least we have to get away from Zygor. Maybe go somewhere uninhabited."

"I know. We could go and get the last egg. Beat this An Kohli to it."

An Kohli's face lit up. "Hey, that's not a bad idea. At least the GCIE will get one real egg."

"You think this An Kohli's been giving the eggs to Blur?"

"Do you think that Mumu's shit in the woods?"*

"We know from the last universe that the An Kohli there didn't collect the eggs in the same order as we did. How do find out which ones she's collected here?"

"Computer, answer that question please."

"The last egg not collected here is the one on the planet of Aragan."

"That was the planet that wasn't supposed to be inhabited, but had some primitive tribes living on it." Den reminded her.

"Yes, I remember. They caught us and got us to help them attack their enemies." *(See Cloning Around)*

"It was also the place where we nearly got killed by Attila, aka Lessar Fro."

"I think we rule that out this time. The Fell won't be chasing around after either the eggs or An Kohli, not with Tiny Blur protecting her. But we'll still have to deal with those tribes."

"They took us by surprise last time. We didn't even know they existed. This time we can use that knowledge to get inside their cave and out again without them even knowing."

"You're looking forward to this, aren't you Den?"

He smiled broadly. "I like to keep my hand in when it comes to some skills. But really I just fancy putting one over on you."

"In your dreams." But she, too, smiled. "But I know what you mean."

\* They do.

## Glossary

Glof - A pointless game that involves hitting a small ball with a big stick until the ball takes refuge in a hole. The whole process then starts all over again until the ball successfully escapes into some deep water or hides in bushes or woodland, after which there is much swearing and the participants retire to a place of refreshment to brag about how well they hit the ball. There is no recognisable scoring system, which makes it highly suitable for the elderly, who always forget how many times they have hit the ball anyway. This game should not be confused with golf, which is played by athletic young men and women who can hit a ball 300 yards without effort.

GSTC - Galactic Space Traffic Control. Each inhabited star system with space travel capability, and some uninhabited systems, has a traffic control system to prevent collisions between space craft and between spacecraft and orbiting satellites and to monitor space activity within its system. These individual systems are linked together through the galacticnet to provide galaxy wide traffic control information.

No Bell Prize - The highest accolade in the galaxy for contributions in specific academic and scientific fields, with an additional Peace prize for beings that have made a significant contribution to the ending of the divisions that create wars. Several members of the Magi have been awarded the No Bell Peace Prize. When the awards were first created, the name of the nominee was read out, followed by the sounding of a bell as a symbol of acclamation. However, at one ceremony the bell failed to sound, leading to that year's prize for Literature being called the No Bell Prize. The name later became synonymous with all the awards and the reason for the prizes now carrying that name.

PMD - Portable Memory Device. They come in a range of shapes and sizes and use a variety of different technologies to store information, but they all perform the same basic function. They are all fully compatible with each other except for those produced by the Banana Computing Corporation.

# 9 - Return to Aragan

Van Golden cursed silently as his communicator buzzed. He should have turned it off, he knew, but the idea of being incommunicado didn't appeal to his vanity. But that came at a price and, in this case, the price was him being disturbed in the middle of a delicate operation to fuse two strands of optical fibre that were so thin he had to use a microscope to aid him in the task.

He tried to ignore the noise, but the caller was persistent. Cursing again, he abandoned his work and retrieved his communicator from his pocket. He was surprised to see the face of Janus Jones, the University's Head of Security.

"Sorry to disturb you, Professor, but I thought you should know. There's been someone making inquiries about your whereabouts. Normally that wouldn't attract my interest, but this being was very persistent. She threatened to blow the head off of the reception droid if she wasn't given the information. Do you know this person?"

An image of An Kohli appeared on the screen. "Yes I do. In fact I'm working ..." He stopped himself just in time. The first reason why he stopped was that the Head of Security had no need to know that he was working with An Kohli. That knowledge itself could be dangerous. The second reason was that An Kohli didn't need to go around threatening to blow the head off of reception droids. She knew where he lived. In fact she had even stood in this very workshop while he showed her the wide range of engineering resources at his disposal, and agreed the purchase of many others that he didn't have to hand. Which meant ..."

"That person is very dangerous, Jones." He said. "If she finds out what I am working on it could be very dangerous for me and my family." That much was true, in relation to the An Kohli who belonged in this universe.

"I thought as much. She looked familiar though."

"Her name is An Kohli. She's a bounty hunter."

"Yeah, I know about her. She's the one looking for the Magi eggs, isn't she?"

"That's the one."

"So why is she going around threatening droids?"

"That I can't answer. Let's just say that she isn't all that she seems. She has some very dubious friends and they have an unhealthy interest in what I'm working on."

Janus Jones knew better than to ask questions of scientists about their work. "So, I take it that you don't want her to know where you live."

"Yes, but more than that. Can you arrange access to the High Energy physics labs for me? I think I'd rather work somewhere where she can't gain access to me." It would be a pain to have to stop his work and transfer all his equipment to the labs, but the alternative was to leave himself open to kidnapping or worse. He would also have to send his family away somewhere safe for a while, which would take some explaining, but it couldn't be helped. The prize was proof that his theories were correct. It could lead to a No Bell prize and he wasn't about to jeopardise that.

"Well, strictly speaking, you aren't working for the University right now …"

"I'll square that with the Bursar." 'I'll stuff his mouth with gold, so to speak,' Van Golden thought. 'Money is one thing I don't have to worry about right now.'

"Well, I can't argue with the Bursar. I'll set it all up and as soon as I get his say-so I'll let you have the access codes. In the meantime, what do I do if An Kohli comes back?"

"I'll leave that to your discretion. All I ask is that she can't get at me."

* * *

The Sunray's smaller shuttle settled onto the surface of Aragan, in a clearing in the middle of a forest. There was no way that An Kohli was going to allow them to be captured the way they had when they visited the same planet in their own universe. They would still have a short walk to the hidden entrance that would take them to the tribe's underground village.

Forewarned is forearmed, so this time both she and Den carried night vision goggles that would allow them to see what lay ahead of them in the tunnels that served the village. They also carried zappers, so that they could fight the beings that lived there, without having to kill them.

"It's still going to be almost impossible to get the egg without them seeing us. We only got it last time because Attilla had already stolen it. This time the tribe will all be at home, because we won't helping them to attack their enemies."

"One step at a time, Den." An Kohli replied as they walked down the shuttle's ramp. "First we have to find out if the egg is in the same place. This is a parallel universe, after all. Not everything is identical to our own. Who knows what differences we might find."

She led the way through the forest, using mapping information transmitted from the Sunray to show their location relative to their objective. While the going was difficult, it wasn't the sort of rain forest they had encountered elsewhere. It was possible to pick a path through the trees so long as they were prepared to climb over fallen trunks, duck under branches and make detours around clumps of thicker vegetation. However, the going was slower than she had anticipated and she soon realised that they might have to stay on the planet overnight.

The sun was starting to set when they found themselves on the path that they recalled from their earlier visit. The last time they had been on it was on their return from the village that they had attacked, forced to do so by their captors who seemed to have some sort of vendetta going.

An Kohli's communicator told them that they needed to turn left, so they did. The way ahead was partially hidden by a curve in the path, so they almost stumbled into a party of natives walking towards them.

Den's senses kicked in first and he grabbed An Kohli by the arm and pulled her off the path and into the trees. As the figures appeared ahead of them, they crouched down in a thick patch of broad leaved plants that took advantage of the increased light levels closer to the path.

The natives were carrying spears and had bows slung over their back. They moved forward in silence. An Kohli counted six.

"Scouting party?" Den whispered.

"Maybe. Or hunters perhaps." They continued to watch as the party passed by barely two met away, eventually vanishing around the curve in the path.

An Kohli stood up, stretching her legs, which had started to ache with the crouching. "We'll need to take extra care. We don't know how far they're going. They may be away for hours, or they may be back in minutes."

"We don't even know if they're from the same tribe. They could be from the other tribe, the one we attacked last time. Maybe they're a reconnaissance group, gathering information ahead of an attack."

An Kohli considered this for a few moments. History was different here. In their own Universe it had been a couple of years earlier that they had landed here, causing one group of natives to attack another group. At that time, she had thought that the tribe that had captured her and Den might be hiding from the other tribe, that they lived in fear of them. Their arrival, with their pulsars, had changed the balance of power, allowing the tribe to attack. In this Universe that hadn't, so far as they knew, happened. Two years later, who knew what else had happened in the meantime.

It wasn't possible to speculate on the state of relations between the tribe they were trying to rob and their neighbours, who may or may not still be enemies. It also wasn't possible to identify the group of natives that had just passed by. Neither side were friendly anyway.

"OK. Point taken, but we carry on. Whoever they are, they will be hostile to us just because we're unknown."

She pushed her way through the vegetation and back onto the path.

"You know, I can't shake off the feeling that we're being watched." Den said after they had walked for a few minutes.

That was something that An Kohli couldn't ignore. Den seemed to have a heightened awareness of danger, almost a seventh sense.*

"How sure are you?"

"Pretty sure."

An Kohli placed her hand on the butt of her pulsar and scanned the edges of the forest. She could see nothing. She placed her hand on Den's arm, bringing him to a stop. The dying of their footsteps allowed them to hear other sounds. The birds called in the tree tops, readying themselves for roosting. Something snuffled in the undergrowth not far from them, but it was a natural sound; not something to alarm them. A puff of wind caught the tree tops, causing them to rustle, drowning out other noises. But if they were being watched, it was by something that they could neither see nor hear.

She cast a questioning look in Den's direction, but all he could do was shrug. An Kohli pulled out her pulsar, but walked on, taking care not to make too much noise herself. Den followed, pulsar in hand, turning occasionally to look back down the path to make sure they weren't being followed.

They reached the point on the path where the forest opened out to give a clear view across the valley to the right of them. This was it, the place where the concealed entrance to the tunnel should be. An Kohli peered through the thicker vegetation, trying to identify the camouflaged frame that hid the way in. She noticed a few dying leaves and stepped towards them. That was the giveaway.

Pushing her hand in, she found the latticework and gave a heave, pulling it towards her. Den leant a hand and they soon had an opening large enough for them to squeeze through. They pulled the framework closed behind them, worried that any unseen watchers might follow them in. The darkness wasn't total, but it was deep enough to prevent them seeing where they were going. An Kohli fished around in her back pack for her night vision glasses and slipped them over her head. At once the way ahead was clear, showing up as shades of grey as the minimal light was magnified several hundred times to reach a point where her retinae could distinguish features.

Still with their pulsars in their hands, they crept forward. The slightest sound would seem loud in the tunnels and would echo along the sides to alert any villagers close enough to the end of the tunnel to hear. In this environment hearing was the most valued sense, not sight.

Working from memory, An Kohli knew that this tunnel wasn't very long; perhaps no more than five hundred met, but it still took them several minutes to creep along it. A turn in the path revealed light ahead of them, as well as sounds. The high-pitched voices of younglings reached them first, as they squealed and shouted as they played. Then they picked out the deeper notes of adults. There were no sounds of alarm, however.

The smell of cooking food drifted towards them, making An Kohli's mouth water. Her stomach grumbled, reminding her that it was several hours since she had last eaten. She had some dried rations in her back pack, but this wasn't the time nor the place to eat them.

An Kohli stopped, hugging the wall, but signalled Den to go forward to do a reconnaissance. For their plan to work he had to be able to adopt the right shape and appearance, which meant seeing the beings that he was to impersonate. He returned a few minutes later.

"About a hundred of them." He whispered into An Kohli's ear. That was about the number they had expected. "They seem to be having their evening meal. I'm guessing they'll settle down to sleep soon after."

"The egg?"

"No guards, but there is a family close by."

"OK, we'll go back to the entrance. There's less chance of us being discovered by accident.

They spent an uncomfortable few hours hunched on the ground just inside the tunnel entrance, before An Kohli judged it to be late enough for them to attempt an approach to the underground village.

This time An Kohli also crept to the very perimeter of the large open space occupied by the native tribe.

The torches had burned low, leaving deep pools of shadow. There didn't seem to be any sort of guard. That was very lax of them, An Kohli thought. While the tunnel entrance was well concealed, it was still possible for someone to discover it by accident. But that wasn't her problem.

Behind her, Den clambered out of his clothing, replacing it with a simple loin cloth, fashioned from an old towel taken from the Sunray. It wouldn't stand up under close scrutiny, but it wasn't intended to. It was similar enough to the native's scant clothing to pass muster from a couple of met away, which was as close as Den intended getting to any of the sleeping figures.

The cave was by no means silent. The sounds of people sleeping could be heard bouncing off the walls and the high ceiling. Children whimpered, adults snored, there was the occasional muttered word. Also heard were the sounds of muted passion as a member of the next generation of the tribe was conceived. But, even with all that, Den was going to have to be very silent indeed as he approached the niche in which the Magus egg was housed.

He looked towards An Kohli, who gave him a nod to proceed. In one hand he held an unprogrammed egg, identical to the one he was about to steal. That served two purposes. If the villagers saw an egg in its correct place they would have no suspicion that the real one had been stolen and therefore no reason to give chase.

The second reason was that it would thwart the An Kohli in this parallel universe, who would be handing over a fake egg to Tiny Blur as well as to the GCIE. The real egg would be sent anonymously to the Guild of Bounty Hunters with a request to forward it to the authorities. They could do with it as they saw fit, but it might cause some confusion when the other An Kohli turned up with the egg from this hiding place which, in turn, might cast some suspicion on her. At least it might cause the GCIE in this universe to examine the eggs that they had more closely.

Den stepped out into the cave, keeping as much to the shadows as he could. But in the shadows danger also lurked, as that was where the families had chosen for their sleeping areas.

The minimal light allowed Den to select a path through the sleeping figures, placing one foot carefully on the ground, testing it to see that it wouldn't inadvertently move a stone or other small piece of debris, before transferring his weight and moving his other foot.

An Kohli turned, suddenly alert to a new danger, and looked back down the tunnel towards its entrance, five hundred met behind her. Was she just spooked, or had she really just heard the sound of a footstep? She strained her ears to listen for the sound again, but there was nothing.

She turned back just in time to see Den slip into the small area where the egg was housed. The opening was barely his height and he had to crouch to avoid hitting his head. For a few seconds he was silhouetted by the flames of the torches inside the niche, kept burning brighter in reverence for the item that had been dug up after being buried by Su Mali so long ago. Su Mali, who had come from above and must therefore be some sort of God. A God who had left them a gift and who would one day return to collect it. And when she did she would lead the tribe to victory over their enemies. Well, that was how An Kohli had interpreted their actions when they had visited the same planet in their own universe.

She started again, turning and pointing her pulsar back along the tunnel. She was more sure this time. It had sounded like the slap of a bare foot against smooth rock. She was sure there was at least one being in the tunnel behind her. Some being that would be blocking their exit route.

She pulled her night vision googles down over her eyes and switched them on. The tunnel appeared in shades of grey, just as before. It seemed to be empty, but ... but was that the reflection of light off of an eye?

It was just the tiniest sparkle in the darkness, it wouldn't have been visible at all without the goggles to amplify it. It disappeared for an instant and then re-appeared. Something had blinked. Now, was it an animal or was it an armed enemy? If it was an animal, the height above ground level suggested that it was a very big one. It was far more likely to be something that walked upright, on two legs.

So, Den had been right. They had been being watched and then they had been followed. They had led the enemy to the place where they could attack *their* enemies as they slept.

She gulped, throwing a look back over her shoulder towards Den. He was halfway back across the cave, the real egg now held in his hand; at least she assumed it was the real egg. He was also, An Kohli noticed, unarmed. A pulsar would have given away the fact that he wasn't a member of the tribe, so he had left it behind. If he was spotted and challenged, he would have to rely on his speed and covering fire from An Kohli, to get him back inside the tunnel.

Turning back to watch the tunnel once again An Kohli's mouth dropped open. There was no doubt now. The tunnel was filled from one wall to the other with figures. They stepped carefully forward, their spears thrust out ahead of them. Without the advantage of An Kohli's goggles they were having to take care not to make any noise in case they alerted the villagers and gave them time to wake and organise a defence. In a few more paces they would be able to erupt from the mouth of the tunnel, taking their prey by surprise and inflicting death with those spears.

Could they see her? It was unlikely, there wasn't enough light. On the other hand she was backlit by the flickering torches mounted around the cave walls, so maybe they could see her. Could they hear her? In her ears her heart pounded loud enough to drown out other sounds, but it was very unlikely that they could also hear that. Her imagination was working overtime.

Patting her hand around on the ground An Kohli found Den's clothes, his pulsar lying on top of them. She picked up the weapon and edged backwards, away from the attackers and towards the cave.

The figures in the tunnel stopped dead. Her movement had been detected, possibly as the light behind her betrayed her presence.

What to do? If she fired, the whip crack of the pulsar would waken the village, giving them an enemy in front and another in the tunnel. If she didn't fire, the attackers would overcome their caution and move forward to take the village by surprise once more. They would be no better off, caught between two sides.

But a pulsar was a fearsome weapon to someone who had never seen one before. Its very presence might scare the attackers off. But then what? With the villagers roused they would have to run for it and the only direction they could take was to follow the beings that were intent on killing in the first place. Beings that would eventually stop running and look round to see if they were being followed, at which point they would see her and Den.

Too much to think about right now, she told herself. First get out of the tunnel and try to find some cover. Perhaps they could hide and just wait for the attackers to finish what they had come to do. Could she do that? Could she hide and watch as the villagers were slaughtered?

Another question there was no time to answer right then. She could feel that the tunnel walls were no longer close to her and An Kohli realised she was now actually in the cave. She slid to one side, no longer forming a silhouette in the tunnel's mouth. Looking over her shoulder she could see Den watching her, a puzzled look on his face.

She used her fingers to indicate beings walking, then pointed to the tunnel. Den nodded his understanding. She held up her hands, bunching and opening her fist several times to indicate numbers. A worried look crossed Den's face as the total got to twenty.

That was an underestimate, An Kohli knew. She had only been able to make out the front ranks of the attackers. She had no idea how many more there might be following behind.

Den changed course and slid against the cave wall beside her. She passed him his pulsar.

"You could have brought my clothes as well." He hissed in her ear.

"You're lucky to have that. If you want your clothes, you go and get them." She hissed back. "Have you seen anywhere we can hide?"

"Only the niche where the egg was."

"Too far. We'd never get there. They must only be about twenty met away by now."

"What about the place they kept us last time?"

Of course. While they had been prisoners of this tribe they had been kept in a small side cave, more of a hollow cut into the wall. It hadn't been far from where they were now crouching.

An Kohli scanned the wall of the cave until she spotted it, about ten met away. In front of it a family lay sleeping, unaware of the danger they were in. There were two adults, spooned together under some sort of covering and three younglings of various ages.

An Kohli nodded towards it and they edged backwards, clinging to the wall so as to make the best use of the shadows. Den kept a watchful eye on the family, willing them not to wake up, then they were inside the hollow.

A figure sat up, crying out in alarm. Damn, the hollow, once their prison cell, was now being used as a bedroom.

The figure was wizened, an old female. Seeing the strangers, one dressed in clothing of a type never seen before, the female screamed again. At once the village was roused. Males jumped up, grabbing at spears and bows. Females gathered younglings to them, protecting them as best they could.

Realising that the element of surprise was lost, the attackers burst into the cave, running towards the nearest figures, their spears held ahead of them ready to puncture flesh.

Confusing the cause of the scream with the appearance of the attackers, the village males rushed forward to counter the threat. The old female jumped up, surprisingly nimble for one of her age, and ran out of the hollow, screaming and waving her arms in panic. No one paid her any attention, because now she wasn't the only panicked figure in the cave. Mothers hurried to take their younglings to safety, getting behind their warriors and heading for the other tunnel, the very long one by which An Kohli and Den had been brought into the village on their previous visit.

An Kohli took a cautious peep out from their hiding place. She had been right about underestimating the strength of the attacking force. There were at least sixty of them, outnumbering the male defenders by a generous margin. The opposing forces were now strung out across the cave in single rank long ranks that faced each other. Bolder figures would step forward and stab at their enemies but the forays were easy to deflect, so the attackers had to step back into the safety of the line once again before they became isolated.

The two lines shrieked insults at each other, brandishing their weapons and jumping up and down. Whether they were challenging their enemies to fight or telling them to run away it wasn't clear. The tension mounted, who would be the first to break, or to overcome their fear of death?

Something streaked across An Kohli's eyeline. A warrior from the attacking side fell back, an arrow projecting from his chest. She searched for the source. Shadows moved, higher up the cavern wall. She made out a figure, a female, drawing a bow and loosing another arrow. She wasn't alone, other shadows moved to gain positions on a narrow ledge, from where they could shoot their arrows over the heads of their male folk.

It decided the issue of who would attack whom. The attackers from the tunnel charged forward into the villagers, thrusting their spears. It was single combat, male on male and with the attackers having the greater numbers they were bound to win in the end. With combat joined, the archers were no longer able to fire, for fear of hitting their own side.

Four of the attackers broke away from the distant flank and started to climb the rough walls of the cave. The females rained arrows down on them and one climber fell to the ground, dead. The others continued to climb, however and in their panic the women just wasted their arrows. An attacker grabbed the ankle of a female and gave a heave, pulling her off of the ledge and casting her down to fall at the base of the wall. She was injured, but still managed to get to her feet. Limping, she tried to run, but two more warriors broke from the end of the line and stabbed her to death with their spears.

Seeing the danger, the remaining women backed along the ledge, giving the attackers free rein to continue climbing.

"We're going to have to do something." An Kohli said, having to raise her voice to make herself heard above the noise of war cries, the clash of weapons and screams of pain.

"They aren't our problem, An Kohli." Den shouted back. "If we intervene we'll attract attention to ourselves. It could get us killed."

An Kohli's Menafield would be good for about twenty shots, she knew, before it would need recharging. Den's smaller weapon would probably be good for another fifteen. It would be enough to tip the balance in favour of the defenders. But why should she help one side against the other?

There was no right or wrong here. It was just another battle in a tribal war that had probably been fought for centuries. There was no *right* side to back, or if there was she had no way of knowing which it was. If they helped the villagers her decision would be made on the dubious moral basis that they had just stolen a Magus egg from the defending side, an egg that they had stolen from Su Mali who, in turn, had bought it from someone who had stolen it from a space ship attacked by pirates. Her possession of the egg was morally justifiable, but that conferred no morality on the villagers who were now under attack. For all she knew, they had previously been the aggressors and the attackers were just there to take some revenge for previous killings.

Den could see her wrestling with the problem. He took a more simplistic view. "If we don't get out if here, it's only a matter of time before we're discovered. If the villagers win, that old female's going to come back and tell her story. If the attackers win, they're going to search the whole cave looking for anything they can take away with them, whether it be women or cooking pots."

This didn't help An Kohli in any way. If they broke cover, there was a real chance they would be seen. Someone, attacker or defender, might come after them and they'd be forced to fight anyway.

The decision was taken out of her hands. From the tunnel mouth came some new arrivals. Six of them. It must be the party they had seen the previous day, An Kohli realised, the ones that had forced them to take cover in the deep undergrowth. But whose side were they on?

That question was soon answered. They started to stab at the rearmost attackers, meaning that they were trapped between two forces. It also evened up the numbers, though not by much.

"This is our chance." Den didn't wait for An Kohli to agree. He just grabbed her arm and pulled her out of the hollow. In a crouching run they headed for the tunnel. They had just reached its dubious safety when a spear clattered against the wall. They had been seen, but did it mean they would now be pursued?

No time to stop and think about that. As they rushed past his clothes, Den grabbed what he could, then went into a full-scale sprint. An Kohli stretched her stride to keep up, but it was difficult. Den, in flight mode, seemed to find extra speed.

With An Kohli's night vision goggles to guide them they made it to the end of the tunnel very quickly. The latticework frame was pushed back, so it didn't slow them down at all. They turned right to exit the tunnel. An Kohli winced with pain as her goggles flooded with light. Dawn had broken while they had been inside. She pulled them from her head with her free hand and ran on.

Casting a look backwards she saw that they weren't being followed. At least, not yet, the dark of the tunnel would slow any pursuers, then the bend in the path hid her rearward view.

"No stopping for anything." She called at Den's back.

"No need to tell me." Den threw over his shoulder.

They ran for ten minutes, then their breath gave out on them. They stood, bent double and heaving to get air into their lungs.

"Remind me again whose idea it was to come here." Den gasped.

"This time it was all down to you." An Kohli reminded him

"Oh shit, so it was."

"Hey, we had nothing else going on at the time. It seemed like a good idea."

That didn't mollify Den. "Who do you think those other six were, that came in at the end?"

"The ones we saw yesterday. Maybe a hunting party, maybe scouts going to take a look at what the enemy were up to. I think we walked through an ambush intended for them; that was what spooked you. Then the ambushers followed us to see who we were and where we were going. We led them to that village."

"Not our war, An Kohli." He reminded her. "Where are we, anyway?" he asked, between sucking in gulps of air.

An Kohli checked the map on her communicator as Den started to pull his clothes on.

"Damn, I've left a boot behind." He complained.

"Lucky you aren't lying there with it." An Kohli retorted. "We're about a thousand met from the shuttle. We stay on the path for about another five hundred met, then cut off through the trees. Shouldn't take us more than half an hour."

They started jogging along the path, eating up the distance with ease.

\* The ability of Gau to sense the presence of other Gau other counts as their sixth sense.

## Glossary

Menafield - The Menafield Arms Corporation (part of the Gargantua Enterprises Corporation) produces a wide range of pulsar and projectile weapons for military, business and family use. The Menafield Pulsar, as used by An Kohli, is reputed to be the most powerful hand held weapon in the galaxy and can punch a hole through ¼ inch steel plate.

Zapper - A small device used by law enforcement officers to pacify beings who might try to resist arrest. The device administers a high voltage electrical charge which disables the victim for long enough for the officer to apply restraints. Most bounty hunters don't bother using them.

# 10 - A Visit To Barnard's Star

Despite Professor Van Golden's warning that it might be dangerous to do so, An Kohli decided that she wanted to check up on progress with the device she hoped would allow her to get back to her own universe. Over the galacticnet the Professor was being vague and, in An Kohli's opinion, evasive.

The journey from Aragan to Zygor took just over a week. As they exited the wormhole the local galacticnet node registered their presence and started to feed news bulletins to the Sunray.

"I don't know why Gala spends so much time watching this stuff." Den grumped as it appeared on a viewing screen. "There's never anything but doom and gloom on the news."

"She likes to keep herself informed." An Kohli defended her friend. "It wouldn't do you any harm to take more of an interest."

Den was unimpressed. "See what I mean, look at this. Every channel is showing the same report of a fire. How many different ways can they say 'just look at this huge fire'?"

An Kohli looked up at the screen to see it filled with a shot of the conflagration taken from above, probably from a camera mounted in a drone. She was just about to look away again when she realised that the burning building looked familiar. "Where is that Den?" she asked as she reached for the volume control to turn the sound level up.

"I don't know. Why, do you recognise it?"

"I'm pretty sure that's the university." She said.

Her fears were confirmed as the voice of the news anchor became audible. "... today when pirates attacked the university, causing the fire to break out."

The image switched to shaky camera footage of a craft descending towards the roof of the high energy physics building. It was of a type that An Kohli had seen before, when it had attacked the clones on the planet that was now called Hope (*see Cloning*

*Around*). The occasional erratic movement of the camera indicated that it was amateur video taken on a personal communicator.

The large beetle shaped craft fired its pulsars, ripping open the roof of the building. The ramp was lowered and figures were seen running down it to exploit the opening.

"Talk about using a sledge hammer to crack a nut." Den observed.

"I don't think subtlety has ever been a pirate thing." An Kohli replied. The images on screen returned to coverage of the fire.

"What the pirates wanted …" The anchor continued, "isn't yet clear. All of the physicists working inside the building, except for one, have been accounted for. In a statement put out by the Vice Chancellor of the university, he said that the research being carried out inside the High Energy Building was only theoretical and, as yet, had no practical applications."

"He probably doesn't know about the work Van Golden was doing for us, though." An Kohli said.

"You think the missing scientist might be Van Golden?" Den asked.

"I'd stake your life on it." An Kohli answered grimly. "When we called him from Aragan he told us he'd had to move back here."

"Are we going down to take a look?"

"Not me. If the other An Kohli is down there and sees me, there'll be trouble. No, you disguise yourself and sniff around for me. By the look of things, that fire isn't going to burn out any time soon, so there will be plenty of rubber-neckers around that you can hide amongst.

\* \* \*

The disguise of a Zygorian wasn't one that Den felt comfortable in. They had very long legs, but short bodies which mean that none of his clothes fitted properly. His trouser cuffs were up by his knees while his shirt hung down to the same level. After some bickering with An Kohli he decided to go as a Prinkosian instead. They were from a neighbouring star system and many of them worked on Zygor.

It was a good choice, he decided, as he forced his way between a knot of Prinkosians to reach the crush barrier that the police had set up to keep people back out of danger from the fire.

There were dozens of fire appliances present, operated mainly by droids, but under sentient direction from beings who stayed safely within the vehicles. Why the fire was so big and was taking so long to extinguish, Den had no idea. Being a building where experiments were being carried out probably had something to do with it. Who knew what the scientists had been keeping in their laboratories.

He made to squeeze through the gap between two barriers but he found his way barred by a large hand placed squarely on the middle of his chest.

"You can't come in 'ere, Sir." Den followed the hand to where it joined an arm and then followed that until he found it was attached to a broad shoulder above which a head seemed to be attached directly to the body, without benefit of a neck.

"Er, I work here." Den protested. "I need to …"

"Don't matter, Sir. For your own protection you aren't allowed in." The meaty hand gave Den a gentle shove backwards and it was only the press of bodies that prevented him from falling.

Undeterred, Den moved further along the line of barriers, heading for one of the large fire trucks. He smiled as he saw how the security guards had been a little lazier here. They had decided that the truck itself represented a barrier, the line of barriers stopped where it met one side of the fire truck and didn't start again until the other side.

Den dropped onto his belly and wriggled under the truck, which had a high clearance to enable it to traverse rough ground. His ears were pounded by the noise of the pumps propelling fire suppression fluid along the snaking lines of hoses and up to the droids working at the tops of the ladders. A few seconds later he emerged at the front of the vehicle, just below the driving position.

A few met in front of him, sweating in the heat, stood a lone figure, its face twisted in anguish as he watched the building burn.

The cheap suit told him that the being was a minor functionary, not senior management. But if he was inside the security perimeter it meant he must be important in terms of his work, if not his status. Besides, there didn't seem to be anyone else Den could talk to.

A hover car pulled up near the line of security barriers, red, amber and green lights flashing on its roof. A bulky figure climbed out and hurried towards a box like vehicle that might be some sort of command post.

Den could spot a copper at a thousand li and that being had been a copper, he knew. He wasn't wearing a uniform jacket, but the stripe down the side of the being's trouser leg said he was wearing a uniform.

Den sidled up to the car, still bobbing on its anti-grav cushion. Sure enough, there on the passenger seat sat a jacket with plenty of gold badges attached, on top of which was a cap, its peak encrusted with braid. Den leaned in and grabbed the two items.

If you're going to pretend to be a senior police officer, you have to also pretend to be an arrogant prick, Den told himself. He marched straight up to the anguished figure and spoke loudly.

"You're not supposed to be here, Sir. Far too dangerous." He barked.

The being turned and showed Den the badge pinned to his chest. "Janus Jones." He announced. "I'm the Security Officer here."

"Oh, right. So it was your job to make sure this didn't happen, right?" It would do no harm to put Jones on the defensive.

"I'm supposed to stop petty criminals from getting in and stealing the lab equipment and the sandwiches in the canteen. There's nothing in my job description about repelling pirate attacks." Jones snapped back. He was clearly a man under severe pressure.

"Well, someone should have been, quite clearly." Den rubbed salt into the wound. "Have all the staff been accounted for?"

"All except for Professor Van Golden. He was using one of the labs for a project of his own. It was all above board. The Bursar had agreed a proper rent and everything."

"I'm not suggesting that the Professor was up to anything untoward, Sir. I'm sure that the University was managed quite ethically, even if it wasn't that secure. Did they get away with any equipment?"

The Security Officer turned to give Jones a quizzical look. "I've told one of your officers all that." He said.

"But my officers haven't told me and I haven't got time to go scouring this campus looking for the one that you spoke to. On the other hand, you are here and you can answer my questions. Or maybe things aren't quite what they seem and you need to come down to the station to answer them instead."

Jones went pale. "No, that's not a problem, officer."

"It's Colonel, actually." Den improvised. All that gold had to count for something, he considered.

"OK, Colonel. Look, I don't know what equipment they might have got out with. The fire started not long after they broke in. I'm guessing the pulsars on their craft were pretty powerful and hit something flammable. They had to get out quite quickly. As the staff were coming out of the fire exits on the ground floor, they were leaving through the roof. I've seen some of the camera footage and none of them seem to be carrying anything though, except for their weapons."

"Is it possible they kidnapped Professor Van Golden?"

"Quite possible. I didn't count bodies, so I don't know how many arrived and how many left."

"OK, Sir. We can check the footage ourselves and see what we make of it."

At that moment a wall collapsed, sending up a shower of sparks and a blast of heat hit them. "I think we better move a little further back, Jones." Den said, retreating towards the police hover car. Jones ignored him and just stood staring at the flames, like a man in a dream.

Den replaced the jacket and cap in the police car and left the scene the same way he had entered.

Thirty minutes later he was back on board the Sunray.

\* \* \*

When it came to puzzling things out, An Kohli had always preferred to have Gala to bounce her ideas off. Gala had an engineers' ability to see the essentials of a problem, sweeping away the dross of speculation and theorising, and winkling out the hard evidence on which action could be based. But this time An Kohli was relying on Den Gau, which was like relying on quicksand to support the weight of an elephant.

"I think we can assume that An Kohli is behind this. It wouldn't take long to Moogle the Professor's name and discover his main field of research. That tells her where we've come from and what we were doing hanging around Zygor."

"But what can she hope to do with him?" Den slurred, half way down his third glass of An Kohli's Grovian, the reward he had claimed for getting his scalp singed. "Surely, her best bet is to let him finish his work and send us on our way."

"I would agree with you, if it wasn't for the fact that she's in bed with Tiny Blur. Quite literally in bed with him, so far as we can see."

"But what good is the device to him? In our universe he uses it to get rid of An Kohli, but here, he wants An Kohli next to him."

"Yes, and that's why he wants it. A being like Blur has many enemies. What better way of getting rid of them than sending them into a parallel universe where they can't do him any harm. It leaves no bodies, no blood stains and, if he does it right, no suspicion. In our universe, I've got rid of the Fell by putting them onto a planet, from where they can't escape. This is his equivalent, but with far less risk of them ever being found."

"But what about all that business with too much matter, or too little matter?"

"Well, first we have to assume that he knows or even cares about any of that, but assuming he does, it's not too hard to get something back from the parallel universe to balance things out. You put one hundred and twenty ziku of being in and you take the same amount of space dust out. It can't be the that hard. Neither is getting rid of his enemy. You invite them somewhere, telling them to keep quiet about it, they walk through a door and instead of meeting Tiny Blur, they find themselves in an empty room with no way back. It's pretty much what they did to us."

"OK, so Tiny Blur wants this device to get rid of his own enemies. But knowing that doesn't help us at all."

"Yes it does, because it tells us where An Kohli took the Professor after the pirates snatched him. He must be at Barnard's Star. Which is why we have to go there."

"You can't be serious. That would be walking up to a tigger and putting your head in its mouth."

"Well, if we don't do that, we're stuck here forever. It's either that or go and find a deserted planet to live on, because the An Kohli in this universe isn't going to be too happy about having competition."

* * *

An Kohli snuggled up to Tiny Blur, a drip of sweat falling from her nose onto his chest hair. "Whoo, that was good." She murmured, her tone of voice suggesting that it was anything but good.

Blur didn't reply.

"You seem distracted." An Kohli said. "Even just now, when we were … you didn't seem to be paying that much attention." The dissatisfied feelings in her loins made her sound more critical than Blur was used to.

"It's Van Golden. He's not talking."

"Have you tried all the usual …" An Kohli had always detested torture until she met Blur, but close contact with him over several years had anesthetised her feelings to some extent.

"Of course, but nothing will budge him. I've done things to him that would make a Jackon break down and cry for its mother, but he just keeps saying that he can't tell me anything."

"I told the pirates to make sure they grabbed anything of interest from his lab, wasn't there anything of use?"

"Some random components, that was all. My science guys tell me they could be used to build anything from an electric toothbrush to a time machine. The clumsy bustards destroyed everything else."

"I should have gone myself. At least I would have had some idea of what to look for."

"You would have risked giving yourself away, which I couldn't allow. The galaxy has to believe in An Kohli the hero and she doesn't go smashing her way into university buildings and kidnapping professors."

"What is Van Golden saying? University professors aren't known for their ability to resist torture so he must have said something."

"He admits he has met an An Kohli from a parallel universe, so you were right about that. He admits he was trying to build a device to help her get back home. But he says that his copy of the plans were all on his computer back in his lab and we know that was destroyed by the fire. He says he now understands the principles on which the device was built back in An Kohli's universe but, without the schematics, it would take him years of trial and error to replicate the device. He even laughed at me, told me that he was just about ready to start testing the one he had built when those pirates broke in."

"So why didn't they find it?"

"Because they didn't know what they were looking for. It looked just like most of the other bits of equipment that were in the lab. When they grabbed him, they knocked it off the work bench and it smashed when it hit the floor. The pirates could have picked it up and it might have been repaired, but that's when the fire alarms went off. The pirates decided not to hang around investigating all the stuff that was there, they just got out."

"All that trouble we went to for nothing."

"Not for nothing, at least not totally. We have Van Golden and we will put him to work on the device, but it won't be a quick process."

"That worries you?"

"Yes, my wife is becoming more difficult by the day. She thinks she should have more power than I am willing to grant her. I think it is time for her to go on an extended holiday, but without Van Golden's device that can't be arranged. Well, there's that planet of yours, but I've kind of gone off that idea. Too much chance of someone stumbling on her by accident. And then there's my colleagues in the Fell, well they're always scheming. I'm sure that they would replace me if they could."

"We could go back to more direct methods. After all, I have rid you of several of the Fell already."

"It may come to that."

"Do you think that the other An Kohli will try to rescue Van Golden?"

"She might try. After all, she needs him even more than me."

"In that case I think we should encourage her. That will bring about a terminal solution."

"Would you, my sweet?" Blur looked relieved.

"Anything for you, my love."

"Well, be careful how you do it. She still has the original set of plans. Van Golden told me they were stored on a small PMD which she kept in her belt. If you kill her, make sure it survives the death."

"It limits my options a little, but nothing is impossible. Now, why don't I ..." she reached up and pulled his head down until she could whisper in his ear. He let out a moan of anticipation.

\* \* \*

The second planet of Barnard's Star had once been a pleasant place made up of pretty little islands organised into archipelagos that formed a necklace around the tropical zones of the planet. It had been under so many protection orders that no one was allowed to erect a dog kennel without completing a million pages of application forms, and then the answer would still be "No!". The population was unassuming, made up of primitive tribes that lived by fishing and showing the occasional tourists around. The tourists were forced by the building regulations to be day trippers. Consequently they were rare and the ones that did visit tended to have strong ecologically sound reasons for doing so. There had been no proper shuttle port, but a continual broadcast had told tourists to "Take nothing but images, leave nothing but footprints."

But that was before Tiny Blur had decided it would be the ideal place for the seat of his new government. Now the planet was one vast building site, surrounded by a swarm of supply vessels.

The first building to be completed was his own palace, naturally, followed by accommodation for the vast number of bodyguards and household staff that he employed. That was on one of the neighbouring islands. He was soon followed by the remaining Fell members, who wanted to stay close to the seat of power, and to remind Blur who was really in charge. Now the sounds of cranes and cement mixers, drills, hammers, shouting labourers and poorly maintained droids echoed across the islands, turning paradise into a passable imitation of Dante's inferno.

Plenty of tourists came to stare in awe at Blur's palace and the variety of government buildings that were under construction and the signs of their infestation were everywhere, even in the oceans. The islands that housed the palaces of the Fell were strictly off limits to all but the owners and their staff. The tribespeople had been shipped off to the smaller islands, or were employed by the occupants of the palaces. Not many of them saw it as an improvement on their previous existences. Unfortunately, the new arrivals had pulsars and grenade launchers, while the tribes had fishing rods and canoes, so there was little that the natives could do but pray to their Gods. The Gods failed to answer, but that's Gods for you.

It didn't take long for An Kohli to become bored with the images of building sites that were being beamed up to her from the miniature camera concealed in the brim of Den's sun hat. He followed the tour guide obediently, but there was nothing of value to be seen.

Looking for some sort of distraction, she scanned the local GSTC displays to see what ships were coming and going. Most were the giant freighters that carried all the building materials necessary to construct a new city and its suburbs, but there were also a couple of passenger craft, carrying tourists of the sort that Den was imitating.

Unlike the majority of star systems, this planet had an orbiting space terminal where visiting cruise liners were required to dock. The passengers then transferred down to the planet's surface using shuttles that were pre-programmed to land at one specific shuttle port. The rented ship where she was currently sitting was parked on one of the docks reserved for privately owned craft.

The only exceptions to these parking arrangements that An Kohli had seen were the freighters and the luxury craft owned by the Fell. The latter were largely over-priced space-borne gin palaces, glittering with the sort of exterior finish that only the very wealthy can afford to replace when it becomes chipped and scarred by the billions of motes of space dust and tiny meteorites that were capable of stripping the exterior within a few years of a ship's launch.

Ships such as An Kohli's Adastra had the functional hardened exterior paintwork of a working ship, but even that required replacing from time to time.

But it was the arrival of a Quasar class ship that attracted An Kohli's attention. She recognised it at once as the Sunray, the ship owned by The Grand Master of the Guild of Bounty Hunters and on loan to the An Kohli that belonged in this universe. It was identical to the one she had borrowed in every detail. An Kohli imagined that if she were on board even the wardrobes would be organised the way she and Gala organised theirs.

She felt a stab of pain cross her heart as she thought about her friend, wondering where she might be right now. Was she still a hostage, or had she been killed? It was unlikely that she had been set free.

She opened a communications channel to the surface. "Den, how much longer has that tour got to go?"

"Just the usual jewellery factory and leather goods outlet to go. I think I'll skip those. Why, do you want me to do something else?"

"Yes. The other An Kohli's just arrived. I want you to follow her and see where she goes."

"No problem. Where will she land?"

"She's docked at the passenger terminal, just like us, so I'm guessing she will be using one of the regular shuttles."

"That makes sense. According to the tour guide, they're the only shuttles that are allowed to land in the Capital area. Even then they arrive on a neighbouring island and transfer on what they call helicopters."

"What's a helicopter?"

"I'll get you an image, but you can look it up on the galacticnet. They're very primitive and very noisy. It's like travelling inside a blender."

"Like everything else from Earth. Anyway, I expect An Kohli will be on the ground in about an hour."

"If she's a guest of Blur I would expect him to send his private helicopter for her. I may not be able to follow."

"Just do your best."

* * *

It was something of a surprise when Den saw An Kohli boarding a regular helicopter, just like the handful of other tourists that had alighted from the shuttle. He mingled with them and boarded the same aircraft just a few places behind An Kohli.

Once full, the craft lurched upwards in a thunder of displaced air, its rotor blades making a thud-thud-thud sound which caused the interior to vibrate in sympathy. Den's teeth chattered and his hearing gave up trying to filter out the blast of sound so he could pay attention to the safety briefing. For the third time that day he failed to hear what he should do in the unlikely event of the helicopter landing on water.

He tried to avoid looking at the back of An Kohli's head. In their disguised state Gau were forced to reveal their true identity, if stared at for more than ten seconds. It was assumed that it was some sort of penalty imposed by evolution to prevent them from deceiving beings. Not that it worked. In most civilisations it was considered rude to stare, especially for as long as ten seconds. But knowledge that beings sometimes reacted to being stared at kept Den's eyes away from the An Kohli that was sitting two rows in front of him.

The helicopter landed with a thump and the engines whined down as power was reduced, allowing the travellers to rub at their numbed ears to try to restore some semblance of hearing. The passengers undid their seatbelts, stood up and ambled along the aisle to the ramp that was being lowered at the rear, which allowed them to disembark.

Den waited until An Kohli had passed him, allowed another couple of beings to go in front of him, then rose and followed the crowd.

The crowd all headed for the one place, the meeting point for the guided tours, but not An Kohli. She took a different direction, one heading towards the Presidential Palace, just visible through the forest of crane towers.

Bereft of his cover, Den had to resort to hurrying between stacks of building materials and machinery, using what cover he could to avoid An Kohli noticing him. Although in disguise, it wouldn't take more than two sightings of him for An Kohli to realise she was being followed.

Perhaps she felt safe on this planet, so close to the person who protected her, but An Kohli didn't use any counter surveillance techniques. Not once did she look behind her, making it easier for Den to keep up, though he did do his best to stay in what meagre cover he could find. He was taken a bit by surprise when she diverted from her expected course. Instead of heading towards the small, well guarded gate where visitors entered and departed the Palace, An Kohli veered away, across the open square where the tourists gathered to capture their images, heading towards one of the neighbouring building sites.

"Where's she going?" An Kohli asked from her observation point, high above the planet.

"There's only one finished building in that direction." Den replied, ducking behind a mechanical digger parked at the roadside.

"It's the gatehouse for a new building. It doesn't appear to be occupied."

"Is there anywhere you can watch without being seen?"

"No. It's so open here that I feel like a pimple on the end of a nose."

"A charming description. Look, is there anywhere you can leave your hat, so it's covering the gatehouse?"

"I can leave it where I am, on this digger. It might look a bit odd if someone comes along, but the worst that can happen is they'll steal it."

"We'll take that risk. You position the hat and then get yourself back up here."

An Kohli knew that the battery powering the camera, with its in-built transmitter, was good for another dozen or so hours if no one disturbed it. She helped Den to position it so that the gatehouse was in view.

\* \* \*

"I was followed here." An Kohli said as she slid back up the bed from under the sheets.

"Did you recognise who it was?"

"No, but if it was a Gau then I wouldn't recognise them unless they were stupid enough to choose a form with which I was familiar. I spotted him as we I left the shuttle port. He was the only one, apart from me, that didn't head for the tour guides' meeting point. He wasn't nearly as good at surveillance as he thought he was."

"Was it the Den Gau from the other universe, do you think?"

"Most likely. I think the bait has been taken. Now all I have to do is reel in my fish."

\* \* \*

The image played on for about six hours, showing no more than a few builders' droids moving to and from the building site, passing the gatehouse without pausing. Then An Kohli appeared in shot. She seemed to emerge from the gatehouse, though she might have approached it from behind, at an angle that kept her hidden.

"Who is that with her?" An Kohli asked.

"I have no idea. She was alone when she went in there. Whoever he is, she's keeping a tight grip on his arm."

It was true that An Kohli seemed to be guiding her companion, holding his arm and steering him past obstructions.

"Damn that fixed lens camera. I can't get a close-up."

"It looks like the Professor to me." Den peered at the image, his eyes screwed up as though that might help in the identification.

"Could be, but … He's the right height and build, but his face is covered by something. I can't see what she would want in that gatehouse." An Kohli said, almost to herself.

"Maybe she didn't go into it. Maybe wherever she was going is behind it."

"But what? There's nothing there except a half-finished office block."

"Maybe there's another way in to the palace, one we can't see. Or maybe that isn't a gatehouse. Maybe it's a small prison."

An Kohli wished that she had a surveillance camera, like the ones on board both the Sunray and the Adastra. They would have allowed her to observe An Kohli's movements better than Den could ever have hoped to do. But the little rented craft came without any helpful extras such as that.

They watched as An Kohli and her companion walked past the hat lying on the fender of the machine, disappearing from view. Even close up it hadn't been possible to identify the male that had been with her.

"Did you notice the way he seemed to stumble, as though he wasn't too sure where he was walking?" Den asked.

"I did. Whatever is covering his face seems to be restricting his vision. And the way she was holding him, as though she expected him to make a run for it at any moment."

"Yes, like he was a prisoner. But his hands weren't shackled."

"No, but he may have been drugged to keep him compliant. Shackles attract attention and she's taking him to a public shuttle port."

An Kohli chewed at the inside of her cheek for a moment. "OK. Let's see how the facts fit. Either she or the pirates took the Professor to Tiny Blur and he was questioned, possibly threatened with torture even if he wasn't actually tortured. They've got what they want from him, or at least as much as they're going to get, so now, why would they take him somewhere else?"

"Because he's a scientist and if they want him to work on the device for opening up parallel universes, then he's going to need access to a proper lab, which they don't have in Blur's palace."

"That's good, Den. Well done. Yes, that fits."

"So the question now, is where are they going?"

"Well we have just as much a need for the professor's services as Tiny Blur, so I have a feeling that we're going to have to try and track them down once they leave here."

Forty minutes later GSTC reported that the Sunray had left orbit, destination unknown.

## Glossary

Tigger - A large stripey animal normally found in zoos but occasionally kept as guard animals. Once prevalent in the wild but now almost extinct.

# 11 - The Death Of An Kohli

"You seem to be pretty sure that they've come here to Xantos." Den observed as the ship entered orbit around the planet, the twin of Zygor.

"It's logical. There are other universities where they might have gone, but Xantos is the only one that could possibly rival Zygor in terms of its facilities. If I wanted the professor to get the fastest results, now that Zygor has lost its best laboratories, this is where I would come."

They drifted into orbit. "Computer, search GSTC records for traces of the other Sunray."

The answer wasn't long in coming. "The Sunray is in orbit on the other side of the planet." The computer pronounced.

"That's going to confuse the heck out of GSTC, having two ships in orbit with the same ID." Den sniggered, always happiest when bureaucracy was being disrupted.

"The question is, is An Kohli down on the planet, or is she in her ship?"

"Down on the planet."

"You sound pretty sure Den."

"She can't risk the Professor doing a runner first chance he gets. She'll sit in the corner of his lab and keep an eye on him."

"No, she can't do that. She has other fish to fry. According to the galacticnet, the Magi are about to be restored. The Guild will want her to be there when it happens. In fact the GCIE may even need her to confirm the provenance of the eggs. There will be accusations from the doubters that the GCIE may try to substitute fakes."

"It makes no difference, does it?" Den challenged her. "We know she's been passing the eggs to Tiny Blur."

"No, we only suspect that she has. But she can't stay away if the Guild want her to be present. It would prompt too many awkward questions. She'll have to go. If the eggs turn out to be fake, then she'll have to talk her way out of it. I dare say that she and Blur have already concocted a story that it's the GCIE's fault."

"So how do they prevent the Professor from escaping?"

"Hired muscle. He'll be escorted to the lab each day and then escorted back to wherever he's staying. An Kohli will check in from time to time to see if he's making progress. That's probably why she hasn't left yet, she's making sure that professor is properly motivated. Without the plans it's going to take him a long time to recreate the device."

"Has he any chance of success?"

"I don't know. We know he had done all the maths to prove the concept and we also know that he has some understanding of how the device works in practice. The rest is down to his ability to move from first principles to practical application."

"And what's your plan?"

"We walk in the front door, find the professor, deal with his guards and then walk out again."

"As simple as that!"

"Yup."

\* \* \*

The reception droid refused them access to the campus of the University of Xantos on the not unreasonable grounds that, according to all its logs, An Kohli was already inside the campus. Despite all her best efforts, and her fingerprint, retina and DNA scans, the droid's logic circuits couldn't be defeated. An Kohli had to fall back on the methods used by all beings when confronted with unbending bureaucracy.

"Can I speak to your supervisor, please?" she said through gritted teeth.

The droid did a passable imitation of a being taking umbrage over its competence being questioned, but it had no alternative but to summon its supervisor.

"Hello." Said a harassed looking being dressed in a shabby suit. "I'm Jonas Janes, and I'm Head of Security here. How can I be of assistance?"

"You look just like …" Den started to say.

"I look nothing like him!" snapped Janes, anticipating Den's comparison with another Head of Security at another university.

An Kohli felt it was time to remind them both that she was present. "We're having a little trouble gaining access to the laboratories that I have rented from the university. Your droid seems to think that I'm already inside and therefore can't be here requesting access." She explained.

Beings tend to see what they expect to see, so when An Kohli said that, contrary to the computer records, she wasn't actually inside the campus, the security officer took her at face value. At least he did after checking all the data and scans that the droid had already checked.

"I can't fathom how this has happened." Janes sort of apologised, "But of course you can come in. You'll find Professor Van Golden in the laboratory you have rented from us." He turned to leave.

"Erm, I'm sorry." An Kohli blustered, "But I have only been here once before. Can you remind me which way to go?"

The harassed security officer wasn't prepared to be delayed any longer. "Across the campus to the High Energy Physics labs. Top Floor." He called over his shoulder. He waved in the general direction of a map of the campus mounted on the wall of the reception area, as though that would answer any other questions.

It is a general law of the universe that when entering certain types of buildings, the room where you need to be is always the one furthest from the entrance. When visiting a hospital, the ward in which your sick relative is residing is the one furthest from the main entrance. When turning up for a job interview the Sentient Being Resources Department will, likewise, be the furthest department from the entrance. When visiting a library, the book stack housing the mystery thriller that you want to read will be in the deepest bowels of the building - and will be misfiled under 'Bee Keeping for Beginners'.

The campus at Xantos was no different from any of those others. Being a thoroughly modern establishment there were moving walkways to whisk staff and visitors around speedily. But it is another universal law that the moving walkway that you need to use to get to your destination is the one that is closed for maintenance. Which was the case for An Kohli and Den.

They trudged their way across the campus, the High Energy Physics Building in the distance seeming to get no closer. When, eventually, they did arrive, An Kohli felt that she had crossed a major desert.

There was no reception for the building. The passes that An Kohli and Den had been given by the harassed Jonas Janes opened the main door for them and they found themselves studying a floor plan of the building.

Den touched one of the rooms on the display and a name appeared. "Dr Gestalt. Faculty of Very Complicated Sciencey Things" it read.

"Looks like we've only got to touch the rooms on the top floor to find out which one they're in." Den observed.

The floor plan showed a dozen rooms, each sub divided into two or three smaller spaces. An Kohli started at one end while Den worked from the other. All were empty but for room nine oh one, A and B, which suggested that the higher up the rooms, the less in demand they were. These rooms were booked out in the name of Professor Van Golden.

They exchanged a glance and headed for the elevator. The doors swished shut behind them as An Kohli drew her pulsar in readiness for whatever waited for them when the doors opened again.

As they were whisked upwards Den began to rub his temples. "There's a Gau here." He said, as the lift came to a halt and the doors slid open with a self-satisfied 'ping'.

"OK. I assume the Gau knows you're here as well."

"One hundred percent. It isn't the me from this universe though. I'd recognise my own brain patterns. It must be someone An Kohli has hired."

The doors of room nine oh one A and B stood facing them, side by side, just a thin strip of metal separating them. Behind the doors An Kohli guessed that a moveable partition separated the two spaces. She led them a short way along the corridor, away from the entrance to the rooms.

"Which room was the Gau in?" An Kohli asked.

"The right hand one, as best I could tell. He's near the partition though, so I might be wrong. Why?"

"This is one of those puzzles you get in certain types of game. You know the ones; one door is guarded by someone who always tells the truth and the other by a guard that always tells lies. You have one question with which to decide which door to use. Choose the right one and you live, choose the wrong one and …"

"OK, I get the picture. So, you think this is a trap and the Gau represents the guard that tells lies."

"Something like that. Certainly it's a trap; it explains why An Kohli hasn't left yet. We're expected. I think we must have been spotted at Barnard's Star and the professor, or a Gau looking like the professor, was used as bait to get us here. Remember, I am the other An Kohli and the other An Kohli is me. We think the same way, so she knew I would work out where to go. I'm now supposed to blunder into that right hand room and grab the Gau, who will look like Van Golden. The first time my back is turned he will kill me."

"And if you go through the other door?"

"Which I would if I'm with you, because you will detect the presence of the Gau. That's where I'll find the real Van Golden and someone else, probably An Kohli, who will also kill me."

"In that case you can't go in there, An Kohli. Look, I'm not always the bravest, but let me go in first."

An Kohli allowed herself a small smile. Who would have thought that Den Gau would ever offer to make the ultimate sacrifice to save the life of another. "No Den. Thank you for the offer, but I can't let you take a pulsar blast for me. You stay back and let me deal with this."

An Kohli raised her pulsar and strode purposefully back along the corridor. She pressed her hand onto the door lock, which recognised her handprint. The door slid open with barely a sigh. An Kohli searched out her target and shot herself.

Den gasped in surprise. It was unthinkable for An Kohli ever to fire first. She always offered a chance for surrender.

"I know." An Kohli snapped, before Den could say anything. "We'll talk later." She turned to address the Professor, who was sat at a work bench, eyes still pressed to a microscope while he manipulated the controls of a miniaturised robotic tool.

"Time to go, Professor." Was all she said.

He raised his eyes from the microscope and wiped away a bead of sweat from his brow. He seemed to be unsurprised to see the body of An Kohli lying slumped in the corner of the room, her eyes glazed over in death. He turned to take in the new arrivals.

"And if I choose not to? I am getting rather fed up with being kidnapped and tortured."

"Then I'll be forced to do it the hard way. You are my only way to get home, Professor. I can't leave you here to work for Tiny Blur."

"You have just said the only words that might persuade me to leave. What that man did to me ..." As he rose from his high stool An Kohli noted the stiffness in his movements. He walked across the room towards her with a noticeable limp that he hadn't had the last time they had met. An Kohli needed no further explanation.

As they left the room a second Van Golden appeared, but at once morphed itself into a Gau as Den threatened him with a pulsar. "I've got no beef with you and your employer is now dead, so I hope you got paid up front." Den said, keeping the pulsar levelled as they backed across the corridor towards the elevator doors.

"I ain't no hero." The Gau replied, backing towards the door he had emerged from.

"Do you want me to kill him?" Den asked An Kohli. "After all, he would have killed you."

"No, leave him." She said as she stepped inside the elevator with van Golden. "Come on, let's get out of here."

# 12 - Unparalleled

Den waited to broach the subject of An Kohli's unexpected behaviour until they were safely inside a wormhole, being taken as far from Xantos as the navi-com could take them without running out of fuel.

"I couldn't believe what I was seeing." Den was unable to mask his incredulity. "An Kohli firing without giving a warning."

"It was the only thing I could do to avoid being shot." An Kohli said, focusing all her attention on the glass of Grovian whisky in her hands. "As I said in that corridor, I am, or was, the other An Kohli and she was me. She expected me to say something, even if it was only 'So, An Kohli, we meet at last'. Or maybe just 'stick 'em up.' Whatever it was, it would give her time to raise her pulsar and kill me. So, I did the only thing I could to avoid that. I had to shoot first, which meant there was no time to issue a warning." She paused, a tear running down her cheek to land with a splash in her drink. "I'm not proud of what I did, but I had to do the one thing that she could never imagine herself doing, which was to shoot without giving a warning. In this universe she might be faking it, but she would still be doing it. I really didn't want to have to do it, but it was either her or me. Whatever else happened, only one An Kohli was ever going to come out of that room."

"But what about the repercussions, like the Professor has talked about. You've changed the course of history in this universe, which means you will have spawned another universe where you didn't shoot her."

"That is true, but it will be a universe in which she shot me. It was always going to happen eventually. The instant that the Professor fell into her hands and told the other An Kohli about us, it became inevitable that one of us would die. We couldn't get home without the Professor and the other An Kohli couldn't let us live in case we exposed her relationship with Tiny Blur."

"An Kohli is quite correct." Professor Van Golden had been sat quietly, listening to them argue. "If your presence here had remained undetected, the ending might have been different, but once the other An Kohli found out that you were here it was inevitable. I was just a useful by-product for Tiny Blur to use and to act as bait for the trap. But if she didn't have me she would have found another sort of bait."

"But to not give a warning …" Den seemed so disappointed in An Kohli. "To not give her a chance of surrender …"

"I know. I'm under no illusion, Den. I'm going to have to live with this for the rest of my life. It would have been bad enough to have done it to some other being, but to have to do it to myself … I'm sorry, I can't talk about it anymore."

An Kohli left the room, almost running, heading for the privacy of her own cabin. As she lay down she was overcome by a violent shivering that wracked her body for several minutes. Eventually it eased off, but not before it had reduced An Kohli to silent, fearful tears.

*  *  *

The rest of the journey was spent with An Kohli avoiding the company of her fellow travellers, taking her meals in her cabin and only emerging to stand her watch on the Sunray's spacious command deck. Den gave her the space she needed, exchanging only the briefest of greetings as they completed the watch handover.

For his part, Professor Van Golden immersed himself in study, utilising the ship's extensive library to keep his mind occupied.

It was with a collective sigh of relief that they eventually emerged from their wormhole and took up orbit around a red dwarf star, which was surrounded by a cloud of asteroids that were slowly but surely losing the battle with the star's gravity. So isolated was their destination that it didn't even have a galacticnet node which might give away their position as it detected the presence of the Sunray and automatically logged it onto its systems.

"We could do with a news round-up." Den observed, as they gathered in the Sunray's lounge to discuss their next move. "We don't know how the news media will treat the death of An Kohli."

An Kohli grunted an acknowledgement. "I don't think we need to see a news feed to know that we have just become the galaxy's most wanted. The Guild will put up a bounty for whoever brings us in and we can expect the likes of Gib Dander to boost the amount. With bounties so few and far between these days, it will be a magnet for every Guild member, as well as the freebooters."

"But how will they report the incident? They can hardly announce that An Kohli killed herself and then walked out of the university. That security bloke, Janus Jones …"

"Jonas Janes" An Kohli corrected.

"Yes, him. He'll tell the police how he spoke to us just minutes before and let us into the university despite the security logs showing that you were already inside. They'll review all the security camera images …"

"And conclude that I was a Gau, or a Sutran."

"The same thing, really." Den grunted. "Mind you, there's no record of a Sutran ever having committed murder."

An Kohli was just about to snap a defence of herself at Den, but changed her mind. It had been murder by any reasonable definition of the word. She had opened the door intending to shoot whoever was guarding the Professor and that intent was what made the difference between murder and self-defence. Any court in the galaxy would reach that conclusion. She felt a tremor start up in her right hand and clenched her fist to suppress it before Den noticed.

"Gau, Sutran, it doesn't matter." She continued. "They won't circulate any images because they will assume that we can't be identified because of our ability to change shape. Which means, Professor," She turned to look at him, "You have just become the best known being in the galaxy. If they find you, they find us, or so they believe."

"Based on the fact that I'm sitting here in your company, their beliefs are well founded." The Professor said sardonically.

"Which means that we can't approach any university or commercial laboratory to find you facilities in which to continue your work to build the parallel universe portal."

The Professor steepled his fingers and rested his chin upon them, deep in thought. Time ticked by as they each grappled with the problem in their own minds.

"The Endeavour!" He said the words so suddenly that he made them all jump.

"What's the Endeavour?" An Kohli asked.

"Oh, it must have been thirty years ago now. Maybe more. I had just graduated and was working as a research assistant for … oh, what's her name? Professor D'Arcy Spanks. Yes, that was her; a brilliant physicist. Anyway, she was working with a team on research into sub-particle dihesion. The team needed to build a huge sub-particle accelerator to test their theories. The trouble was, it was such a high risk device that if anything had gone wrong it might have destroyed any planet on which it was built; possibly even its star as well."

"But what's that got to do with …"

"I'm getting to that." The Professor snapped, irritably. "Because of the risks they decided to build a huge space station to house the accelerator. They called it the Endeavour. It had a staff of over three hundred including crew and they sent it out into an empty patch of space where it couldn't do any harm if it went bang. Well, the crew would all have died, but they knew the risks."

The professor could see that his audience's eyes were starting to glaze over with boredom. "Anyway, the research proved to be a waste of resources because they didn't find anything worth finding and after about ten years the station was abandoned. The amount of money wasted was enormous, enough to pay off the debts of several star systems. That made it an embarrassment and after that, hardly anyone ever mentioned it again. Well, I say abandoned, but the technical term was 'care and maintenance', just in case anyone needed to use it again in the future. The crew and the scientists all went home and droids were put in to keep it maintained. So it's still out there, just waiting for someone to come along and use it again."

"Were you one of the crew?"

"No. I was too junior to get a place. Professor Spanks left me back at Zygor to do the number crunching when they started sending back data. By the time they abandoned the Endeavour I had my first Phd and was working on my second, which was research into parallel universes. I think Professor Spanks retired about then. But the thing is, the Endeavour has wonderfully well-equipped laboratories. If I can just pop home and get a few things from my workshop …"

"Oh, no. You're not going anywhere near Zygor, or anywhere else you might be recognised. Den, will you go?"

"Sure. If the Professor gives me a shopping list and images to show me what he means, because I doubt if I would know the difference between a mass spectrometer and an electric egg whisk. Is there anyone who has legitimate access to your house that I can disguise myself as?"

"My own lab assistant, Phrumph. He's always popping around to borrow stuff. The door lock is programmed to accept his handprint … oh, you won't be able to replicate that. No matter. I'll tell you how to by-pass it. It isn't difficult."

"That's settled then. How will you source raw materials and components without giving away our location?" An Kohli asked.

"They'll be delivered by automated drones, so that won't be a problem. If I spread the orders around several different suppliers in different star systems, there's no reason for anyone to be suspicious. The purchasing and logistics systems are all automated these days, so my orders will just be hidden in with a million others unless I try to buy something that's on a restricted list. That might be a difficulty, but again, if we can use Den to go and buy in person, the clearance processes can be circumvented as well. There's just one other thing …"

"Go on." An Kohli said cautiously.

"I'd like my family to join me. I miss them so much and there will be plenty of room on the Endeavour for them."

"I see no problem in that. We just have to make sure that they aren't under surveillance. There's no point in hiding out on an abandoned space station if your wife just leads a posse of bounty hunters to us."

"Very true, but there's no reason to believe that anyone knows where my family are right now."

\* \* \*

The air on board the Endeavour smelt musty, despite its air conditioning systems being fully functional. Perhaps it was An Kohli's mind playing tricks on her, recalling memories of how other abandoned places smelt.

When Professor Van Golden had described the Endeavour as a space station, she had imagined something the size of a small office building. It had to be to house three hundred staff. Its actual size was closer to that of a small city. The only artificial structure in space she had ever seen that could rival it was New Earth, but that was exceptional.

"It's the size of the accelerator, you see." The Professor explained as they boarded it. "It's several thousand met long, arranged in a spiral. Everything else, the offices, labs, engines and so on, are just bolted to the outside of it."

The station was so large it didn't need shuttle ports. There was room for several full sized space craft to dock directly onto ports built into the hull.

Sensing the presence of a ship, the automated systems on the space station powered up, providing heat, light and fresh air. The service droids hadn't needed such luxuries. The first thing An Kohli did was to find a computer terminal and use it to locate a map of the station which they could download onto their communicators. She also used it to check the state of the supplies. Food and water levels were both adequate for a long stay, though the thought of eating food that had been in storage for some twenty years didn't offer much appeal. Den, when he arrived, would be disappointed to find that there was no alcohol on board. He'd have to return to the Sunray for that.

A few weeks after their arrival, the Professor's family also arrived. What should have been a happy reunion was anything but. Stuck out in a remote cabin hidden on a sparsely populated planet, Mrs Van Golden, Minnie to her friends, was anything but happy. Neither were her two younglings, having missed the many opportunities to inhabit the cyber world of their friends due to the lack of galacticnet connections. Professor Van Golden's holiday cabin had been so far off the grid that the grid was just a distant memory.

"It isn't going to get any better here, either, kids." The Professor warned them. "You can't do anything that might give away our location."

"But it's so boooooring here." They protested. How they knew that, it was difficult to tell, seeing as they had only been on board the Endeavour for a few minutes and hadn't even been shown their rooms, let alone the other excellent facilities that the space station offered, but they were typical of most teenagers to be found across the galaxy.

"Well, you can try going on Spacebook and telling your friends where we are, and then see how exciting it gets when a bunch of bounty hunters come storming out of space to try and take me prisoner." He had retorted.

There was more in that vein, so much more that An Kohli decided that the less time she spent in the company of the younglings the better. She went off to find the communications console and block access to all the social media sites, because she knew, without having to be told, that whatever you tell teenagers not to do, they will immediately do it, regardless of the potential consequences.

"There is an incoming call from a spacecraft called The Laurel." The space station's computer informed her a few days later.

An Kohli was immediately on her guard. Damn! Merkaloy must have managed to track down the Professor's family and followed them here. It wouldn't have been difficult. Den had been sent to a variety of planets to make purchases of components and specialist tools for Van Goldon. While he was down on one of them it wouldn't have been difficult for someone to plant a tracking device on the hull of the Sunray. Once it emerged from its wormhole on arrival at the Endeavour it would have started beeping its location, piggybacking on the galacticnet connection within the space station.

Merkaloy would be first amongst the Guild of Bounty Hunters to want to track down An Kohli's murderer and seek revenge.

"Put it on screen, but don't allow video from this end." She instructed. "Oh, and feed my voice through a synthesiser." An Kohli's one hope was to convince Merkaloy that she wasn't of any interest to him, which meant not exciting his curiosity by allowing him to hear her real voice.

"An Kohli, is that you?" Merkaloy's familiar boom came across the airwaves.

"Everyone knows An Kohli is dead." She replied, non-committedly.

"Well, an An Kohli died, that's for sure, but we don't know which one. I'm guessing that you are the An Kohli that doesn't belong in this universe."

That gave her pause for thought. It was unlikely that the other An Kohli had spread the news about parallel universes, so how could Merkaloy possibly know about that? Unless he, too, was working for Tiny Blur. Well, if the An Kohli in this universe had been sleeping with him, then it was more than possible that she might have corrupted some of the other bounty hunters.

"I have no idea what you're talking about." She bluffed.

"Look, I'm not here to do you any harm, An Kohli."

"What makes you think I'm An Kohli?"

"Because I've come a long way to find you. A very, very long way, if you get my meaning."

Now he was speaking in riddles. That wasn't his normal manner. But then he didn't know which An Kohli had survived and which hadn't. Or was he stalling for time, waiting for reinforcements to arrive?

"You're going to have to speak more plainly than that. Look, we're on ship to ship radio. It will take these signals years to reach an inhabited planet, so you may as well say your piece."

"OK. Look, I have someone on board who you might be better talking to." There was a pause before the image on the screen changed to show Professor Van Golden.

"Er, I … I mean …"

"Yes, it is me, An Kohli. I assume that it is An Kohli, despite the distinctly male voice we are hearing at this end. In our universe we never met, but I'm very sorry to have done what I did to you."

"Which was?"

"To send you through into a parallel universe. Believe me, I have spent the last several months trying to track you down, with your friend Merkaloy here, so I can make amends and get you back home."

At that moment Den wandered into the control room, scratching his backside and yawning. He stopped short when he saw Van Golden's face on the screen.

"Erm, I just saw him going into the shower." He said, pointing at the screen.

"Ah, is that Den? Yes, sorry for the confusion, but I'm not the Van Golden in the shower. In fact, I'm not even the Van Golden from this universe."

Den owed his survival to being very suspicious and this was an occasion which he considered merited a little of that quality. "He could be a Gau, An Kohli." He whispered. "Where is he? He might be too far away for me to sense him."

"My colleague is suspicious of your credentials, Professor." It wasn't just Den who was suspicious. It would be an elaborate plan, but an effective one if it worked. Convince An Kohli that they were from her own universe, get her to let them on board the space station and then grab her while her guard was down.

"What can we do to convince you?"

"Keep the Laurel at a distance. Come over in a shuttle by yourself. If you are a Gau, Den will be able to sense you without you leaving the shuttle. If you are, you don't get on board. Come alone, I'll be scanning the shuttle to count bodies."

"Sounds fair. Which dock do you want me to go to. There are several."

An Kohli picked one far enough away from the control room for her to able to keep space between them and the real Van Golden if they managed to get aboard.

\* \* \*

This time the reunions were as joyous as they were supposed to be. Having established that the newly arrived Professor Van Golden wasn't a Gau, he was allowed to board the Endeavour, where he continually apologised for having marooned An Kohli and begging forgiveness, until An Kohli had to threaten to kick him off the space station in order to get him to shut up.

By which time Merkaloy had docked the Laurel and bounded on board the Endeavour to envelop An Kohli in a huge hug that threatened to crush her ribs. Den kept a safe distance between himself and the Arthurid, offering a hand to be shaken and wincing in pain as it was squeezed in Merkaloy's tight grip.

Then followed Laurel, Merkaloy's wife, after whom he had renamed his ship. As a Sabik she was less physical in her hugs, but no less emotional as tears of joy streamed down her face.

Hearing the commotion, the other Professor Van Golden arrived with his family. It took him several attempts to explain to his younglings what was going on, realising in the process that the two were probably never going to be candidates for a No Bell Prize. The two scientists at once closeted themselves away and started comparing scientific notes. Minnie Van Golden and her children lost interest in the new arrivals and drifted off to find something else with which to divert themselves, leaving Merkaloy, Laurel, An Kohli and Den to settle down with large glasses of Grovian while they caught up with events.

"The Guild contacted scientists to try to work out what had happened to you and their conclusion was that you had, somehow, crossed into a parallel universe." Merkaloy explained. "That led us to Professor Van Golden. He was distraught about what he had done, but we knew that he had no alternative. Unlike the Van Golden in this universe, his family were taken hostage. He would have lost them had he not complied with Tiny Blur's orders."

An Kohli nodded her head in understanding. "We sort of guessed it must have been something like that."

"Anyway, the Professor couldn't do enough to make amends, so we followed you from one universe to another, always arriving too late, or not being able to track you down. We followed you around this universe for weeks, trying to make sense of your movements and never being able to catch you up. Then we heard that An Kohli was dead and we didn't know what to make of that."

Laurel took up the story. "We guessed that you were involved somehow, but couldn't work out how and we didn't know which An Kohli was dead; you or the one from this universe. So, we staked out Barnard's Star for a while, expecting the other An Kohli to turn up there. We knew you had been there, as well as the other An Kohli, so it was obvious that she had some connection to Blur, but we didn't know what."

"In this universe she was Blur's lover." An Kohli revealed.

"Wow, I wasn't expecting that." Merkaloy admitted.

Laurel dismissed the detail. "Anyway, when she didn't turn up we came to the conclusion that it was you that survived. That led our Professor to work out that you might have come here. The same space station exists in our universe."

"I'd never heard of it." Merkaloy admitted.

"Me neither." An Kohli confirmed. "Apparently it's an embarrassing sort of secret. No one ever talks about it; a bit like an uncle getting sent to prison for stealing underwear."

They laughed. "Anyway, we turned up here and here you are."

"We thought you might have got a tracker on our ship when Den was away buying parts."

"We didn't need to. The Endeavour is in the same place in both universes. All we had to do was work out that you'd come here. With both Zygor and Xantos ruled out, there weren't many other options."

"So, what happens now?" An Kohli asked. "Can we all get back to where we belong?"

"The professor thinks it won't be a problem. He says the portal always uses the same set of space-time co-ordinates when it opens a portal and they work in both directions. He will use his device, we take both ships through and then the portal closes behind us. We reposition the ships and repeat until we get back home. All we have to do is go to New Earth, which is where he opened the first portal, and we're good to go."

* * *

"What becomes of me now?" The Professor Van Golden from the universe they were in asked after the two returned to join the group.

"You haven't committed any criminal offence, so far as I know." An Kohli said. "You can go back to Zygor and take up your life where you left off. The police will have a lot of questions for you, but you can answer most of those truthfully. The An Kohli from this universe wasn't the goody two shoes that she seemed and kidnapped you and took you to Tiny Blur. The only lie you have to tell is that you don't know who rescued you, but you're glad they did. You can even tell them that you came here. There will be questions you can't answer, not if you don't want to be considered insane, but the police will have to treat you as a victim."

"Or I could stay here and continue working on the device, just as I was."

"I would like to stop you from doing that, but I can't, so it isn't even worth discussing. You have a copy of the plans now, so short of taking them off you at pulsar point there's nothing I can do. That's your choice. But I think your family might have something to say about staying here."

"That is true. My dear wife is already giving me a hard time about being cooped up here. Honestly, it's more luxurious than any hotel where we could afford to stay. You would think she would just kick back and enjoy it."

"Perhaps she's homesick." Laurel suggested.

"Perhaps. OK, let's say we go back to Zygor. How do we get there?"

"None of us dare been seen around Zygor. After the fire they'll be ultra-hot on security, if you'll pardon the pun. It's always the same after the event. Merkaloy can take Den somewhere to rent you a commercial ship and bring it back here. You can use that to get back to Zygor. The rental company will pick it up from there."

"So we're stuck here for a bit longer."

"A few days, not much longer than that. It's better than the months you were going to be here."

\* \* \*

Just as promised, a few days later the Professor and his family boarded a rented ship and were ready to leave. At the docking port, the Professor remained behind for a few moments to say his goodbyes. Much to An Kohli's surprise he handed over the PMD with his copy of the plans stored on it.

"To tell you the truth, An Kohli, I've discovered that being able to prove that there are parallel universes isn't as much fun as it sounds. I think that this sort of technology could be very dangerous and a No Bell Prize is no compensation for opening Diadora's Box."

Giving An Kohli a light peck on the check, and Den a hearty handshake, he boarded the rental ship and left their lives.

An Kohli found the nearest garbage disposal and flushed the PMD into the space station's incinerator.

\* \* \*

The Sunray and the Laurel drifted in space, waiting for the local area to clear of space traffic. The Professor was most insistent that the occupants of no other ship should see what happened to them.

"I have worked out why you came to this universe rather than returning to ours when you last went through the portal." Van Golden said. "It seems that direction of travel is important when opening the portal. When you left the last universe you approached the co-ordinates from the same direction, which meant that you went forward one further iteration of the universe, rather than going back to ours. If you think of it in two dimensions, if you want to go forwards you need to travel right to left and if you want to go backwards you need to travel left to right."

It seemed to make sense, An Kohli agreed. After all, if you go into a room, you have to reverse your direction if you want to leave by the same door.

"Five thousand li to go, then we're in position." Professor Van Golden announced, watching the co-ordinates shown on the navi-com display.

"OK, about two minutes then, at our current speed. Did you get that Merkaloy?" An Kohli called over the ship-to-ship radio.

"I'm right on your tail An Kohli."

"OK. When we get into position we'll have to go through side by side to make sure one of us doesn't get left behind."

"We've been through this, An Kohli." Merkaloy reminded her as gently as he could.

"Sorry, Merkaloy. I drive Gala up the wall with that sort of thing."

"Not just Gala." Den muttered.

No reply came back, but An Kohli could imagine the big Arthurid chuckling to himself.

"Two thousand li." Van Golden said, from his position in the co-pilot's chair.

Without warning, another voice came across the airways. "Sunray, heave to and stand-by to be boarded."

"Oh shit. This doesn't sound good." Den muttered from behind her.

"Merkaloy, did you hear that?" An Kohli asked.

From the command deck of his own ship, Merkaloy replied. "Yeah, I heard it An Kohli. I'm guessing that the message came from that big Orion class ship that's approaching."

"How did he get here?" She brought up a viewing screen and searched for the ship. There it was, coming from the direction of the giant space station called New Earth.

"It's in Space Force colours." Den observed.

"Looks like they've been warned to expect us."

"My alter ego probably told them that to get back to where you came from, you'll have to be in the same place as you arrived. Anywhere else and you'll probably just go through to the nearest parallel universe, which might not be the one you want."

"Turns out that the professor was a bit more of a blabbermouth than he let on." Den said, "Oh, sorry Professor. No offence meant."

"But plenty taken." Replied the Professor. "No, you're right, but you can hardly blame him, given what Blur's torturers were doing to him. I've met Blur, remember."

A pulsar blast zapped past the nose of the Sunray, so close that it caused the ship to rock. "I won't warn you again, Sunray. Heave to or it's over."

"Apart from me, they can't know who's on board." The Professor stated. "And it's me they want; well, my device at least. It means they can't attack us. They can only warn us."

"OK, I agree. We keep going." She accelerated the Sunray a little, closing the gap on the tiny patch of space that they were heading towards. "Captain of the Orion class ship. Stop firing or you will destroy your target."

By way of reply another blast of pulsar fire set the Sunray rocking once again.

"Seems they're prepared to play chicken, anyway." Den muttered through gritted teeth.

"Activating portal." The professor announced.

"You hear that Merkaloy?"

"I did. I'm right with you."

In front of them the planet Saturn faded out, as did the stars behind it. A grey area of space formed.

"That Orion is speeding up. Looks like he's intending to cut us off, An Kohli." Merkaloy warned.

"He can try. Keep up with me, Merkaloy."

The two ships accelerated towards the grey area of space, the Orion class ship on an intercepting course and closing fast. Trying to force the Sunray into changing course it fired another pulsar blast. This time there was a hit on the nose of the ship, setting alarms sounding. But Newton's laws of motion must be observed and the Sunray maintained its course and speed as the universe flickered around it. There was the briefest of vibrations, but that could have been caused by the damage done to the ship.

"We're through." The professor announced.

"Are we in the right one?" An Kohli asked.

"Difficult to tell until we do some computer analysis."

"What the freak is going on?" The voice of the captain of the Orion class ship came blasting across the airwaves. "What happened to New Earth?"

"I think that may be a fair indication." The Professor smiled. "In the universe we needed to cross into there was no New Earth."

"So the captain of that ship is now a long way from home." Chuckled Den.

"Captain of the Orion. Who am I talking to?" An Kohli called across the ship-to-ship channel.

"My name is Captain Garoo, of the Space Force of Earth and New Earth. Who am I talking to?"

"I am An Kohli. If you ever want to get home, I suggest that you stop firing on us."

"An Kohli is dead."

"No, *an* An Kohli is dead. I am An Kohli from a parallel universe. If you doubt me, ask yourself what has happened to New Earth. It was there one moment and gone the next. When you tried to force me to change course, you crossed into a parallel universe alongside me."

There was a lengthy silence as the Orion's captain tried to take in this wealth of information.

"This is some kind of trick." The denial finally came back.

"OK, if it's some kind of trick, tell me what I've done with New Earth. Also tell me why this planet Earth doesn't have the chain of space elevators around its equator that it had a few moments ago."

Silence returned once more. An Kohli could imagine the captain interrogating his ship's computers, trying to work out what was going on.

"You are still under arrest, An Kohli. I'm still a Captain in the Space Force."

"Which doesn't exist in this universe. If you try to take me down to Earth they won't know what you are talking about and they will probably lock you up in a room with rubber walls. I hate to think what they'll do to me when they see that I'm not human. No, Captain Garoo, you have only one chance. Do as I say and I'll help you get back to your own universe. If not, I'll leave you here to fend for yourself. If you try to stop me, my friend in the Meteor class ship, that has just moved round behind you, will join me in blasting you into atoms.

The captain of the Orion class ship seemed to realise that he was both outnumbered and bemused by events. He admitted defeat.

"What do I tell them when I get back? They were tracking you from New Earth. That was how I was able to find you."

"Tell them anything you like, it won't be my problem anymore. No, hang on. Tell them that all traces of the device that's used to open the parallel universe portal have been destroyed, so there's no point in harassing Professor Van Golden anymore. All he has now is some mathematics. Tell them I wiped his memory before I left."

"That isn't possible." The captain sounded doubtful which, given his circumstances, was to be expected.

"It is in my universe." An Kohli lied. "He won't remember anything about me or the device he was working on."

"OK. I'll tell them. Just get me back where I belong."

"I'm sending you some co-ordinates. Head towards them at orbital speed. You'll feel a slight vibration and then you'll see New Earth again, which means you'll be back home."

An Kohli nodded at the Professor, who fed the co-ordinates into the communications system and transmitted them to the Orion class ship.

"We've moved quite a long way from there ourselves, An Kohli." He reminded her. "We'll need to go back as well. We would have had to anyway, as we can only approach the portal from one side. If we approach from this side we'll just follow that ship back to its own universe again."

"OK, just tell me where to go." An Kohli replied.

A few minutes later the Orion entered a patch of grey space that shimmered against a faint background of stars. First its nose disappeared, then the rest of the hull then, finally, the red glow of its engines. The Professor operated a switch and the stars returned to full brightness once more.

"OK. Let's do it one more time and see if we've made it home." An Kohli said.

\* \* \*

"Welcome back, An Kohli." The reassuring image of the Grand Master of the Guild of Bounty Hunters appeared on the viewing screen.

"Thank you, Grand Master, but I couldn't have done it without Merkaloy's help. We would have been there for months more if he hadn't arrived when he did. Even then we'd have probably gone through the portal in the wrong direction and ended up in yet another parallel universe."

"You'll have to tell me all about it when you get here."

"Sorry, Grand Master, but I've still got to find Gala. Is there any news?"

"Every bounty hunter in the guild has been looking for her. Every informant they have has been shaken till their teeth rattle. We now know that this being was the one who carried out the kidnapping."

The Grand Master's image was replaced by that of a Rastabanian. If it hadn't been for the sneer that seemed to be glued into place he might have been considered good looking.

"Jaffa the Hurt." An Kohli exclaimed. "I caught him years ago and he went to prison."

"That's right. He was released by Tiny Blur, along with so many of the other criminals in the galaxy. The price of his release seems to be having to kidnap Gala for him, so that he could set the trap that sent you wandering around parallel universes for the past few weeks."

"Any idea where he is right now?"

"Not yet. If I get any news I'll let you know. In the meantime, what are your plans?"

"I think Merkaloy is going to Sabik, but I have to drop our guest off back home. After that, I'm not sure. Given that we still don't know where Gala is, I may come to Guild HQ. It's as good a place as any to gather new information."

"My thoughts exactly. I'll let you get on. Oh, by the way, the Adastra has been delivered here. Apparently it was taking up valuable space once it had been cleaned up, so they sent it here as this is where it is registered."

"That's great news, Grand Master. Another reason for me to come to HQ." She cut the connection. "Set course for Zygor." An Kohli commanded.

## Glossary

Diadora's Box - In ancient galactic mythology there lived a beautiful woman called Diadora. She inadvertently married a God, who gave her a box as a wedding gift, on the condition that she never opened it. It seems like a stupid sort of gift, but gods are like that. Unsurprisingly, Diadora's curiosity got the better of her and she opened the box, which she found was full of the god's dirty underwear. As a punishment for disobeying him, Diadora was condemned to spend the rest of eternity washing his pants; a punishment that has plagued females across the galaxy ever since. Not to be confused with Pandora's Box, which was a whole different thing altogether. According to legend, the last thing left in Pandora's Box was hope. According to a different legend, the last thing left in Diadora's Box was belly button fluff.

Freebooters - Unlicensed bounty hunters. While the Guild manages licensed bounty hunters and holds them to a strict code of ethics, there is no galaxy wide law to prevent anyone from going after a fugitive in order to claim the reward. While licensed bounty hunters are obliged by their code of ethics to try to bring their quarry to justice alive, Freebooters are more likely to bring them in dead providing the arrest warrant doesn't actually stipulate that they must be alive.

Grovian Whisky - While Scotland may have invented whisky, the planet of Grovia perfected it. From a mountain spring that produces only a few gallons of water per year, the most divine whisky in the galaxy, perhaps even the universe, is distilled. It is very rare and therefore very expensive. Most bars charge for it by the droplet.

Navi-com - Navigational computer. Nobody knows how it works, but it does.

Spacebook - A galacticnet social networking site where people who have no discernible social life of their own spend a lot of time reading about other people with no discernible lives, while being bombarded with advertising. The method by which most of the inaccuracies inherent on the galacticnet are disseminated, especially by people who are too lazy to Moogle the correct information for themselves.

# 13 - Jaffa The Hurt

They stood at the shuttle airlock, the Professor once again apologising for his part in sending An Kohli into the parallel universes. An Kohli was doing her best, once again, to tell him that apologies weren't necessary.

"What you did, you did for the love of your family. I wish you hadn't done it, but I can't blame you for it. What happened to me happened because of my love for my friend. I knew I was heading into a trap. I just didn't understand the nature of the trap. I was expecting Jackon thugs with pulsars and a villain stroking a white cat saying something like 'Ah, An Kohli, so we meet at last'. Instead I got a doorway in space and a place where a whole giant space station didn't exist, and another place where the you that was there hadn't advanced with his research because of a lack of funds."

"I know, but I feel so …"

"And you can't let it ruin your life, or your family's lives."

"But there is a way I can make amends. On my bed in my cabin I have left the portal device. Do with it what you want. When I get back to my lab, I will be deleting all traces of my research into parallel universes. I can't get rid of my published work, more's the pity, but at least that is only theoretical."

"That means no No Bell Prize."

"I have to agree with my alter ego on board the Endeavour. The prize isn't worth the cost. If some of our forefathers had considered the cost of their scientific breakthroughs, perhaps they might never have carried on working on them and the galaxy might be a better place because of it." He shook his head, dismissing his own thoughts. "Who am I kidding. Scientists are no different from any other profession. Fame and fortune are like the air we breathe, just like it is to actors or politicians. With it comes money and with money comes power. The best I can do is slow things down, which I am happy to do. I will know that my theories were correct; for me, that is enough."

He turned and entered the shuttle. "Goodbye, An Kohli. I hope you find your friend."

"Goodbye Professor."

The airlock door slid shut and a few seconds later there was a muffled thump as the shuttle disengaged, carrying the Professor back down to Zygor and to his family. An Kohli found herself wondering if the Professor really would destroy his research. It was hard to imagine. Narian, in the galaxy they knew as Messier 14, had supposedly destroyed his time machine but it turned out that he hadn't. And if Van Golden did, would it make any difference? Tiny Blur knew about it now. Could the genie really be put back in the bottle?

After the shuttle had returned. she went into his empty cabin and found the device lying on his bed, just as he had said it would be. Such a small thing, no bigger than a pair of her boots, but capable of causing such mayhem.

From her belt she pulled out the small PMD that housed her copy of the schematics for the device. Picking the device up she took them both to the auxiliary airlock.

"Computer, take us as close to the star of this system as is safely possible." She commanded. She felt the ships engines power up in response. A short while later she ejected the device, along with the PMD, and watched through the armoured glass port as it drifted out into space. It started to accelerate as the star's intense gravity acted on it. The extreme heat would destroy it long before it got anywhere near the star's exploding surface.

"Set course for Artemis Beta." She commanded, turning her back on the airlock and dismissing parallel universes from her mind. They would return in her dreams, or nightmares, but at least they would play no more part in her waking life.

\* \* \*

The Adastra gleamed like a new ship. The shipwrights of Skopos may not be too fussy about who they built their ships for, but they did a good job, An Kohli had to admit. She searched high and low but couldn't find a single trace of the vikes that had been the cause of the ship having to go in for cleaning *(see Robinson Kohli)*. Now every surface seemed to have been polished to a point where it hurt her eyes to look at it.

"Lazarus, are you still here?" She asked, stepping onto the command deck.

"I am Captain. How can I be of service?"

"Just wanted to hear your voice." An Kohli lied. "Oh, but now I come to think of it, open a communications channel to the Grand Master of the Guild for me."

"On the screen now." Came the almost instant reply.

"Ah, An Kohli, I've been expecting your call."

"Good day, Grand Master. I just wanted to let you know that I've brought the Sunray back."

"Is it in good order?"

"Almost. We took a pulsar hit when we left the place we were." She was reluctant to use the term 'parallel universe' over an open channel. It was too dangerous a reality to be bandied about lightly. "Nothing serious. The maintenance droids patched it up. I'll pay for the full repairs, of course."

"No need, An Kohli. Just file a report that doesn't sound too incredible and I'll claim off the insurance. Now, I have some good news. Two of our colleagues have managed to trace Jaffa the Hurt."

"That's great. Where is he?"

"He's on Towie. Judging by what they told me, he always was. He took Gala there and never left."

"So that video of her …"

"Theatre, by the look of it. His job was to send you to New Earth. He had no need to go there himself."

"Any sign of Gala?"

"Not so far. The two bounty hunters that found her are called Boo and Toprik. They've got him under surveillance. They want to know whether to bring him in or not."

"Can't say I know them. Are they reliable?"

"They've got a good record, both pretty experienced. Steady, but not quite in your league."

"Well, Jaffa the Hurt is a slippery one. Best ask them to keep an eye on him. I'll get over to Towie and give them a hand."

"There's never any hanging around with you, is there An Kohli?"

"Certainly not this time. How long has Gala been missing now? Three months? Four? Who knows what sort of conditions she's being kept in, or how she's being treated. The sooner I get to her the better." She couldn't even bring herself to think that her friend might no longer even be alive.

"I won't detain you any longer, An Kohli. Good luck."

An Kohli didn't believe in luck. She believed in being prepared to deal with whatever she came up against. Bad luck was for people who didn't think ahead and who didn't keep their eyes and ears open. She just hoped that Jaffa the Hurt was one of those.

* * *

From her similarity in features to Laurel, An Kohli assumed that Boo was from Sabik. She had a good firm handshake without trying to prove a point by exerting undue pressure. Her smile was warm and sincere. Toprik appeared to be a Cebalrain. He was tall and stocky, looking as though he could take care of himself in fight.

"Do you two normally work together?" An Kohli asked, taking a seat in the bar across the street from the last known location of Jaffa the Hurt. Den was currently keeping watch, to allow An Kohli the opportunity to quiz her new allies.

"Not really." Toprik answered for them both. "We both got the information that led us here separately, then we spotted each other keeping a close eye on the hotel across the road. It didn't take a genius to work it out. It was handy though. It meant we didn't both have to stay awake twenty hours a day while we waited for you to arrive."

"What's his routine?"

Boo took up the commentary. "Nothing unusual, if you don't count not having any visible work to do unusual. He appears in the late morning, wanders around most of the day looking for some form of amusement, sports and gambling mainly, watching the first and participating in the second. In the evening, he goes to the same Rastabanian restaurant for dinner, before hitting the clubs and the bars. He gets back to his hotel in the small hours, usually with company. The females he brings back all seem to be professional and we've never seen him with the same female twice."

"Nothing to indicate that he knows Gala's whereabouts?"

"No. But he could have accomplices. We know that he didn't snatch her from Canarias by himself."

"Yes, I know. I showed Den his image, he recognised him, but he wasn't the one who had followed them around the island. It looks like he had booked himself a room and was posing as just another guest. It probably allowed him to check out the security and find the right people to pay-off."

"That's what the intelligence has been suggesting."

"How did his name come up in the investigation."

"Someone in Ops was going over the security footage from the hotel. All the stuff that you requested but which wasn't sent over until after you left the island. There was so much of it that it took several weeks to review it all. Anyway, this retired bounty hunter that works in Ops, he recognised Jaffa the Hurt. Apparently, their paths had crossed at some point, before you sent Jaffa the Hurt to prison. Given that he was in prison for kidnapping and extortion, it seemed too much of a coincidence. Anyway, he was booked into the hotel for the week, but no one saw him after Gala was snatched. His bill was paid up front by some corporation or other. There was no way of tracing the money. But we've run a check here. The same corporation is picking up his tab for Blondie's."

Blondie's was the name of the hotel across the street where Jaffa the Hurt was now known to be staying.

"How did you find him?" She looked to both of them for answers, but it was Toprik who spoke first.

"Once we had a name to work with it wasn't too hard. We all just squeezed our informants for any information. Mine happened to see him here a couple of weeks ago. So I took the chance and came here."

"Same story for me, really. Different informer on a different planet, but Jaffa the Hurt seems to be pretty well known. And he's splashing a lot of cash around. That gets him noticed." Boo replied.

"When would be the best time to grab him?"

"If we want to do it quietly, without any fuss, then I'd wait in his hotel room until he came back after his night out." Toprik answered.

"I've already checked the hotel out." Boo continued. "It's reasonably high class, for Towie, but their security isn't good. The night porter spends all his time in the office behind reception, unless he has to deliver room service. Guests come and go using their room keys to access the front door. Both that and the door to his room are so weak a youngling could get in without any trouble."

"What about security cameras?"

"Are we bothered? I don't think anyone will be too worried about reporting him missing. At least, not until we're long gone."

"I'd still like to avoid them if possible."

"Well, we can use a jammer. That's one thing about Towie. Anything you might want is available if you can afford it."

Toprik laughed. "Basically we'll be doing to Jaffa the Hurt what he did to Gala."

An Kohli didn't feel like laughing, but didn't say anything to Toprik. He wasn't as emotionally engaged as she was. For him this was just another case.

"OK, we'll do it tonight." Was all she said.

\* \* \*

The room was unremarkable by hotel standards. Although Blondie's classed itself as five star, An Kohli considered there to be at least three stars missing from the room. Whoever was bankrolling Jaffa the Hurt wasn't exactly splashing out. There were handprints on the walls and the tiny bathroom displayed signs of damp and a poor sewage system. Most of the furniture had scratches and dents in it, the sheets and towels were more grey than white and the entertainment system was a basic model with only five hundred channels and twenty thousand movies and games.

With time to spare before Jaffa the Hurt would return, An Kohli searched the room from top to bottom to see if she could find any clue as to Gala's whereabouts, but there was nothing to be found. Jaffa the Hurt seemed to be someone who travelled light. Den applied himself to the room's small safe, succeeding in identifying the code for the lock within a few minutes, but it held nothing but a roll of cash. Towie was the sort of place where, for a variety of reasons, not everyone had a bank account, so it was one of the few places in the galaxy where cash was still king.

Time dragged slowly by as An Kohli waited, the boredom almost visible in the room. Stakeouts were something that they were both used to and which they had learnt to tolerate.

After what seemed like an eternity, but in fact was less than an hour, Boo's voice sounded in An Kohli's ear. "He's on his way up. One female with him, no sign of any weapons."

"Lights off." An Kohli commanded and darkness fell in the room. Toprik was already in position in a neighbouring room, rented for the night, ready to emerge and block the escape route.

The silence was oppressive, but useful. They heard the elevator whine into life, then stop again after a few seconds. There was a bing as the doors rattled open, then the sound of footsteps. Just two pairs, as Boo had predicted.

An Kohli heard the sound of muffled voices in the corridor. One, a higher pitch, giggled. The door slid open and a voice, deeper than that of the giggler, commanded the lights to come on.

The room lit up to reveal An Kohli standing opposite the entrance, her big Menafield pulsar pointed squarely at Jaffa the Hurt's chest. Also visible, slumped in one of the room's chairs, was Den. His pulsar was also levelled at Jaffa's chest.

"Don't try anything, Jaffa." An Kohli barked, but he was quick. He grabbed his female companion and hauled her around in front of him, blocking any sort of pulsar shot. But no weapon appeared in his hand.

"I'll kill her." Jaffa threatened.

"How?" An Kohli smiled. "It will take a while, but you can probably bore her to death."

Toprik stepped across the room's threshold and pressed his pulsar firmly against the back of Jaffa's head. "Be a good boy now, Jaffa. Let her go." Toprik's voice was barely audible to anyone other than Jaffa.

Pushing the female hard, Jaffa propelled her across the room, preventing An Kohli and Den from pursuing, at the same time he turned to launch a roundhouse punch at Toprik's head. Toprik swayed out of the path of the blow and a howl rent the air as Jaffa's hand connected with the wall with full force. It punched a hole in the thin partition. An Kohli thought she heard the sound of bones crunching.

Pulling his hand out of the hole, Jaffa gripped his injured hand with his uninjured one, He did a sort of folk dance, punctuated with yelps of pain, around the narrow entrance passage, before falling through the door into the bathroom. Water was heard running as he ran his hand under the taps to try to ease the pain and the swelling.

"That hurt." Jaffa's voice could be heard complaining.

"I didn't feel a thing." Toprik chuckled through the door at him.

"Bastard." Came the only word of reply.

"OK, get him out of there before he wakes up the whole hotel." An Kohli said. She turned to the female who had slumped onto the bed, fear in her eyes.

"Has he paid you?" An Kohli asked.

The female whimpered a reply, making it positive by nodding her head.

An Kohli handed her the wad of cash that Den had removed from the safe. It was considerably more than Jaffa the Hurt had paid her. "Stop the night." An Kohli said. "Order room service, watch a move, anything you want, just charge it to the room. Jaffa won't mind, I'm sure. But don't leave before daylight. We'll have someone watching the hotel. OK?"

The female gave a fearful nod of her head.

An Kohli held her hand out. "Communicator" she said. The female reached into her bag and took out the slim card, passing it to An Kohli.

"We'll leave it at the shuttle port." An Kohli told her, before pushing the female from her mind.

Toprik pushed Jaffa the Hurt ahead of him along the corridor to the fire escape stairs. They had agreed not to use the elevator in case its motion alerted the night porter. When they reached the ground floor level they left by a rear exit, where Boo was waiting with a rented hover car. The shuttle port wasn't far, but to try to hustle a noisy Jaffa the Hurt along the silent, deserted streets wasn't a good idea.

Den took control of their prisoner and pushed him on board the Adastra's shuttle, while An Kohli gave her thanks to Boo and Toprik for their assistance.

"I'll make sure you get a good share of the bounty money being offered for Gala's return." She promised.

Boo held her hands up in protest. "There's no need for that. I'm doing this for Gala, not for the bounty. She would have done the same for me."

"Is that the way you feel as well?" An Kohli asked Toprik.

"Absolutely. Besides, hearing Jaffa the Hurt's bones breaking was all the bounty I needed. Tell you what, when you find Gala, you can both take us out to dinner. How does that sound?"

"You've got a deal." An Kohli smiled, offering her hand to seal it. "And thanks again for finding him. Let's hope that he can lead us to

Gala now that we have him. Look, if you won't take a share of the bounty, at least let me cover your expenses." She pleaded. They nodded their agreement.

Boo and Toprik turned in opposite directions, heading towards their own shuttles. An Kohli watched their departing backs for a moment, then went on board her own shuttle.

* * *

"I've told you a dozen times. I have no idea where she is right now. I was just paid to lift her and lay the trail. That's all I had to do." Jaffa the Hurt was shackled to a chair in the Adastra's small lounge, where he been since the ship's medi-sys had finished setting the broken bones in his hand. An Kohli and Den had been taking turns to interrogate him, but so far they had been told nothing of any use.

Right at that moment it was Den's turn again. "What about your accomplices?"

"Just a couple of guys I knew from the old days, back before she took me in for trial." Jaffa jerked his head in An Kohli's general direction. "I paid them off as soon as we got to Towie and I haven't seen them since."

"Where did you keep her on Towie?"

"Like I told you, we had a small apartment, low rent, cheap and nasty, but we only used it for a couple of days. That was it."

"So what happened to Gala after we left for New Earth."

"Not this again! This guy came along, handed me a whole load of cash, told me there was a room at Blondie's I could use for as long as I wanted, and told me to get lost. So I went to Blondie's and I never saw Gala or him again."

"Who was the guy?"

"I told you, he never gave me a name."

"Would you recognise him if you saw him again?"

"Of course I would. You see him on TV all the time."

"What?" An Kohli intervened, leaning across the small gap between them to put her face directly in front of Jaffa's. This, finally, was some new information "What do you mean, he's on TV all the time?"

"Whenever you see that Blur guy on TV, one of the other guys that's usually with him. That's the guy who took Gala and gave me my money."

"Lazarus. Find me a recent media broadcast by Tiny Blur." An Kohli commanded.

"On screen now." Came the almost instantaneous reply. The viewing screen in the lounge lit up to show Tiny Blur entering a room full of media representatives. He took his place behind a battery of microphones, flanked by a half dozen of his aides.

"Freeze the image." An Kohli said. "OK, Jaffa, can you see him there?"

"Yeah, the one immediately behind and to the President's right."

"You mean this one?" She pointed at a tall human.

"Yeah, that's him. Really bad personality. Just gives orders, no please or thank you."

Touching the screen, An Kohli addressed the computer again. "Lazarus, can you identify that figure?"

"I can, An Kohli. He is Alison Fakescotsman. He is one of President Blur's most trusted advisors."

"At last, we're getting somewhere. Thank you, Lazarus."

"There is no need to thank a humble computer, Captain."

An Kohli could swear she could hear the computer smirking. "Did he say anything that might give us some sort of clue as to where he was taking Gala?"

"Nothing. He said nothing. Besides, why should I help you?"

"Because helping me will make a big difference to which prison you eventually end up in."

"You know I won't be in prison for more than five minutes." An Kohli had a very strong urge to wipe the triumphant smirk off of Jaffa the Hurt's face.

"There's more than one type of prison, and not all of them have guards that can be bribed or governors that can be given release orders."

"Oh yeah, like where?"

"Well, there's always Xantia."

The smirk disappeared from Jaffa's face. "You wouldn't!"

"Do you really want to find out if I would?" It was now An Kohli's turn to smirk.

"OK, look, it probably doesn't mean much, but he did say one thing before he left. I did ask him where he was taking Gala. All he said he was that he was taking her to a place that no bounty hunter would ever think of looking."

"What the heck does that mean? "Den asked.

"How should I know?" Jaffa the Hurt protested. "Honestly, that was all he said. He was sort of laughing at the same time. He walked out the door and that was the last I saw of him."

"OK, Jaffa, that's earnt you a reprieve from Xantia. We'll take you to a lovely place we know where you can while away the time until we can start to trust the courts again."

Den unlocked the shackles that secured Jaffa the Hurt and escorted him to the Adastra's holding cell.

"Do you think he's telling the truth?" he asked when he returned.

"Hard to tell, but yes, I think so. We know that Blur was behind us being sent to a parallel universe, so it would make sense for one of his aides to have set the whole thing up."

Den went to the drinks dispenser, his finger hovering over the button marked 'Grovian Whisky'. When An Kohli didn't pay any attention he pressed the button twice, to give himself a double. He took it over to the couch and sat down, cradling the glass in his hands to warm the spirit and release its rich aroma. "I know you don't want to hear this, but I can't help wondering if Gala is still alive. After all, why keep her if he doesn't need her anymore?"

"You're right, Den, I don't want to hear it, but you're right to ask. But I think she is still alive. If Blur wanted her dead, she would never have been taken from Towie. As soon as he sent us to that parallel universe, Gala would have been disposed of. She would hardly be the first dead body to be found on Towie."

"We don't know that she was, taken from Towie I mean."

"She must have been. We would think to look there, so it doesn't fit in with Alison Fakescotsman's cryptic comment."

"Assuming he ever made it. Jaffa could have been lying to save his own skin."

"I know it sounds stupid, but I think he was actually telling the truth. With the threat of Xantia hanging over him, I don't think he would risk lying."

"So where is the place that a bounty hunter would never think of looking?"

"A very good question, the answer to which I don't have the foggiest. I think we need more brains working on this. Let's go to Sabik and see what Merkaloy and Laurel make of it."

\* \* \*

The atmosphere of dejection in the Three Moons Bar was so heavy it was threatening to turn the beer sour. Four figures stood in front of a star map displayed on the massive media screen that was more often used to show sporting events.

"How about Algieba." Merkaloy suggested.

"We already ruled that out." An Kohli replied. "I can think of a dozen fugitives that have been arrested there over the years.

"No one has ever been arrested in the Dubhe system." Laurel said, looking up from her communicator, which she was using to search the Guild records for arrests.

"But I know that bounty hunters have looked for fugitives there, even if they haven't found any." An Kohli reminded them. "Veritan went there after a tip off. He was furious when there was no trace of whoever it was that he was after."

"There must be an easier way of doing this than sticking pins in a star map." Den said, picking up a fresh beer from the service droid that had just rolled across the room to them.

"Lazarus is good at probability maths." Laurel said, almost to herself. "Have you tried him with the problem?"

An Kohli's hand hit her forehead with an audible slap. "Of course. Why didn't I think of that?" She pulled her communicator from her belt and opened a channel to the Adastra. "Lazarus. A question that I need answering. Where in the galaxy has there never been a search made for fugitives?"

"I cannot answer that as I can't account for the movements of all law enforcement agencies."

"OK. How about if you give me a list of all star systems where there has never been an arrest recorded for fugitives. Specifically search for arrests of beings on planets where the crime wasn't committed, or where the fugitive didn't live."

The channel went quiet while Lazarus considered the question.

"Why don't you want to include the planets where the crimes were committed?" Laurel asked.

"That's always the place that bounty hunters look first, right before they knock on the door of the fugitive's house." Her husband replied. "There's no point chasing halfway across the galaxy if the perp is hiding under their own bed."

Laurel nodded her head in understanding.

"There are seven million, two hundred thousand, three hundred and fifty nine planets that meet your criteria." Lazarus's voice interrupted them.

Den let out a groan, but An Kohli raised a hand to silence him. "Lazarus, exclude all those planets where humans would be unable to survive without space suits."

"The list is reduced to four hundred and fifty six thousand, eight hundred and nineteen possible planets."

"That's still an awful lot. It would take years to search them all." Den said.

"But some have to be more probable than others." Laurel reminded them.

"Lazarus, given a start point of Towie, which are the three most probable destinations for planets where bounty hunters are least likely to search for a fugitive." An Kohli instructed.

"I can't give you three." Lazarus replied.

"Why not?"

"Because there is only one."

"Are you sure?" An Kohli silently cursed herself for asking the question. Of course the computer was sure.

"I am absolutely sure. To forestall your next question, the place where no bounty hunter is likely to search for a fugitive is Artemis Beta."

They sat in stunned silence. Of course they would never think of looking there. Artemis Beta, also known as Acme, was the planet that hosted the Headquarters of the Guild of Bounty Hunters. A criminal would have to be insane to seek refuge there; insane … or a genius.

"When you have eliminated the impossible, whatever remains, no matter how improbable, must be the truth." An Kohli quoted. *

"Lazarus, why is that the only possible location?" Den was still unconvinced.

"Based of the logic that no criminal would ever consider taking refuge there because there are so many bounty hunters. The risk of being identified and arrested is too high. However, if a crime is committed on Artemis Beta, the local police would initiate the search for the perpetrator, but they would only hand the case over to a bounty hunter once they were satisfied that the perpetrator was no longer within their jurisdiction, and therefore was no longer to be found on Artemis Beta."

The logic was flawless, An Kohli had to concede that. It was the last place that a bounty hunter would think of looking. In fact, it was the place where a bounty hunter would never even think of looking, last or not.

"It looks like we're off to Artemis Beta then." Merkaloy said what they were all thinking.

"I'll warn the Let Bynch to lay in extra stocks of beer at The Bounty Hunter's Lair." Den grinned.

* Sherlock Holmes in *The Sign of Four* (1890) by Sir Arthur Conan Doyle.

\* \* \*

"It's a big planet." Merkaloy said, looking at it on the viewing screen in the Adastra's lounge. "Where do we start?"

"With GSTC." An Kohli replied. "Unlike Towie, the staff here take their duties very seriously and you can't just park a spaceship anywhere you want."

She typed some commands into the computer and a long list of space craft appeared. "Given the date we were on Towie and the fact that Jaffa the Hurt said that Alison Fakescotsman arrived a couple of days after we left, we can make a rough guess at when he arrived here." That's assuming he came here in the first place, she didn't say. They were staking a lot on the results of a computer's probability calculations. "Lazarus, eliminate all ships that are known to be owned by, or registered to, bounty hunters."

The list was immediately cut to about a quarter of its original length. "We need to reduce it some more." Merkaloy said. "He's a human, from Earth, isn't he? Is there any ship with Earth connections?"

"Lazarus, did you hear that?" An Kohli asked.

"I did. There are no ships registered on Earth. However, there is one that was built there. It is a Jupiter Class ship called The Forum.

"Who is the registered owner of the ship?"

"It is registered to a company called Benefit Enterprises Corporation."

"That sounds familiar." Den said.

"Yes, I thought so as well. Lazarus, can you make a connection between that company and any other ships we have encountered recently."

"The company is also the owner of the Shogun, Captain. As well as several other ships." *(see Cloning Around)*

"Of course! The Shogun. In my book that makes it a ship owned by the Fell."

"The evidence is starting to rack up." Laurel observed.

"It is indeed. Lazarus, can you track where The Forum's shuttle landed?"

"Nothing could be easier." The computer replied. "It landed at the commercial shuttle port at Mysore."

"What do we know about Mysore?" An Kohli asked the room in general.

"Mysore is the third largest city on Artemis Beta." Lazarus provided. "It is approximately eight thousand li from the Headquarters of the Guild of Bounty Hunters, in the southern hemisphere, on the continent known as Antipodes. It has a population of approximately one million three hundred thousand beings, the majority of whom are native Artemians. Its chief industries are …"

"OK, thank you, Lazarus." An Kohli said, regretting that she had asked the question. The computer took things far too literally at times. "Has anyone ever been there?"

Her three companions shook their heads. She wasn't surprised. While bounty hunters came and went from the planet at frequent and regular intervals, they rarely ventured beyond the confines of the Guild's HQ and The Bounty Hunter's Lair. It wasn't that there was anything wrong with the rest of the planet, it was just that they felt no need to explore further.

"There must be someone who has. Lazarus, post a message on the Guild's Spacebook page asking for anyone who has been to Mysore to get in contact."

"What shall we do while we wait?"

"It may be a big haystack, but we might as well start looking for the noodle. We'll start by seeing if we can get a look at the security camera footage at the shuttle port and see where we go from there."

\* \* \*

Like many commercial shuttle ports across the galaxy, the one at Mysore was almost fully automated. Owners or pilots landed, recorded a credit card against which their parking charges would be made, then left to get on with their business. When they returned their departure was noted and their parking bill charged against their card and their account closed. So it took some persuading for An

Kohli to arrange for a manager to meet with them and then some time for him to arrive.

Persuading the manager to let them see the security camera footage wasn't such a difficult task. The inhabitants of Artemis Beta knew that having the Headquarters of the Guild of Bounty Hunters on their planet gave them a measure of protection from the ever present Meklons and other organised criminal gangs, so everyone, including businesses, went out of their way to help as much as possible, even if it meant bending the privacy laws.

Unfortunately the security footage didn't reveal much. Alison Fakescotsman could be seen walking to the payment point, recording his credit card and then walking to the area where rented hover cars were collected. The hover car appeared again next to the shuttle, but there was no camera angle that showed what happened once it was there. Then it left.

"Can we trace the hover car's movements?" An Kohli asked.

"Probably not." The manager answered. "The data is over-written after thirty days, unless the vehicle is involved in an accident or there is a police report of a traffic violation. Then the data would be downloaded and stored until we get clearance from the insurance company or the police. Hang on, I'll check."

He entered some commands into the computer. "Sorry, nothing. The driver seems to be have been both law abiding and careful."

"I don't think he was very law abiding, at least, not in the way you mean. What about his credit card? Can we get details of that?"

"Of course." The manager carried out another search and sent the data to An Kohli's communicator. "The only other thing I can tell you is that the shuttle departed four days after it arrived."

"Thank you, that has helped us." Not a lot, An Kohli thought, leading her friends out of the manager's office, but the credit card information had given them another lead they could follow.

"Four days." Merkaloy noted. "Just enough time to rent somewhere and then hire some goons to babysit Gala until he decides what to do with her."

"That's what I thought." An Kohli replied. "Well, let's see if his credit card can tell us anything."

Connecting to the Guild's computers, she was able to run a check on the credit card and the transactions it was used for. The card also turned out to be belong to the Benefits Enterprise Corporation, the owners of Alison Fakescotsman's ship.

"It was used for several transactions while it was here." An Kohli told her companions. "If we can find the locations of those transactions then we can narrow down our search area. Oh, and we've had a reply to our Spacebook post. There is someone who has visited Mysore quite a lot. He's agreed to meet us and is on his way over by sub-orbital. He's told us to meet him at a bar called Gallifrey's."

\* \* \*

Gallifrey's was a timeless sort of place. Its décor was tasteful but subdued, designed not to overpower the senses. The bar was circular and surrounded by high stools to allow customers to sit in casual comfort. Around the outer walls were a series of booths with curving bench seats that allowed half a dozen beings to be seated in comfort, maintaining eye contact but also allowing them to see around the room. Each booth had its own automated service point, which did away with the need to go to the bar to top up drinks.

Between the bar and the alcoves were tables surrounded by comfortable chairs. These were served by droids.

At the end of the room furthest from the door was a small dance floor, behind which was a low stage. Musical instruments were arranged around the stage, waiting for the musicians to arrive. It was too early in the day for that.

When An Kohli and her friends arrived there was only one other couple present, sitting in one of the booths having a tight lipped argument. They gave them some space and chose a booth nearer to the door.

Their contact identified them as soon as he walked through the door. He was a Prathian, so not from that planet, but accompanied by a pretty female who was identifiable as being Artemian.

He extended his hand and greeted each of the bounty hunters in turn. "I'm York Boston." He said. "I work in Ops. I wanted to be a bounty hunter, once upon a time, but I sort of got sidetracked. This is my wife, Thea, and she's the reason I know Mysore so well. She was born and raised here, so I thought I'd bring her along. She will probably be of more use than I will."

"Thank you for coming. Do you know why we're here?" An Kohli asked.

"I assume that you're still looking for Gala, though why you should come to Mysore I can't think."

"Let's just say that we've had some information that pointed us in this direction. Now, we have some addresses where a certain credit card has been used. It would be really helpful if you could tell us where they are."

An Kohli had transcribed the list of addresses to remove the credit card details and she showed them to York and Thea.

"I only know one of those." Thea said, frowning. "Gabba Street. If she's in that area then I wouldn't recommend going there at night."

"Why?" Asked Merkaloy. "I think you can assume that we're capable of taking care of ourselves."

"Forgive me." Thea smiled an apology. "I'll rephrase that. Most Mysoreans wouldn't go there at night. We don't have a lot of crime in this city, but most of what he have originates from this area. It's a very old part of town, very run down, so it only attracts people who have nowhere else they can go. That includes many of the criminal elements, of course."

"Actually, from our point of view, that would make a lot of sense. I wouldn't think that Gala would be being kept in the lap of luxury." Laurel observed.

Thea got busy with her communicator and brought up an image. "This is a street view of Gabba Street. The address you have seems to be some sort of convenience store."

"Why didn't he just order over the galacticnet and get his groceries delivered?" Den asked.

Thea laughed, a pleasant, tinkling sound. "I'm sorry, I shouldn't laugh, but I can assure you that any delivery droid would require an armed escort and drones would be shot out of the sky. In the Gabba Street area the weak prey on the weaker and anything that can be stolen probably will be."

"Can you check out these other addresses?" An Kohli asked, not really bothered about how Alison Fakescotsman arranged for his groceries to be delivered.

"Of course." She changed her communicator from street view mode to mapping. "Yes, I thought as much. All those addresses are in the Gabba Street area."

Switching back to street view she showed them a couple of seedy looking bars, what might once have had pretensions to being a restaurant and a shop that sold security equipment.

"Hold on. What was that last one?" An Kohli asked as the last image disappeared from view.

Thea called it up again. "Seems to be a letting agency." She answered. "Is that important?"

"I'll say it is. He needed somewhere to lock Gala up. Put that letting agency together with the security equipment supplier and you have a house or an apartment with new locks on its doors. I guess he made the arrangements over the galacticnet, then went to the agency to pick up the keys and pay the security deposit."

"That's our in, then." Merkaloy said. "If we go there and ask nicely, I'm sure they'll give us the address."

"Not in Gabba Street." Thea said. "People in Gabba Street don't take kindly to strangers. I'd better go with you. At least if I speak to them in Artemian they might not be so reluctant to talk."

"Thea isn't going anywhere without me." York staked his claim to tag along.

An Kohli recognised the logic of Thea's argument. She had encountered similar prejudices before. "OK, we all go together." She announced.

* * *

The scene had played out much as Thea had predicted. The letting agent had been very reluctant to provide any information at first, even when offered a substantial bribe. But some lengthy chatter in Artemian had brought the agent to the point where the wad of cash disappeared into a pocket and the information flood gates opened,

They also paid a visit to the security equipment provider, where they discovered that as well as stout locks and dead bolts, the purchaser had bought security cameras, pressure mats and other fittings for an alarm system.

Den snorted in derision. "There's nothing there that will keep anyone out for long." He declared. "The alarm sensors all have to be routed to the controller by radio signal, one channel for each sensor. If you let me buy the right stuff I can make it think that nothing's wrong while a marching band climbs through all the windows."

The owner of the security equipment supply shop grimaced at Den's poor opinion of his products but didn't deny their weaknesses. Besides, he also sold the sort of equipment that Den had described.

Den's capabilities never ceased to surprise An Kohli. "So where did you learn how to do that?"

He grinned. "As you well know, An Kohli, I spent a little time in prison. Through no fault of my own, I might add. My name was cleared - eventually. Anyway, it's amazing what you can pick up if you're nice to the right beings when you're inside. Most prisons could open their doors as universities of crime, if they wanted to make some extra money. Businesses could certainly improve their security systems if they were to speak to criminals instead of punishing them so severely."

"OK, buy what you need." An Kohli agreed. "Is there anywhere round here where we can lay up while we plan our approach?" She asked Thea.

"Nowhere where you won't come out scratching yourself for weeks. I suggest we move down the street a few hundred met. The boundary between the reputable and disreputable areas is only a couple of streets wide. There's a pretty good hotel within walking distance."

"With six of us wandering around the way we have, we're bound to have been noticed." Merkaloy observed. "It isn't a bad idea to be seen leaving the area. When we come back later we can be a lot more covert about it."

\* \* \*

The only light on Gabba Street came from behind the security grills of the convenience store, which stayed open late to accommodate the nocturnal lifestyles of some of the area's inhabitants. What street lighting there might once have been was broken and most of the windows were covered by shutters. The business premises were all secured with stout metal doors and very large locks.

Despite their protests, York and Thea had been left behind at the hotel. They would bring a hover car to get them out of the area once Gala had been rescued, assuming that she was in the room that Alison Fakescotsman had rented.

Although he worked for the Guild of Bounty Hunters, York Boston revealed that he had never been a bounty hunter himself. He had arrived at Guild HQ wanting to become one, but couldn't find anyone to take him on as an apprentice. His build, small for a Prathian, had worked against him. Instead he had taken a job working in the Guild's technology department, before eventually moving into Ops, where he had remained ever since. He had met Thea while travelling back from a visit to his family, when the two had found themselves sitting side by side on the lengthy journey from the commercial spaceship interchange station back to Artmenis Beta. York was smitten and spent every hour of his free time in Mysore, courting Thea until she agreed to marry him.

"He wore me down." Thea laughed. "Or at least he wore my parents down. They said he had to either marry me or buy a new sofa to sleep on, because he'd worn the old one out."

"Not that I spent much time on the sofa once Thea's parents went to bed." York grinned.

"York!" Thea let out a mock protest at his revelation, giving the back of his hand a light slap of reproof.

But with neither of them having the sort of experience that the bounty hunters could amass between them, a night operation in the Gabba Street area was no place for them.

The building had once been a large family house, with room for servants, but had long ago had been divided into smaller apartments, with some being even further sub-divided. The letting agent had provided them with a floor plan of the building, along with the information that the apartment they wanted was on the top floor at the rear. There were two ways up. The internal stairs provided the main route, but at the rear of the building there was a rarely used fire escape.

"If you use it, take care." The letting agent had advised. "It's as rusty as heck and is as likely to kill you as save your life."

Den was first to go back into the Gabba Street area. They had visited a second hand clothes shop to kit him out in a suitable style and he borrowed the face of the Artemian that had served him, so that he wasn't marked out as a stranger. The zapper and pulsar he barely concealed under his jacket made sure he wasn't marked out as a victim.

The building stood by itself on a side road, separated from its neighbours by a narrow alley on either side. Across the road, in the darkest of the dark places on the street, Den took up a position where he could see the comings and goings. There were many. At regular intervals male Artemians approached the house, pressed one of the row of call buttons and spoke a few words, before going through the open door. Den was a being of many worlds and knew the purpose of such places. If it wasn't drugs it would be females and quite possibly it was both.

He relayed his findings back to An Kohli, Merkaloy and Laurel who were sitting in a bar, one of the last buildings which was still outside what Thea regarded as the disreputable part of town.

"No sign of any movement down the alleys." He reported. "If there's a back way in then it's not being used."

A female arrived and went straight inside without using the call buttons. After a few minutes a different female came out. Shift change, Den concluded. It made sense, keeping the maximum amount of revenue passing through the building around the clock.

"Go inside and check out the approach to the top floor." An Kohli instructed.

Den crossed the street, his eyes adjusting as he approached the lit doorway. There was no sign of anyone else, but he play acted an exchange of conversation over the intercom. Taking a second look to check behind him, Den went through into the hallway. Doors stood shut on either side, but the corridor stretched away from him. On his left was a flight of stairs leading upwards. He strolled along the corridor to the back of the building to find two more doors at the rear, before returning to climb the stairs. The layout was the same on the next floor and the next. He stopped as he heard a door open on the floor above him. Feet descended the stairs, moving quickly.

A being hurried past, head down, not wanting to make eye contact. Den brushed past him as though in a hurry to get to an appointment. Reaching the top floor he saw the same arrangement of doors at the front, but without any stairs going upwards he could see that there was only a single door at the end of the shortened corridor. So only three apartments on this floor, rather than four, just as the floor plan had indicated. Outside the door was a chair, but it was empty. The door behind it stood slightly ajar, suggesting that the chair's occupant had gone inside.

"Top floor, target room guarded, one guard position outside but he's not there right now." Den reported quickly.

The door to his right opened and another male figure emerged, surprised to see Den there. He ducked his head and almost ran down the stairs. In the doorway a female stood, clasping a robe closed to cover her chest. Den wondered why she bothered, observing that the robe was almost as see-through as glass.

The female said something, but Den didn't understand what she said. It was always the disadvantage of disguising himself as a member of the local species. It was assumed, not unnaturally, that he spoke the language.

"Sorry." He said in Common Tongue. "I didn't understand you."

The female gave him a curious look, which was unsurprising. She probably didn't speak Common Tongue more than half a dozen times a year.

"You looking for someone?" She asked.

"I might be." Den decided to take a chance. Once inside the female's apartment he might be able to buy some information. If not, it would still give him a good vantage point from which to observe the rear apartment.

"Fifty nuks and I don't do any of that strange stuff." The female stated, extending her had to accept payment. Den wondered what counted as strange for her but didn't ask.

"OK." He said, fishing in his pocket and pulling out a wad of notes. He peeled off enough to cover her fee and put the rest away. Her eyes watched the bulk of the notes disappear back into Den's pocket like a hungry being watching a butcher carve a steak.

Standing back from the door, the female allowed Den to enter her apartment, before closing the door behind her. Leaving Den standing in the middle of the small room she walked over to a rumpled bed and stretched herself out, arranging her flimsy robe so that it revealed more, if that were possible. "My name's Petra, if you're the sort that's bothered with names." She said. Boredom almost dripped off of her.

"That's not what I'm here for, Pertra." Den said.

"I told you, I don't …"

A wave of Den's hand cut her off. "It's nothing like that. How much do you want for me to use your apartment for about thirty minutes?"

"You've just paid for an hour. How you use it is up to you." The female appeared indifferent. "I'll just go next door and …"

"No, you have to stay here. By next door, do you mean across the hall," he pointed back through the door by which he had entered, "or along the corridor." He pointed towards the rear of the building.

"Across the hall. My friend works there. I don't have anything to do with them along the corridor. They ain't too friendly."

"Well, it's them I'm interested in." He pulled out his wad of notes again and peeled several off. "I'd be interested in whatever you can tell me about them."

The female shrugged, pulling herself upright and closing the robe around her. She stretched out her hand to take the money. Den separated the notes and gave her half of them. "If what you tell me is useful, you get the other half." He said, keeping the rest of notes visible.

"What do you want to know?"

"How many of them, what they do, when they come and go. Have you seen any weapons, that sort of thing? You talk and I'll ask questions if I want to know more."

"Well, there seems to be about eight or nine of them altogether, but they aren't all here at the same time. Usually three turn up and then three leave, changing over every few hours."

"What time are the changeovers?"

"Midnight, seven in the morning and two in the afternoon. I usually hear the afternoon and midnight changeovers, but the other girl that works here told me about the morning change."

"OK, how many guarding the door at any time?"

"Just the one. But they get bored. They'll be away for maybe half an hour at a time sometimes. I guess they go inside to watch the media or whatever."

"Are they all Artemians?"

"All the ones I've seen. I think they're local. I recognised one of them at least and a couple of the others looked familiar."

"Do you know what they're guarding?"

"No. I heard a female voice one time, that was all. I've never seen her though. I thought maybe they've kidnapped someone and were holding her for ransom, but kidnappers don't usually hold onto beings for this long."

"You would know, would you?" Den doubted that she would.

"I know beings who have, sort of …"

"I get the picture. Have you talked about her to anyone else?"

"Just my boyfriend. It was him that suggested it wasn't kidnapping, but we can't work out what it might be. Maybe she's hiding out and they're looking after her."

"What about weapons. Have you seen any?"

"The guards all carry guns stashed in their belts. The one on guard usually has his in his hand."

"Guns, not pulsars?"

"I've never seen any pulsars."

Den handed the remaining notes to her and she hurried across the room to put them into a drawer, as though frightened that Den might take them back.

A plan started to form in Den's mind. "Would you like to earn a whole lot more money?" He asked.

"How much more?"

Den took out his diminishing reserve of cash and counted it. "I've got five hundred nuks here. You can have it all if you do what I ask."

"I take it that you don't want to …"

"No, you just have to do a bit of play acting for me."

She gave a short laugh. "What I do for a living is always play acting, but I get your meaning. What would I have to do."

"First of all, can you tell your friend next door that if she hears anything she should stay in her room and lock the doors."

"Sure, that's no problem."

"OK. Then I want to stage a fight between us. Lots of shouting and crashing about. Then I want you to yell for help, scream, you know, really make it sound like you're in trouble."

"You think the guard will come to help me?"

"I hope so. If he does, then I'll take him out. There's something you don't know. I'm a Gau. I don't usually look like this, and if I can disable that guard I can assume his appearance."

"I've heard of Gau. Sneaky bastards if you ask me, being able to look like other beings."

"Well, it comes in handy sometimes, like now. Well, are you willing to do it?"

"For five hundred nuks I'd probably let you beat me up for real, so I guess I'm in."

"OK. Look, I've just got to contact some friends, so they know what I'm going to do. If they agree then we'll start in about ten minutes."

\* \* \*

Walking across to the rear of the room, Den removed his backpack and extracted a small electronic device. A series of red lights came on as the device started to search the local area for radio signals. As it locked on to one, a red light stopped flashing and shone steadily, until the search concluded and seven of them were lit up. Den touched a small sensor, increasing the transmitting power of his device until the lights turned green, indicating that the alarm system of the apartment next door was now reacting to Den's signals and not the ones of the sensing devices. Any security camera images would remain frozen until Den switched off the device.

"If you ever get a burglar alarm, Petra," Den smiled at her, "Make sure the connections use old fashioned wires and not radio signals. They're far too easy to interfere with."

"I'll bear that in mind." She replied, sarcasm heavy in her voice.

"OK then. Let's get the show on the road."

Den took up his position just inside the door of the apartment, his zapper in his hand. "You bitch!" he shouted at the top of his voice, at the same time slapping his fist hard into the palm of his hand.

Petra replied with a stream of obscenities that made even Den blush, all the time smacking her hands together to make it sound like a fight was in progress. She grabbed a chair and threw it across the room, sending it crashing against the wall.

Den shouted some more meaningless phrases, banging his hand against the door and then thumping the wall. From outside the room it would sound like a full-scale bar brawl was in progress.

As a finale, Petra let out a blood curdling scream then threw herself to the ground, making the floor shudder. It was so effective that Den worried that she might really have injured herself, but she immediately scrambled back to her feet.

A male voice could be heard shouting, but it was in Artemian, so Den couldn't understand it. It was followed by the sound of heavy footsteps approaching. The door crashed back and a figure barged across the threshold, arm extended ready to fire the gun he was holding.

Ducking inside the arm, so that the gun couldn't be used against him, Den wrapped the male up in one arm and while his other hand pressed his zapper hard into the flabby skin at the being's neck. There was a crackling of electricity discharging and the figure went limp, hanging in Den's arms.

While Perta shut the door once again, Den dragged the unconscious figure into the centre of the room. With well-practiced movements Petra undid buckles and fastenings, stripping the outer layers of clothing off their victim.

A voice shouted a query from the hallway.

"You're up, Petra." Den said, as he started to remove his own clothing. Petra stepped through the door and into the corridor to start a lengthy conversation in Artmenian. She was supposed to convince whoever it was that the unconscious guard was giving Den a pounding in retaliation for the attack on her. To help with authenticity, Den let out a few loud grunts and bellows of pain while he banged on the floor a couple of times.

Handcuffing the being to a water pipe, Den morphed into character, picked up the being's gun and emerged into the corridor. About half way along the passage a tearful Petra stood, acting her heart out. A large male figure stood in the doorway of the rear apartment, a gun hanging in his hand. He shouted something at Den then backed into the apartment, closing the door behind him.

"He said don't leave your post again. Let the whore die next time." Petra said with a look of disgust. "Give him a kick for me if you get a chance."

"Well done Petra. You're a natural actress." Den smiled at her as he passed.

"Goes with the territory." She said, turning to retreat to her own apartment.

Already Den could hear feet on the stairs, distant, still not yet on the first floor landing, but the heavy tread of Merkaloy was unmistakable, with the lighter pattering that was An Kohli and Laurel. Den held his breath, hoping that anyone inside the apartment would wait a few more seconds before emerging.

Merkaloy's large frame appeared at the top of the stairs, soon followed by the lighter forms of An Kohli and Laurel. Taking more care now, they approached the apartment almost on tip toe. Den let them get into position.

As they stood poised, Den banged the butt of his pistol against the door. "*Agh mota far goen.*" He called, using the Artemian phrase that Petra had coached him in; 'I need to take a leak'.

The door opened a crack, but it was all Merkaloy needed. He launched himself at it from a range of two met, sending it crashing back on its hinges as the guard inside went flying across the room. Laurel leapt after her husband, landing on the prone figure and applying her zapper to his neck. He jerked for a few heartbeats, then lay still as she rolled him over and secured his hands behind him with a pair of handcuffs. Dragging him around she managed to get another pair onto one ankle before securing him to a solid looking bit of furniture.

An Kohli was already at a door inside the apartment, it's sole bedroom. There were loud shouts coming from within. Although the Artemian was meaningless to them, the tone made it clear that it was a demand for information.

An Kohli turned the door handle, threw the door open and stepped through, her pulsar levelled in front of her. Merkaloy followed her before Laurel entered to make up the trio.

Sitting on the bed, one hand shackled to the bedhead, was Gala. Behind her sat the third male that was known to be in the apartment, his gun pressed to Gala's temple. The stream of Artemian he came out with needed no translation.

"We seem to have a stand-off." An Kohli drawled.

"No, we don't." Den said from behind her, stepping through the door and pressing his gun to the back of An Kohli's head. "Drop your weapons or she's dead." He snarled in Common Tongue.

"Well done, Cid." The being on the bed said, switching languages as three pulsars landed heavily on the ground.

"You better pick them up." Den instructed. "If I lower my weapon, she'll make a grab for me."

Smirking, the figure on the bed rose and stepped towards the three helpless figures. His hands were soon full with two of the pulsars, plus his own gun. Which meant that when he bent over in front of Merkaloy to pick up the final weapon, he was unable to defend himself when the Arthurid's meaty fists smashed into either side of his head. Pulsars clattered to the ground for a second time, followed by the heavy thud of the being's unconscious body. Den lowered his gun.

"That went well." He said, a bright smile on his face.

"Sometimes it's easy to forget which side you're on, Den." An Kohli grinned in reply.

"All part of my charm. But this isn't the time for trading compliments."

Taking the hint, An Kohli hurried over to Gala. "You look like shit." She said, taking her friend in her arms and giving her a huge hug.

"Nice of you to notice." Tears were streaming down her face as weeks of pent up emotions were finally released. "The key to the cuffs is on the dresser." She gulped between sobs, pointing with her free hand. Laurel picked it up and tossed it over to An Kohli.

"I'm OK." Gala protested as Laurel and An Kohli tried to support her weight on either side. "I can walk well enough."

An Kohli let go and Laurel followed her lead. They followed Gala out of the apartment and into the corridor. Behind them Merkaloy finished securing the third guard with the handcuffs that had been removed from Gala, then followed. Den was the last to leave the apartment. At the top of the stairs Petra stood, in company with another scantily clad female; her friend from across the hall.

As they passed Den stopped to give Petra a hug. "Thanks, you made it a whole lot easier for us. If you want to get your kick in, they aren't in much of a position to resist right now. But I recommend that you get some clothes on and take a bit of a holiday. They won't be too happy with you when they work out what happened."

"No problems. My boyfriend's on his way, with a couple of his friends. They won't mess with them when they see who he is. I may be a whore, but I'm *his* whore." She said with some pride. "Maybe I've changed my mind about Gau. If you're ever in the neighbourhood again, make sure to come and see me." She gave Den a peck on the cheek. "You've still got ten minutes of your hour left."

"That's all he'll need." Merkaloy chuckled. Den ignored him.

Den hurried down the stairs as though he was afraid that he might be left behind. Doors were opened and scared looking females were peering through, then hurrying to close them again as they saw so many armed and strange looking figures. Outside, a hover car stood bobbing at the curb. Along the street, doors were opening, silhouetting figures against the inside lights. Word was already spreading that something interesting had been going on and curiosity was overcoming caution.

Merkaloy squeezed himself into the front of the hover car, alongside Thea and York, while Gala, Laurel, An Kohli and Den had to cram themselves into the rear. The vehicle dipped under their weight, briefly touching the ground before its antigravity generators could compensate for the heavy load.

"Where too?" York asked, spinning the car in its own length and heading it towards Gabba Street.

"Where is the sub-orbital port in relation to the shuttle port?" An Kohli asked.

"Opposite directions." Thea replied.

"OK, go to Gallifrey's and that's where you two get out. Those thugs haven't seen you, so they won't be looking for you. Get a taxi and get yourself back to the Guild on the next available sub-orbital."

"But ..." York was about to protest.

"We're very grateful for all you've done," An Kohli cut him off, "but I don't want to risk your lives. It won't take long for word to get out that we've rescued Gala and I'm guessing that whoever is in charge will come looking for us. They'll guess we arrived by shuttle, but they don't know about you two."

York admitted defeat and took a turn to take the hover car towards Gallifrey's. When they arrived, he and Thea got out and stood forlornly on the curb while Merkaloy replaced York behind the controls and Den relieved the pressure in the back seat of the car by moving into the front. The copious amount of tears still being shed, now by An Kohli and Laurel as well as Gala, was starting to make him feel damp at the edges. With a short exchange of goodbyes, Merkaloy steered the hover car back into the light night-time traffic.

It was a few minutes later that An Kohli, peering through the rear window, announced that they seemed to be being followed.

"How close?" Merkaloy asked.

"Two vehicles by the look of them, maybe still a hundred and fifty met behind."

Ahead of them they could see the lights of the shuttle port in the distance, but it still seemed to be a long way away.

They sped closer, but the gap between them and their pursuers closed relentlessly. The hover car was speed limited, which was something that the pursuers probably didn't have to contend with.

Not bothering with such niceties as the entrance gate, Merkaloy pulled back on the steering column and took the car upwards to clear the shuttle port's perimeter fence. He then headed downwards again, towards the gap between his own ship's shuttle and that of the

Adastra. He applied reverse thrusters and the car slid to a halt, rocking wildly.

The car had barely stopped moving before An Kohli was out and rolling across the ground. She came upright onto one knee, levelled her pulsar and fired at the first of the pursuing vehicles, all in one smooth movement. Her Menafield hit it square in the front, sending it spinning around to crash into the perimeter fence before it tilted over and landed on its roof. The second vehicle had to swerve to avoid a collision and went careening across the compound to crash into a shuttle parked on the far side.

She fired at the second vehicle, the power of the blast dislodging it and sending it crashing to the ground. No one inside would be bothering them for a few minutes, at least.

An Kohli had time to lean into their own car and slap the button marked 'auto home'. The car did a sedate about turn before heading towards the regular exit from the compound and taking itself back to the rental depot.

The ramp on Merkaloy's shuttle was already raising itself as An Kohli trotted along the ramp of the Adastra's shuttle. It started to rise as soon as she stepped off the inner end. Den had the controls in his hands and didn't need to be told to get them out of there.

"Back to the Adastra?" He asked.

"No need. The shuttle can take us straight to HQ. I want Gala checked over by a doctor as soon as possible. Besides, if they try to come after us the best place to be is surrounded by bounty hunters. Did they hurt you?" She asked Gala as the shuttle started to rise.

"Not much. A little bit when I fought them off the night they grabbed me, but I was drugged for a lot of the time after that. Then they brought me here. They kept me handcuffed to the bed most of the time, only letting me up to go to the bathroom. That's why I look so bad. They never closed the door so I didn't feel comfortable taking a shower. I just did what I had to then came out again."

"You've lost weight as well." An Kohli observed.

"Yeah, the food they gave me was shit. I only ate enough to keep myself alive." She started sobbing again and An Kohli folded her in her arms once more as Den guided them towards the Guild's HQ.

## Glossary

Meklon - A collective noun for a group of people who live outside the law. They live a wide variety of criminal lifestyles but one of the most common is space piracy. The origin of the term is lost in the mists of time. Some say it is taken from Mik Lon, a legendary figure who robbed from the rich, there being very few sane reasons to rob from the poor. Legend has it that he then shared the proceeds of his robberies with the poor but that is just lunacy as that would make the poor richer and he'd then have to rob them as well. Another version is that a planet called Meklon, location unknown, was a safe haven for a group of these criminals. Neither version is verified by the galacticnet, but then again very little is.

Noodle in a haystack - A metaphor for something that is difficult to find. Sometimes rendered as 'needle in a haystack' but that's absurd. Who would hide a needle in a haystack?

Sub-Orbital - Abbreviation for Sub-Orbital Craft. A generic term used to describe airborne craft that aren't capable of orbital travel. Includes aeroplanes, helicopters and a wide range of rocket and impulse powered craft. Generally considered the worst possible way to travel given the way the passengers are treated, worse than farm animals.

# 14 - Do Drop In

The Guild's doctor gave Gala the all clear, so they went in search of the biggest bath available in the guest accommodation and filled it full of steaming water and frothy bubbles. After Gala had settled herself in, a glass of wine in hand, An Kohli went in and perched herself on the side of the bath.

"Do you feel up to a few questions?" She asked.

"I suppose, while things are still fresh in my mind." Gala answered reluctantly. "Besides, I know you. You'll butter me up for a few minutes than ask them anyway." She smiled.

"Well, it's really all about whether or not they interrogated you and what you told them."

"Not at first; not while Jaffa the Hurt was holding me. They just kept me locked up and fed me from time to time. But after Alison Fakescotsman collected me, he had several goes. He didn't hurt me, or use drugs on me, but he was persistent." She paused to take a sip of her wine.

"First he asked me about the missing members of the Fell. I stuck with the agreed story, which was that they were on Sadr Gamma as far as I knew. He told me he knew they had been moved, so I told him that if that was the case only you knew where they were. That was when he told me about sending you to a parallel universe. I got real pleasure out of telling him that if you were gone, then your secrets went with you. He didn't ask about the Fell again though."

"I think that was just a token thing, so that Tiny Blur could tell the remaining Fell members that they had asked but that you didn't know anything. I don't think Blur really wants the missing ones back."

"Anyway, after that there were lots of questions about Su Mali. I told the same story; that you had put her on Sadr Gamma and if she wasn't there then only you knew where she was. He asked how we had tracked the Magi eggs down and I told him about the navi-com data. There didn't seem to be any point in holding that back. It wasn't any use to him."

"Yes. When we put the Adastra into dry dock you ordered Lazarus to copy the Nav-com data to the Sunray and then wipe the Adastra's navi-com. It was a wise precaution. The Adastra was delivered here a few weeks ago and I'll bet my last nuk that someone had a good look at the navi-com before it got here. They've probably hidden a tracker on her as well."

"So they must be after the last egg."

"Yes. Either that or they want to make sure that no one else gets it. As we've always known, we need all nine eggs if we want the Magi to be restored." An Kohli paused, already suspecting what the answer to her next question might be and not wanting to ask it. "Did he tell you why he was keeping you alive?"

There was a long silence as Gala steeled herself to give the answer. "Yes. He really likes the sound of his own voice, so when he starts talking it's hard to get him to shut up. A bit like his boss in that respect. He told me I was their insurance. If any other bounty hunters went after the egg, he'd start sending bits of me to the Guild as a warning."

"Did those thugs do anything else to you?" An Kohli asked as gently as she could.

"No, but I think if it had come to the cutting bits off phase, then they would take their chances. He told me that the war was going to start soon. Almost all their new fleet has been delivered, from Skopos and the other places they're being built. He said that once the crews have been trained they'll be ready to start. After that I wouldn't be of any further use."

Gala shuddered, sending gentle ripples through the foam. An Kohli laid a reassuring hand on her friend's shoulder. "Well, you're back here, safe and sound."

They drifted into companionable silence for a few minutes. Having spent years together travelling between the stars, they no longer felt the need to talk all the time.

Gala was the first to speak again. "If it came to the crunch, do you think the Grand Master would have stopped any bounty hunters going after the last egg in order to save my life?"

"Do you mean if he had to choose between you and the galaxy?"

"When you put it like that the answer seems pretty obvious."

"It's certainly not a question you should ask the Grand Master next time you see him." She paused for a moment, uncertain whether or not to continue. "Look, I have to tell you something. Something about what happened in the last parallel universe. Den knows all about it, so he's bound to let something slip eventually and I'd rather you heard it from me."

"This sounds serious."

"It is." Taking a big breath, An Kohli told her about the other An Kohli, the one that was Tiny Blur's lover. "I don't know if she had got at your equivalent and Den's, but she might have." She took another big breath. "Anyway, I killed her in cold blood."

Gala's mouth fell open with the shock of the statement.

"I didn't give a warning, I just went through the door and killed her. I told Den it was because I had to do the last thing she would expect and she would expect me to give a warning, which would give her time to kill me. But that wasn't really why I killed her."

She looked down at her almost empty wine glass and swirled the few remaining drops around the bottom. "I killed her because I hated what she had become. I hated her because she was Tiny Blur's lover. I hated her because she had thrown her lot in with the Fell and I hated her because she had become corrupt.

And then, when I had killed her, I realised that I was just like her. I was her and she was me. If I could kill in cold blood like that, then I was capable of anything, just as she had been."

"Come on, An Kohli. Don't beat yourself up over this. We've hunted down so many killers now, we know that anyone can be driven to kill. What's that list of motivations to murder you always give me?"

"Power, greed, love and hate."

"Exactly. How many killers have we brought in where the family have said he or she couldn't have done it, they wouldn't hurt a fly. But all the evidence showed that he or she did do it. Well, now it's just your turn to find out the truth of that."

"Would you have killed her?"

"In a heartbeat. You had no choice."

"The worst thing is, as Professor Van Golden pointed out, I probably just spawned another parallel universe where she killed me."

"Well, there you go then. In the ultimate scheme of things there were no winners and no losers."

"Could I be like her?"

"Even though you killed her? Not a chance. That isn't you An Kohli. It never has been and it never will be. It was a one off, an essential to ensure your survival, and I, for one, am extremely grateful, otherwise I'd still be in that room with those goons."

"Merkaloy would have come for you."

"But he was away looking for you. He might have come back to find me eventually, but by then it might have been too late. We have to deal with what happened, not what might have happened. How many times have you told me that, when an operation has gone wrong?"

"I take your point."

"Now, I'm starting to prune up, so you go back next door while I dry off. Then we're going to party."

Standing up, An Kohli went to leave the bathroom, then stopped. Instead she leant over and kissed her friend on the cheek. "It's good to have you back."

"It's good to be back." She threw a handful of foam at An Kohli and her expression dissolved into an impish grin. "Now get out."

* * *

The party was as epic as everyone had hoped. Gala looked resplendent in borrowed clothes, her hair neatly cut from its straggling collection of rats' tails into the bob she favoured to prevent it getting caught when she was crawling around in the engineering spaces of the Adastra. An Kohli doubted that she had ever looked better.

When they arrived at the entrance to the Bounty Hunter's Lair, An Kohli pushed Gala ahead of her into the crowd. The music was cut and she was greeted with a mighty roar of welcome. Even in the dim light, An Kohli could see Gala's skin blush to a deep purple colour. It took her a long time to get from the door to the bar, with everyone wanting to hug her and shake her hand.

By the time she had reached the bar to be handed a glass of fizzing wine by Let Bynch, she had tears streaming down her face once again, ruining her make-up. As she took her first sip, someone started to sing one of the favoured songs, asking why she was born so beautiful and declaring her to be of no use to anyone. Bounty hunters didn't go in big for complements, but they could give and take insults as well as any rigby players. A huge glass of beer was handed to Gala, replacing the fizzy wine and she was required to drink it down in one as the song continued. The challenge was for the glass to be empty before the song ended. As was often the case, most of the beer ended up soaking Gala's clothes.

An Kohli slipped in quietly. As far as the bounty hunters knew she had been scouring the galaxy to find her friend and she was happy to allow that to become the authorised version of events. She was given a few hearty slaps on the back and firm handshakes, but everyone was just so happy to have Gala back that An Kohli was obliged to take a back seat for the evening; not that she minded.

The music was returned to full blast and Gala found it difficult to get time to drink any more. Everyone wanted to dance with her to celebrate her safe return. Good news was so rare that, for one night at least, everyone was going to celebrate this one little bit.

Den sidled up to her. "When do we go after the last egg?" He shouted in her ear.

"As soon as we sober up enough to take the Adastra safely out of orbit." She shouted back.

"So, about a week then." He threw his head back and laughed, before lurching off into the crowd.

Seeing Laurel across the bar, An Kohli forced herself through the heaving mass of bounty hunters to reach her.

"A bit crazy." Laurel observed. She hadn't been Merkaloy's co-pilot for long and wasn't used to bounty hunters' parties.

"They're celebrating being alive." An Kohli shouted. "Most of the beings here will have lost a friend at some time. To get one back is a rare thing."

"I have to admit, I didn't know being a bounty hunter was so dangerous."

"Most of the time it's not. Most fugitives don't want to exacter … exasher …" An Kohli slurred. She looked at her glass, wondering what was in it. "… make things worse by killing, so they come quietly. But some of them are just bad. They kill for the sake of killing and to have killed a bounty hunter makes them famous when they go to prison."

"I asked Merkaloy if he had ever been seriously injured. He wouldn't tell me."

"Are you asking me to betray a confidence?"

"If you want to put it that way."

An Kohli smiled and hiccoughed. "Merkaloy is flesh and blood like the rest of us. But he's one of the toughest. It takes a lot to put him on the ground."

"But has he ever been on the ground?"

An Kohli frowned, her mind flying back over the years. "We were working together over in the Acrab system, chasing a fraudster. It was a white collar crime and he wasn't reckoned to be dangerous, but we didn't know he was as high as a kite on drugs. He got the drop on me and was just about to put a bullet in me. Merkaloy pushed me out of the way and took it for me. He saved my life. If the perp had been using a pulsar, he wouldn't be here today, and neither would I."

Laurel took a sip of her juice. As someone who had spent several years working in bars and dealing with drunks, she didn't have much of a liking for alcohol. "The four of you go back a long way, don't you? It makes me feel like an outsider."

An Kohli draped a drunken arm around Laurel's slim shoulders. "You're a great kid and you're just what Merkaloy needs." An Kohli said. "And don't worry about fitting in. You did just great back in Mysore. You'll make a good bounty hunter one day. And while you're waiting, just be a good co-pilot, a good wife and a good friend."

A figure erupted through the crowd, stumbled and measured his full length on the floor at Laurel's feet with a mighty crash that could be heard even over the music.

"Ah, my beloved seems to have returned." Laurel grimaced. "Can you give me a hand to get him to the door?"

But Let Bynch had seen the incident and four of her burly bar staff arrived and dragged Merkaloy away. Laurel followed, exchanging rueful comments with bounty hunters as she went. An Kohli also decided that the evening was over. If she stayed any longer she would probably end up in bed with some chancer who just wanted to say he had slept with An Kohli and she decided that she didn't want to be that person anymore.

"Can you keep an eye on Gala for me?" An Kohli shouted to Let Bynch as she passed.

"Like she was my own first born." Let Bynch yelled back. That wasn't too comforting considering the Let Bynch's eldest child had spent some time in prison, but she trusted Let to do as she asked.

\* \* \*

"What are you going to do with Jaffa the Hurt?" Den asked as they prepared to leave Artemis Beta.

An Kohli slapped her hand against her forehead. "I must be losing it. I'd forgotten he was even on board."

"Out of sight, out of mind. He's been pretty quiet. Don't worry, he has everything in there he needs. Except maybe for female company. Are you going to take him to Xantia?"

"No. What he told us helped us find Gala, so he kept his side of the bargain. I was going to take him to Macroterra, but …" She paused, deep in thought. "Actually, I might have something else he can do for us."

"Would he agree?"

"I think he would. I'll offer him the chance to walk away free and clear if he does."

"You'd let that piece of shit walk free after what he did to me." Gala was furious at the thought.

"Calm down. If what I'm thinking of works, I think he could be far more use to us for him to do it." An Kohli saw the look of thunder on Gala's face. "If you want ten minutes alone with him with a big bat, I'll look the other way."

"Don't tempt me. Sometimes, An Kohli, you really confuse me." She stormed from the command deck.

"I deserved that, I suppose. But he really could be useful."

Den just shrugged.

* * *

The Hellenic star system was technically uninhabited, but in fact there was actually quite a lot of life on three out of its nine planets. Two of them shared an orbit, one on either side of the star, while the third was further out, but large enough to be seen as if it were a moon when the planets passed each other every three hundred days. The combined gravitational pull resulted in massive disruption on them, with extremes of tidal and seismic activity.

On one of the twin planets life was limited. It appeared as single cell creatures huddled together in great sponge like blobs along the edges of the oceans. When the tides were high they were submerged and when they were low the were high and dry. They multiplied by splitting cells, forming ever larger blobs until they merged with their neighbours. When this happened the cells from one blob would try to consume the cells from the other. Usually the larger blobs emerged victorious, though smaller blobs made up of very aggressive cells could also win. Large blobs with aggressive cells were always the winners.

Although created at the same time as its twin, the life forms on the second planet were more advanced. Why this should be, scientists were unable to explain. Perhaps the planet's atmosphere was slightly richer in one element than another, or perhaps there were minor temperature differences, but here life crept and crawled on multiple legs both in and out of the seas. Humans would have called these life forms insects, or slugs or centipedes, though in fact they were unique species and wouldn't be categorised as such by any self-respecting scientist.

Finally, on the oldest of the three planets, which had been named Stavros, after a favourite uncle of one of the crew of the ship that had first explored the system, life had evolved into larger animals, though lizards were the dominant species. The largest of these had evolved far enough to start throwing rocks at each other and it was generally accepted that thermo-nuclear warfare was only a few millennia away. This was Hellas epsilon and it was where Su Mali had chosen to hide the final magus egg. Well, it may not have been the final egg for her, as they didn't know in which order they were hidden, but it was the final one for An Kohli and her crew.

The surveillance camera located the tall cairn easily enough. The grassy plain was otherwise featureless and so a very clear marker had been needed if Su Mali had ever wanted to find the egg again.

"Are we ready to go?" Den asked.

"Wait a moment." An Kohli replied, staring at the screen, chewing at the inside of her cheek.

"What's up?" Gala asked from the co-pilot's seat.

There was a long pause before An Kohli replied. "It's too easy." She said at last.

"That suits me." Den replied. "After some of the things we've had to do to recover some of the eggs … You smell a trap, don't you?"

"I'm not sure, but you just said it. 'After some of the things we had to do.' That's just it. Every one of the eggs had some sort of guardian around it. Not necessarily a life form, but something that made it harder to reach the egg."

"Well, I remember that storm that had been raging for two thousand years. That nearly killed us." Den commented.

"And the vikes." Gala added. "Then there was Atlantis. First there was the ice, then there was the size of some of the marine life. We had to get all that special equipment." she reminded them.

"And those tribes on Aragan," Den joined in. "Mind you, we don't know if Su Mali knew about them."

"We don't know that she didn't." An Kohli said, still examining the viewing screen intently. "Everywhere she has hidden an egg, there has been more to do than just go and find it. We even had to rob a bank to get at one of them."

"Not Sadr though." Den said.

"Yes, even Sadr. I think she knew that pirates used that planet as a place to keep their slaves until they had enough to attract buyers. The camp was temporary, which meant they came and went. I'll bet she waited until they left, hid the egg and then relied on them to come back again and provide her with the additional security."

"She nearly got caught herself, remember." Den pointed out.

"But that was because she knew we were after her. I thought at the time she was going to move the eggs somewhere safer, so she didn't have time to think it through and just blundered into the pirates."

Gala took the opportunity to move the conversation on. "OK, if we assume there is some sort of trap, what could it be? There's no signs of any life in that area. Nothing large, anyway."

"I think the clue is in where she landed the shuttle." An Kohli pointed at the screen. "It's at least two hundred and fifty met from the cairn. Why would she land that far away?"

"Unstable ground." Gala answered firmly. "Maybe something concealed by the grass, but which would cause the shuttle to get stuck and unable to lift off again."

"OK, that's sounds plausible." An Kohli said. "Lazarus, what are the possibilities of there being unstable ground near the cairn."

"The proximity of the planets in their orbits creates considerable instability." The computer replied. "The evidence for this is the large numbers of volcanoes present along the junctions of the planet's tectonic plates. As Stavros passes one of the planets on the inner orbit, their combined gravities draw the molten magma to the side closest to the passing planet, which results in eruptions from existing volcanoes and the formation of new volcanoes."

"But this site has no volcanoes close by, which suggests it isn't on the junction of any tectonic plates." An Kohli stated.

"True." Replied the computer. "But it isn't only the magma that reacts in that way. The same gravitational pull will draw water upwards. This causes high tides ..."

"But it isn't near the coast or any rivers."

"... as well as drawing up underground water." The computer wasn't to be deterred. "Underground water mixing with a loose soil will create quicksand, which will be concealed by grass growing on the surface."

That silenced them. They stared at the grass being blown by the gentle breezes on the surface, straining their eyes to try to see what lay beneath. Once again An Kohli wished that they were better equipped for exploration. Ground penetrating radar would have answered a lot of their questions.

"So, she somehow knows that the location is prone to quicksand whenever the planets pass close to each other. It will take time to form, then more time to disperse, making the surface treacherous for several weeks at a time. She lands some way away, then picks out a route to where she builds the cairn. I guess she uses a pole of some sort to test the ground to make sure its firm and marks a route so she can find her way out again." Den suggested.

"That would be how I would do it." An Kohli replied. "Lazarus, what is the current position of Stavros in relation to the other planets?"

Lazarus provided an overhead view which showed that Stavros was currently at right angles to the beta and gamma planets, which were sharing the same orbit but destined never to meet.

"That's good." Den said. "That means we're in the period when they have the minimal amount of gravitational pull on each other."

"Lazarus, how long before the planets get close enough to affect any underground water?" An Kohli asked.

"Approximately fifty days. There will then follow a period of one hundred days of increasing influence, followed by the same period of decreasing influence. The cycle is then repeated as Stavros passes around the other half of its orbit, past the other planet of the pair. The total period of Stavros's orbit is six hundred days."

"Fifty days; that's plenty of time to get down there, grab the egg and get back up here." Den stated.

"That's as maybe." An Kohli said, "But I think that Su Mali will also have been well aware of the planet's positions, so we still exercise maximum caution. "

\* \* \*

To walk to the cairn directly from the landing ground should have taken only a couple of minutes. It took them nearly two hours. Each painful step was preceded by the careful testing of the ground ahead of them, before any weight was committed to the surface.

Although the surface was soft in parts, where water had pooled after recent rain, even there the metal rod that they had brought never penetrated more than a couple of sim into the ground. But they still took their time. An Kohli wasn't going to be rushed into any rash movements.

Behind her, Den waited patiently, a reel of makeshift tape in his hand, made from strips cut from garments that they had all sacrificed. On his back was a pack full of metal spikes made by cutting up lengths of the frame of Den's camp bed. He would either have to sleep on the floor for the return journey, or on the small sofa in the Adastra's lounge. Completing his kit was a hammer borrowed from Gala's tool kit, which he used to drive the stakes into the ground before tying the tape to the top to mark the safe route.

At last An Kohli stood in front of the cairn. Carefully she tested the ground around it, making sure that there was nowhere that she might sink as she moved around the cairn, removing its stones.

"Ready?" She asked Den as he straightened up from driving in the final stake.

"When you are." He replied.

She lifted the topmost rock from the cairn. It was about the size of her head and was quite heavy. She pitched it a few met from her, where it landed with a thud on the ground. She repeated the movement with the next rock. Beneath the grass a thin crack appeared as the second rock landed.

The third and fourth rocks joined the first two and the crack grew longer and wider, snaking towards the base of the cairn.

The next rock wasn't accessible without An Kohli moving around to the other side of the cairn. She was still working at shoulder height, heaving each rock above her head before casting it aside. As the fifth rock landed a new crack appeared, creeping towards the cairn where it might join up with the first.

As the sixth rock landed, the noise it made was more of a boom than a thud. Den's head jerked upwards, instantly alert to the change in pitch.

"An Kohli …"

"What?" she gasped as she threw the seventh rock."

"Did you hear that?"

"Hear what?"

"That sound. It was like someone beating a drum."

She paused, her head cocked. "No, I can't hear anything."

"Not now. I mean when the rock landed. It sounded like you had banged a drum, a big drum."

"You're imagining things, Den."

"You're the one that said we had to be careful; that we might be wandering into some sort of trap."

About to lift the next rock, An Kohli paused with it still in her hands. Den was right. Anything different could be significant.

"OK. Throw the rock and then listen." He suggested.

She pitched it hard to one side, so it landed at right angles to where she was working. Beneath it the ground was solid and she heard nothing more than the sound of a rock landing with a thump. But once again a crack appeared.

"Sounds OK to me." She said.

"Maybe I'm getting paranoid." Den grimaced.

"Paranoia has saved your life more than once Den." An Kohli puffed, pitching another rock into the grass. It landed on top of one previously discarded. The already open crack opened wider and the lower rock sank a few sim as the length of the crack almost reached the base of the cairn. But, of course, the length of the grass concealed the movement.

The cairn had been reduced to waist height when An Kohli pitched the rock that shook their world. The two longest cracks joined together beneath the cairn and the weight of the stones above did the rest. The cairn teetered as soil crumbled away beneath it. An Kohli's foot gave way as she found nothing to support it, then more soil fell from beneath her and her other foot found itself without support. She dropped into the gaping hole that was forming around both her and the cairn. Spreading her arms in panic she managed to support her weight on the edges of the crater that was forming rapidly, as the cairn disintegrated into its constituent rocks and clattered and banged their way into the chasm below.

"Get back Den." She screamed as the edges of the hole crumbled under her weight. Already perilously close to the edge, Den tried to scramble backwards but his feet slipped and slid on the crumbling soil.

Gravity exerted its influence, pulling the soil from beneath An Kohli's arms and she fell downwards. She flailed her arms, trying to stay upright. Soil, stones and rocks fell with her. Hitting the bottom of the hole with a painful thud, stars splintered her vision as a rock hit her on the head in passing. Her knees gave way and she collapsed into a heap.

How long she lay there she couldn't tell, but as she recovered consciousness she heard Den's voice from above her.

"… Kohli, can you hear me?"

"Yeah, hang on a minute. I'm feeling a bit woozy."

"Hanging on is what I'm doing." He snapped back.

She looked up, her eyes dazzled by the sunlight, but she could see Den silhouetted against the sky. At least she could see his legs, dangling in the air, trying and failing to find anything on which to get a grip. The ground around him seemed to be holding, though from time to time a heavier bit would break off and patter to the ground near her.

She became aware of the sound of water, trickling past not far away from her. She tried to make out how big the cavern was. It wasn't quite conical, more sort of bell shaped. She reached her hand out to touch the wall. Solid rock. One part of her mind worked out that the softer ground must have been washed away by the water, while the other part of her mind wondered how the freak she was going to get out.

"Any chance of you climbing out, Den?" She called up.

"Maybe if I'd spent a bit more time in a gym practicing pull-ups, I might stand a chance. Right now all I can do is hang by my fingertips and hope that no more of the ground gives way."

She looked up again, trying to gauge the distance between herself and Den's dangling feet. Fifteen met, she guessed. Not far if he fell, not enough to kill him as her own survival showed. But if he did fall they would both be down here with no way to get out.

So, Su Mali had laid a trap after all. She must have known about the subterranean water and the cave and placed her cairn on the thinnest point, where the heavy landing of the rocks had cracked the ground open. That was why she had landed so far from where she had built the cairn. It wasn't quicksand she was worried about, it was the cave crumbling under the weight of the shuttle.

Rational thought began to return to her and she pulled out her communicator. It would take time to recover the shuttle and for Gala to get down here with a rope to pull them out, but it wouldn't be long enough for them to die of hunger.

"Gala, can you hear me?" She spoke into the device.

"Gala, can you hear me?" She tried again. The silence suggested that the answer was 'no'.

"Den, I don't seem to be able to get a signal down here. Can you get at your communicator?"

"What do you think I am? The amazing Marvo on the flying trapeze? If I let go with one hand then I'm going to be joining you down there sooner, rather than later."

"Can't you change into something with better upper body strength?"

"It doesn't work like that, An Kohli, as I have explained before. I may be able to change my body shape, but I can't change my basic physiology. I'm a weakling regardless of what shape I take on."

"What about something that flies?"

"Same problem. Wings are just another form of arms, so if I let go, I hit the ground before my change is complete."

An Kohli sat down on the ground, cradling her head in her hands while she thought about their predicament. There was no way for her to climb the walls. Even if she found hand and footholds, as she neared the top she would be hanging upside down by her fingertips. Like Den, she just didn't have the upper body strength for that sort of manoeuvre. On the other hand, Den was in grave danger of falling at any moment.

There only hope was if Gala was able to see what had happened, so she could recall the shuttle and then come and get them.

"Any sign of Gala recovering the shuttle?" An Kohli called up to Den.

"No. It's as quiet as a grave up here."

An Kohli wished that Den had chosen a different simile. The sound of a shuttle taking off at a distance of two hundred and fifty met wasn't something that Den could have missed. So what was Gala up to? She always kept a close eye on things when An Kohli was down on a planet's surface. It was the most important part of her job and had saved An Kohli on more than one occasion. And in this case they were already on their guard because of the risk of the non-existent quicksand.

A large lump of soil cut off her thoughts as it broke away under Den's hand and tumbled to the bottom of the cavern, narrowly missing An Kohli.

"It's no good." Den's voice sounded desperate. "I think I'm coming down to join you."

More soil pattered around her, causing her to scuttle backwards towards the side of the cavern, then a large chunk, then the sky went black as Den's falling, flailing body blotted out the sun. He crashed into An Kohli, sending them both to the ground in a painful heap of arms and legs.

"Thanks." Den gasped, picking himself up. "I think I might have broken something if you hadn't been there."

"I think I have!" An Kohli groaned. Tentatively she tried to get up, testing each limb as she did so. She seemed to be intact, though her back and one thigh were a mass of fiery pain.

"Now that you're down here, is it possible for you to turn into some sort of flying creature?"

"I could try a brocolip. I know Gau who have been able to fly in their form." In the gloom An Kohli heard the sound of clothing being removed. Then came a flapping sound followed by a groan of pain.

"Sorry, An Kohli. I've done something to my shoulder. I doubt I could get a sim off the ground in the condition I'm in."

"Well, thanks for trying. I'll try Gala again." An Kohli knew that radio waves travelled in straight lines, so the Adastra would have to be almost directly above the hole above their heads if it was going to pick up their signals. That was where the Adastra should be at that moment as it offered the best angle for their surveillance cameras but judging by the response she was getting to her communications, that was where the Adastra wasn't. Moving around the cavern, trying different angles, An Kohli kept trying to raise the Adastra, but finally gave up. She switched channels and tried to connect to the galacticnet instead, but that was equally unresponsive.

Gala, where are you? An Kohli silently cried out.

\* \* \*

An Kohli, where are you? Gala silently cried out. She could make no sense of the images at which she was looking. Where the shuttle had been standing there now appeared to be a sea of empty grass, swaying in the light breeze and looking like the restless surface of a jade green sea.

"Lazarus, can you find the shuttle?"

"I'm sorry, Gala, but I can find no trace of it."

"What about An Kohli and Den?"

"No trace of them, either."

This didn't make sense. A shuttle and two people couldn't just disappear into thin air.

She had been monitoring their movements closely, watching them as they felt their way towards the cairn. All had seemed to be well. Progress was slow, but that was to be expected. Then she had watched as An Kohli began to dismantle the cairn in search of the egg. Their images were small, even with the surveillance camera turned up to maximum magnification, but they had been visible on about the same scale as she might observe a beetle.

Then there had been some sort of disruption, the camera's image breaking up and when it had been restored there was no sign of the shuttle, An Kohli or Den.

"Lazarus, check again that the camera is directed towards the correct co-ordinates."

Gala was sure she heard the computer give an impatient sigh, but the reply came back as she had expected. "The camera is locked on to the correct co-ordinates, Gala. And before you ask, yes I'm absolutely sure."

Getting more and more frantic, Gala increased the search radius and started an infra-red scan, looking for heat signatures.

"Ship approaching." Lazarus said in a voice that suggested it was no unusual occurrence, despite it being an uninhabited star system.

"Identify." Gala commanded, without looking up from what she was doing.

"Erm …"

Gala's head snapped up. Computers weren't supposed to say 'erm …' and it was the first time that she had ever heard a trace of doubt in Lazarus's voice.

"Erm … I'm not quite sure how to tell you this …"

"Just say it, Lazarus." Gala had no time for shilly-shallying.

"The ship is the Adastra." Lazarus finally admitted.

\* \* \*

After completing her brief tour of the cavern An Kohli sat down again, placing her head between her hands and her elbows on her knees.

"She was very clever." An Kohli conceded. "She's been one jump ahead of us pretty much all of the way."

"She's not that clever." Den tried to mollify her. "You did catch her twice, after all and it's her that's stuck on Macroterra with a whole lot of former Fell members for company."

"Yes, but it's us that's stuck in this hole. The planning she put into this was pure genius. She didn't just pick that spot at random. She knew about this cavern."

"How could she?"

"Exploration ships routinely use ground penetrating radar to try to see what's beneath the surface of planets. It saves a lot of time when choosing where to take core samples, looking for mineral resources. She must have gained access to one of the survey reports and seen this cave in the radar images."

"That would be highly classified information. The exploration companies don't make that sort of data public. They want all the minerals for themselves."

"Which means she got help from somewhere."

Her head slumped lower towards her knees. "Damn, damn and damn again. We didn't see it Den. We didn't see the most obvious clue."

"I'm not with you."

"No, and I wasn't with it either. The cairn! We were so busy looking for quicksand that we didn't ask where she got the rocks to build the cairn. You saw the terrain up there. It's smooth grassland. There's nowhere she could have found the rocks. At least nowhere convenient or without digging them up, which would have left signs."

"But we checked the shuttle data. It came straight here from the Pradua. Well, she didn't call the ship that, but that's how I think of it." Su Mali's Brightstar had been confiscated as part of the bounty for her arrest and An Kohli had renamed it the Pradua, intending to give it to Gala as a gift. (see *The Magi*)

"Precisely. When examining data, it isn't the answers that are the most important thing; it's the questions, and we didn't ask the right question.

We didn't check on where the Pradua had been, did we? We just used the Pradua's navi-com data to bring us to Stavros, then identified the co-ordinates for where the Pradua's shuttle landed. We didn't think to look to see if the Pradua went anywhere else while it was here. It was a Brightstar and they're very aerodynamic, capable of sub-orbital flight. In fact it's quite an effective fighter aircraft if it's flown by a decent pilot. She must have loaded the rocks into a cargo net, then used the Pradua to ferry them here. Then she parked the Pradua in orbit and came back down in the shuttle to build the cairn and hide the egg.

By the way, is there any sign of the egg?"

"Yes, it's over there." Den pointed to where a polyviol bag lay half buried in pile of soil and stones.

An Kohli went over and picked it up. "I wonder if it was damaged in the fall?"

"That's a bit of a moot point if we can't find a way out of here." Den replied morosely.

Den applied some thought to how they might get out of the cavern. He was pretty good at escaping. In fact it was probably his best skill, after getting drunk and having unsuitable sexual liaisons. He stood up, listening, then followed the sounds he heard. On one side of the cavern a trickle of water came in, took a meandering course across the cavern floor, then left through a tunnel on the other side. He looked up at the size of the cavern. No trickle of water that small could have carved something that big, not even over the course of several millennia.

"An Kohli, how was this cavern made?"

"Judging by the smoothness of the rock, I'd say it was erosion, probably from that stream."

"But the stream's so small."

"Yes, it is now, but this is high summer. It's probably fed by a lake, or maybe snow melt from mountains. In winter and spring it would be a raging torrent but it got smaller as the supply dried up. It's a good job for us that it did, or we would have drowned by now. Over time it wore away the softer soil and loose stones, creating this cavern. In a few years' time we might have arrived to find the roof already caved in. It could only have been a matter of time."

"That's just what I thought. So, if that amount of water flows through this cavern in the winter time, the water course itself must be of a reasonable diameter."

"I suppose so. Why?"

"Because that may be our way out … well, my way out at least. Subterranean rivers rarely stay underground for their entire length. Eventually they find their way to lower ground and break out onto the surface. All we have to do is find out where it emerges and that's where we get out."

An Kohli took out her communicator and found the map of the planet she had downloaded. She zoomed in on their current location, then reduced the scale to take in more and more of the local area. A blue line appeared on one side, apparently starting in the middle of the plain. "That looks like it. It's in the right general direction compared to the course of the stream."

"How far?"

"Maybe ten li."

"That's five thousand met, give or take."

"The roof is pretty low, where it disappears. I'm not sure I could stay crouched over for that long. I got pretty banged up when I fell."

"Me neither, at least not in this form. Time for me to earn my wages again, I think. If I choose the right creature to morph into, I can probably make it out in three or four hours. I could be back at the shuttle in five or six."

"It could be dangerous; you know, rock falls, that sort of thing."

"Right now I don't think we have a lot of options. There's still no sign of Gala and I don't believe for a second she's just bugged out and left us here."

"Me neither. There's something wrong up there, which is all the more reason for us to find a way out. Are you sure about this?" An Kohli was well aware that bravery wasn't one of the qualities that Den had in abundance.

"No, but I don't think I have any choice. It's either that or a slow, lingering death made all the slower by listening to you complaining about how clever Su Mali was."

An Kohli let out a snort of laughter. "You have such a way with words, Den. OK. If you want to give it a try. But if things start going wrong, come back here."

"Where else would I go? Just don't forget about me if Gala turns up."

An Kohli stood up and embraced him. As far as Den could remember it was the first time she had ever done such a thing.

"Good luck." She whispered in his ear.

"As I recall, you don't believe in luck." He chuckled.

"No, but you do."

Without a further word, Den turned and made for the side of the cavern where the stream disappeared into its tunnel. Ducking low, he entered the watercourse.

It was lower than he had expected and he wasted no time in choosing a new form. The last vestige of his clothing was removed and he took on the form of a panther like creature. He splashed his way along the trickle of water for what seemed like hours, but he knew that time tended to slow down in darkness such as this. It was total. As he had explained to An Kohli, although he was able to adopt the shape of the creature, he wasn't able to take advantage of many of its physical capabilities, such as enhanced vision in darkness. He was reminded of this every time his head collided with a jutting rock. For a long time after his departure An Kohli heard a range of yelps and growls echoing down the tunnel to her.

The tunnel continued and if it deviated in its line then the changes in direction were too subtle for Den to sense. The ground must have been sloping, because the water continued to flow, but the slope must have been quite gentle.

After a while Den realised that his feet - or paws as he should have thought of them - were now submerged, which meant that the water was getting deeper. Before long he found his elbows getting wet, and then his shoulders. Finally he felt the water splashing against his chin.

He stopped, trying to work out what the change in depth signified. The water was still flowing, he could feel gentle tug of a current against his fur, but the increase in depth meant that there was some sort of obstruction to the flow, causing the water to back up behind it and for this subterranean pond to form. There was no doubt in his mind that he couldn't continue the journey in his present form.

The problem was, what to change into. Some sort of eel made sense, but what sort? There was one hundred and ten ziku of him, which meant that whatever sort of eel he chose also had to be one hundred and ten ziku. He could expand or compress his mass, to some degree, but he couldn't make it disappear. Most of the eels of that size with which he was familiar tended to be quite thick around the middle and that wouldn't be of any use to him. The water course had only been a trickle so the hole had to have quite a narrow diameter for it to form that size of a pond behind it. Either that, or the water course had become blocked by debris. Allowing water to only soak through and no shape he could adopt would work for him.

He searched his memory for every eel he had ever seen on natural history media programmes or in aquariums. Then he remembered that some types of snake could also travel under water for quite long distances. There were several species of snake that were long enough to accommodate his mass without also thickening in the middle. But for what distance would it be necessary for him to swim? There was no way of knowing. Well, An Kohli had wished him good luck, so now was the time to find out how good his luck was.

His legs disappeared, and he felt his skull shrink and his face lengthen. His tongue flicked out, sensing the damp air. He knew he had to make a decision, either to go forward or to retreat. He went forward, his body moving sinuously to propel him beneath the water.

For the time being he was able to keep his head up and continue to breath the air.

Again he lost all sense of time, but at last he felt the walls of the waterway close in around him. The ceiling became lower, finally forcing his head below the level of the water. His nostrils closed automatically.

His body became restricted as the walls closed in to inhibit his ability to bend and he slowed down. Closer and closer the walls, floor and ceiling compressed him. But behind him the force of water kept pushing him along, like trying to push a cork back into a bottle of wine. He felt himself wedged in position, unable to moved forward or to move back. Panic started to set in. He knew he had to stay calm but telling himself that only made the feeling of panic worsen. He began to feel his lungs burning as the last useable oxygen within them was consumed. How long did he have until his body forced him to open his mouth and take in his first mouthful of water; the first of several that would result in him drowning?

Snakes! He cursed himself. Think of what snakes can do!

They can get through holes with a smaller diameter than their own bodies a voice whispered inside his head. Of course they can. But how can they do that?

By compressing their rib cages. The voice replied.

But I'm not a snake. He told the voice. I just look like one right now.

Why not give it a try anyway? The voice encouraged.

Oh, very well. He gave in to the voice. He concentrated hard on his ribs, trying to work out how to compress them. Spots formed behind his eyes as his air supply ran out. He didn't have long. He tried again, but nothing happened. At last his body gave up the unequal fight and he lost consciousness.

* * *

"Communication coming in." Lazarus informed Gala.

"Put it on the screen." Gala's jaw dropped as she came face to face with herself. Not quite herself, though. The other Gala hadn't had the benefit of the services of a top class hairdresser recently, and her longer hair was drawn back into a pony tail. But apart from that, Gala had to admit that her own mother would have been confused.

"Hand over An Kohli." The other Gala commanded.

"That isn't very polite." Gala stalled. "How about telling me how come I'm looking at myself on a ship that shouldn't exist."

The other Gala gave a sigh. "I've no time for this. Just hand her over."

"No. I'm not going to do anything of the sort until I find out what's going on." Gala stalled desperately. She couldn't let them find out that where An Kohli was. It wouldn't be difficult to intercept the Adastra's shuttle and blow it to atoms. It also wouldn't be difficult to fool An Kohli into docking the shuttle with the other Adastra and take her prisoner, if that was their intention.

"Oh, very well. Are you aware that An Kohli has recently visited a parallel universe? A couple of them, in fact."

"I am. She told me all about it."

"Did she tell you that in our universe she killed our An Kohli."

"She did. She wasn't happy about having had to do it, but she didn't have much choice in the matter."

"That is for a court to decide. We've come from that universe to arrest her." At least that suggested that this Gala hadn't been corrupted by the other An Kohli.

"How? An Kohli told me that Professor Van Golden was giving up his research into the subject."

"What can I tell you? He lied. Beings do sometimes." She paused to think. "We tracked him down to the Endeavour. An Kohli thought he had taken his family back to Zygor. In fact he did, which is where we found them and how we found out about the space station. But then he returned to the Endeavour to continue to develop the portal device. We turned up about the time he completed it."

"Did you ask the Professor what had happened to him? How he had ended up on the Endeavour?"

"No, we just asked him if the device was working, grabbed it and left him there. Then we came here, to this universe and opened a portal to let you into it."

So that was how An Kohli and Den had apparently disappeared. The disruption to the surveillance cameras must have been caused by the cross-over. But she still had to dissuade this other Gala not to pursue An Kohli any further.

"Perhaps you should ask the Professor what happened to him."

"Why?"

"Because then you'd have found out that the An Kohli you knew was Tiny Blur's lover and was working against the restoration of the Magi, not towards it. It was your An Kohli who was behind the pirate raid on Zygor University. She took the Professor to Tiny Blur to be tortured."

"You're lying."

"I wish I were." Gala remembered a phrase that An Kohli had used. "I am you and you are me. Do you think I'm capable of lying?"

"The same argument applies to your An Kohli. Is she capable of killing in cold blood the way she did?"

Touché, thought Gala. But there had to be an argument that would convince her. Evidence to back up her claims, that was what she needed. "Back in your universe, have you been harassed by the Fell? Have they tried to kill or capture you? Have they tried to prevent you from finding the Magi?"

"Not really. They've been too busy robbing the galaxy to pay us any attention."

"That's strange, because in our galaxy they've tried several times. They want the Magi eggs for themselves, or for them to be destroyed. Either will do. The reason that An Kohli ended up in your universe was as a result of their latest attempt to stop her finding this last egg. It very nearly worked, as well."

"According to you."

"You don't have to take my word for it. In your universe, do you submit reports to the Guild when you have completed an operation?"

"Of course."

"Then perhaps you had better read some of ours. Lazarus, send the last two years' worth of operational reports to the other Adastra."

"Done." The computer replied.

"You're just stalling for time. Giving An Kohli the chance to escape."

"Where to? If she's on board you would see her leave, but she isn't."

"She's on that planet, isn't she?"

"No, actually she isn't." Gala hoped that the lie didn't show on her face "Den's down there trying to locate the last egg. It was an easy recovery, so An Kohli went off to do something else."

"But it wasn't." The other Gala sounded alarmed. "Su Mali had … You don't know what Su Mali has done, do you?"

"No." Panic gripped Gala, making her voice shrill. "But now you've got to tell me."

"It will do you no good to know. You're staying here and we'll go and find An Kohli for ourselves."

"No, please wait. At least read the reports before you go. They'll give you a very different version of the Fell to the one with which you are familiar."

"Oh, very well." She turned away from the camera to speak to someone out of sight. "Den, you take one half and I'll take the rest."

She cut the communications channel.

It was an hour before the channel opened once again.

"OK, I'll admit you seem to be having far more trouble with the Fell than we have experienced." The other Gala conceded. "But that doesn't prove that our An Kohli has had anything to do with Tiny Blur. She hates him."

"If you go back to your own galaxy and speak to your Professor Van Golden, he'll be able to confirm it. I take it that he's still on board the Endeavour?"

"He may have left by now. Or maybe he's started building a new device. He seems pretty obsessed with it."

"Well, if he isn't on the Endeavour he'll have gone back home, I'm sure. Either way you won't have any trouble finding him. When you do, ask him to tell you what happened after the fire at Zygor, up to the time when An Kohli came back here; well, not here, but back to our universe."

"And while we're away, what will you be doing?"

"Sitting here waiting for you to come back. You said it yourself, I'm not going anywhere." It shouldn't take them that long. Once back in their own universe they would be able to contact Van Golden via the galacticnet and communicate with him that way.

"You might still have your device, the one your Professor built."

"You were off the air for an hour while you read the reports. Yet here I am, just where you left me. I think that proves that I don't have another device."

"Very well. We'll be back when we've spoken to the Professor, but we may be some time."

It was only after they had disappeared through their portal that Gala realised that if they were convinced that her An Kohli was innocent, they didn't have to come back at all.

* * *

Den's body gave up the fight against the lack of oxygen and he lost consciousness.

At which point Den's muscles relaxed and his ribs were pushed inwards by the pressure being applied by the walls of the watercourse. The pressure of the water building up behind him finished the work, driving him through the narrow tube and into the open air.

The pressurised jet of water propelled him through the air, twisting and turning like a length of discarded rope. He landed with a soft thud on dry grass. Reacting both to the lack of oxygen and to the change in environment, Den morphed back to his natural state. Hungry lungs sucked in the fresh, life giving air and he gradually returned to consciousness.

Waking up naked was nothing new to Den but waking up naked in the middle of a broad grassy plain was, so it took him a few moments to re-orient himself. The pains in his body were the greatest help in this. He groaned aloud as he tested the various parts of himself to make sure they were working. Examining the scrapes on his skin he could see that a couple were bleeding, though not much. Strangely his arms were unhurt, then he remembered that snakes don't have arms. He would live, which was good, but he would hurt for several days, which wasn't.

He looked skywards and saw that it was starting to get dark. It had been just after dawn when they had arrived, probably late morning when he had set off along the tunnel, which meant that it had taken much longer than he had anticipated to get to where he was. He would have to hurry. Even in summer the plain might be colder than expected.

He checked the direction of the watercourse to make sure he had his bearings correct, then trotted up the hill, imagining the small trickle of water running deep beneath his feet. It wasn't high and when he got there he could make out the dim silhouette of a ridge, flattening and broadening to form the level ground on which they had parked the shuttle. But it wasn't in view so he had a long way yet to go.

As night fell and the stars came out he tried to keep his mind empty. Thinking would just slow him down, as he learned to his cost in the past. There would be plenty of time for thinking when he got to the shuttle. There were space suits in the shuttle, stowed away in lockers behind the seats. There were also emergency supplies of water and food. An Kohli would be OK for water where she was, but for him it was a more urgent need, or it would be once he got there. Food was important for both of them. He wondered how long they would have to survive on what little there was.

Stavros didn't have a moon. With three planets in such close proximity any moon would have been unable to find a stable orbit, but there was plenty of starlight. He fixed his direction on one prominent one and headed for it. It would move, of course, but not enough to take him off course. In fact it rose steadily skywards, not seeming to drift left or right. But still he almost managed to miss the shuttle in the darkness. Had he been in hilly ground he would have done, but as it was the large egg shape stood out against the horizon to one side of his path.

He activated the external ramp switch. An Kohli had the remote control and he doubted that the infra red signal would carry around corners. As the ramp dropped, the interior lights came on, providing a bright rectangle of illumination.

What to do first? Dress? Eat? Contact Gala? Contact An Kohli? He didn't know which. He imagined An Kohli sitting on the floor of the cavern, alone and not knowing whether he was dead or alive and that made up his mind for him. He opened the emergency locker and started to look through the supplies stored within.

Screw her! It was her fault he was here. He'd been perfectly happy masquerading as a droid bartender until she turned up. Since then she'd nearly got him killed half a dozen times.

But had he been happy? Happy serving beers to morose drovers who were poor conversationalists and worse tippers? Not that he was able to join in the conversations, in his disguise. And not that droids were ever tipped. Had he been happy eating leftover food; bad food at that? No, not really. Had he ever felt more alive than when chasing along in An Kohli's wake, trying to capture someone or escape from someone? No, he hadn't. Perhaps she wasn't that bad after all.

He closed the locker and reached towards the comms panel. "An Kohli, can you hear me?

"Den, is that you?"

"Who do you think it is, the tooth fairy? Of course it's me. How are you doing?"

"Not bad. It's a bit cold down here."

"I'll wrap some food in a blanket for you and drop it down. I don't think there's a rope long enough to pull you out, but I'll check that in the morning. Right now I'm too weak to do anything even if there was one."

"That's fine. I'll manage until then. Any sign of Gala?"

"I haven't tried her."

"OK, if you can't make contact, activate the distress beacon."

"Are you sure you want to do that?" Pirates monitored the distress frequencies, hoping for easy pickings from stranded ships. They would be sitting ducks if they were located by a Meklon ship.

"We don't have any choice Den. If Gala's missing then the only way off this planet is for us to be rescued."

Opening the space suit locker Den pulled one of the bulky, one-size-fits-all suits out. He didn't need the whole thing, just the lining. Tubes ran through it, carrying the heating elements that kept the wearer alive in the absolute zero temperature of space. He unplugged it from the suit's power supply and dragged it out through the opening at the waist. It wasn't an attractive garment, but when An Kohli was eventually pulled from the cavern it would be preferable to have her mocking his fashion sense than his physical attributes.

Opening the food locker again he drew out some of the dehydrated food packets, checking the labels to see what they were. An Kohli and he had different tastes in food, so he may as well make sure that she got the meals she liked and he got the ones he preferred. Satisfied that what he had selected would at least satisfy her hunger, he took one of the thermal blankets out of its vacuum pack and wrapped it around the food packets, before adding a spoon. The food was mixed with water in the packet so there was no need to provide a bowl. Besides, he didn't have a bowl.

Adding a torch as a final gift, he secured the bundle with a cable ties and was ready to go.

The approach to the hole would be the difficult part, he knew. The soil was dry and crumbled to the touch. It wouldn't need much weight to be applied for it to give way under him. He got to within five met and dropped onto his belly and started to crawl forward, pushing the bundle of supplies ahead of him through the grass like the prow of an ice-breaker.

He was about fifty sim from the edge when he heard stones start to patter to the floor of the cavern, evidence that he was starting to upset the stability of the hole. No matter. He was close enough.

"An Kohli, can you hear me?" he called.

"I can hear you. I don't know how close you are, but don't come any closer. You're dropping stones on my head."

"Thanks for the warning." It wasn't necessary, but An Kohli didn't know that and she was trying to be helpful. "I've got food here for about three days. When that runs out there's some more, but I suggest you ration this. We don't know how long we'll be here."

"Ok, send it down."

"Mind your head!" Den shouted, pitching the bundle over the edge and into the cavern. A second passed, maybe a little more, then he heard the soft thump as the bundle hit the ground.

"I hope it isn't all Aludran stew." An Kohli called up, naming the least appetising dish normally to be found in the emergency rations.

"Beggars can't be choosers." He laughed as he called back. He had actually kept that back for himself. There was something about it that reminded him of his mother's cooking; she had been a terrible cook.

"I'll keep the radio channel open. Just call if you need anything." He said as he started to wriggle backwards away from the black circle of the hole. Not that he could think of anything that she might need that he would be able to provide, but it seemed like the right thing to say.

Satisfied that he was safe, he stood up and walked the remaining distance back to the shuttle. At least he had a comfortable seat in which to sleep. An Kohli would have to make do with the hard rock of the cavern floor. No she wouldn't, he decided. He could take some of the cushions from the other seats. It would be better than nothing.

Piling up three of the large cushions, he made his way back to the cavern and pitched them over the edge, before returning to the shuttle for the remainder of the night.

He spent thirty minutes trying to contact Gala, but there was no sign of her. Finally conceding defeat, Den logged the shuttle onto the local galacticnet node, left by the exploration ship that had first visited the planet, and activated the distress beacon. He would have to have a word with Gala about modifying the shuttle's communications system to handle voice calls or mail. That would have allowed him to use the galacticnet to summon help from a friendly source, rather than entering a lottery that included the arrival of Meklon pirates.

Finally he allowed himself to fall into an exhausted sleep.

The following morning he searched the shuttle's toolbox, accessible only from outside the craft, but found nothing that would allow him to pull An Kohli from her rocky prison. His only alternative was to strip some of the electrical cabling from the shuttle to substitute for a rope, but he knew that wouldn't be a good idea. Gala might know which cables weren't needed for a safe return to the Adastra, but he had no idea.

They settled down to wait, either for the return of Gala or for the arrival of a rescue ship.

* * *

Bounty hunters get used to waiting. Even when they know the location of a fugitive, they often have to conduct stakeouts that last for days, waiting for their target to arrive home, or at a hotel or some other place of refuge. Then there was all the space travel. The galaxy was just such an enormously big place. Even using wormholes, journeys could last for months.

There were commercial interchange stations, used by scheduled passenger transports, located at points where the navi-coms calculated that the greatest distance could be travelled in the shortest amount of time, but bounty hunters rarely used commercial stations. They preferred to travel direct and that meant taking whatever route the navi-com selected for them.

But the boredom of waiting was usually tempered by the extensive entertainment library that ships carried. In a shuttle, however, that wasn't something that was available.

For Gala, however, there was always something to do. She was never happier than crawling through the engineering spaces of the Adastra, looking for something that might need the turn of a screw, a drop of oil or just a dab with a cleaning wipe. Tucked into her pocket was her communicator, a channel open to relay any incoming communications to her from the command deck.

At that precise moment, she was lying on her back in a narrow duct, a panel above her head open while she inspected the inner workings of the pulsar guidance system. The last time they had used the weapons it had been a fraction of a sim off and that would never do. She scrutinised the servo for any signs of wear, but she realised that she would have to strip it out and put it under a magnifier if she really wanted to examine it.

"Incoming communication." Lazarus's voice sounded from the pouch pocket of her flight suit.

"This is Gala on the Adastra. Who am I speaking to?" She said, pushing the inspection panel back into position.

"The same, but different." The reply came back.

"I'm not able to take your call on visual." Gala announced.

"I can guess why." The other Gala sounded cheerful. "What is it this time?"

"Inaccurate pulsar fire."

"You suspect the servo?"

"Yes."

"I'll take a look at ours when we get a moment. Anyway, can you please return to your command deck. We want to send you back where you belong."

"You spoke to Professor Van Golden."

"I did. He confirmed everything you told me, right down to providing a description of Tiny Blur's torture chamber."

Gala wriggled free of the duct, dropped to the floor of the corridor and stepped through the door onto the command deck. The other Gala's image was already on the viewing screen.

"What will you do now?"

"I've already sent a report through to the Grand Master. This is going to make things very difficult for us. Our An Kohli must have passed on details of our most secret plans."

"She has also, we suspect, passed on the Magus eggs. The ones you have given the GCIE are either copies or they're empty."

"Yes, that is something else we will have to deal with. Things aren't looking good for us right now."

"Is there anything we can tell you that might be of help?" Gala felt her alter ego's torment. She hadn't just lost a friend, however bad that friend might have been, she had seen everything she believed in betrayed.

"No, I don't think so. But I can tell you something. Su Mali positioned that cairn above a cavern. The roof of the cavern is very fragile and it is likely that you're An Kohli has fallen through it. In our universe that didn't matter too much. It was an inconvenience, but I was able to get her out. But you've been away for over a week. Who knows what might have happened in the interim. I'm sorry for my part in that."

"You were doing what you thought was right. You were being a bounty hunter."

"Not any more. I'm not doing that anymore. Without An Kohli …" Tears started to run down the other Gala's face.

"I know. I would feel the same. What will you do instead?"

"In the short term I'll continue to work with the Guild to stop the Fell. After that … well, there's always someone who needs an engineer.

"The ship builders at Skopos would snap you up in a heartbeat."

"Too corporate for me. No, I'll probably sign on to a mega freighter or something like that. They're so badly maintained they'll keep me occupied for years." She cuffed away the tears from her cheeks. "Now, you need to get into position to return to your universe. If you aren't in exactly the right place who knows where you might end up. I'm sending the co-ordinates over now.

The ship was manoeuvred into the right place, heading in the right direction.

"Goodbye Gala." They said in unison. There was some disruption to the surveillance cameras, the picture breaking up for a few seconds before settling once again and a vibration ran through the ship, then the image on the surveillance camera's viewing screen showed a large hole in the ground where the cairn had previously stood. At the same time, a bleep started up from the communications panel, indicating an incoming distress call.

"Ship approaching." Lazarus said.

"What now, for freak's sake." Gala said. "Identify."

"No identification available."

"Ready pulsars." She snapped, realising that a ship without any identification could only mean it was a pirate. "Put the ship on the viewing screen."

It was a typical looking pirate craft. A converted freighter with an additional engine bolted to its side to improve acceleration and pulsar turrets to intimidate its prey.

"Lazarus, map the fields of fire of those pulsars."

At once the computer sketched cones above and below the ship to show where the danger areas lay. There were two areas where there was a reduced risk of being hit. The largest was, as usual, at the rear of the ship, where the flare of the rocket effluxes formed a screen, but at the same time the rockets themselves provided a back blast of energy. The other one was in front of the ship, but not until the attacker got quite close in, risking being hit on its approach.

"Eenie, meenie…" Gala said aloud, trying decide which way to approach. The ship changed its angle of attack, bringing it towards the Adastra. While the captain would mainly be interested in whoever, or whatever, was emitting the distress signal, he couldn't leave himself open to attack. The Adastra had to be dealt with first.

"That makes the decision easier." Gala said aloud to the otherwise empty command deck. "If I try to go around you I'll open up my flanks for attack, so head on it is."

Pulsar fire erupted from the two turrets as the pirate captain engaged at maximum range. The Adastra rocked, but the shields held. Too much power had been dissipated by the blasts at that range.

"Full speed, Lazarus." Gala commanded. If she was going to do this, she needed to be faster than the gunners aboard the attacking ship.

She jinked the Adastra left and right, up and down, spiralling around, confusing the gunners and preventing them from getting any shots on target. Well, almost preventing them from getting any shots on target. One blast did hit the ship's nose, but it was the best protected part of the ship, both in terms of armour and in its shields. She opened up with her own pulsars, engaging the upper turret, where the better gunner appeared to be. She saw the blasts hit the hull around the turret, but it didn't stop firing. "Damn, I knew that servo was off whack." She muttered to herself.

"Allow me, Gala." Lazarus said, taking control of the pulsars. He let a stream of high energy rip across space between the rapidly closing ships. They hit direct on the turret, silencing it.

As Gala rolled the Adastra upwards, taking her out of sight line of the lower turret and into the new safe zone that had opened up, she heard the computer comment. "I was able to compensate for the error."

Gala lined up her next shot with care. Freighters always had their command decks at the front, so as to leave maximum space between the front and the rear of the ship for cargo. She fired directly into the nose of the larger ship, seeing several of her blasts hitting home before she was over the top and heading for the back of the attacker. She turned back quickly, anxious not to overshoot and allow the lower pulsar turret a target at which to aim.

She was now playing catch-up with the ship below her, but its speed was no match for the Adastra. As she overhauled it she rolled the Adastra so that its pulsars could fire directly downward into the upper surfaces of the ship. A line of strikes lit up brightly. Loose objects started to fly from the hull, indicating that she had breached it. Between the high internal air pressure and the vacuum of space there was no stopping any object, or being, that wasn't secured within the ship.

The pirate craft was still under power, however, even if it was no longer under command. Its path was now taking it towards the edge of the planet's atmosphere. A shuttle popped out of the side as some of the crew decided that the end was nigh. The hunters would now become the hunted.

It was illegal to fire on shuttles escaping from stricken ships, so Gala paid them no heed. She kept her eyes strictly on the bigger craft as it struggled to maintain altitude. But with no one to operate the controls, the huge engines continued to drive it down towards the planet. The nose started to glow as the friction offered by the planet's atmosphere started to make itself felt. The ship wasn't built for the rigours of atmospheric flight, so it started to break up. A second shuttle appeared, but was hit by a chunk of flying debris, puncturing the hull and surely killing anyone inside.

* * *

Den was sitting in the sun outside the shuttle, eating the last half of the last packet of emergency rations. What he would do for food the next day he had no idea. There was wildlife around, he knew. He had even seen some of it, but its reptilian forms were distinctly unappetising.

He heard a double booming sound which made him look up. Above him was a massive fireball, streaking across the sky and heading for the distant horizon.

But what was it? A meteor? An asteroid? A space sh … no, surely not the Adastra?

He hurried towards the edge of the cavern, abandoning all thoughts of safety. At the very last moment he realised the danger and dropped onto his stomach to spread his weight.

"An Kohli, can you see that, above us?"

"No, I can't see anything Den. I heard something though. It sounded a bit like a sonic boom."

"It was. There's a fireball. Something's crashing, but I don't know what."

"You don't think it's the Adastra, do you?"

"I don't know. It could be … hang on, the shuttle's ramp is closing."

"OK, Den, don't panic. Think logically. The fireball can't be the Adastra. If it was then there could be no remote command signals to operate the shuttle. I think whatever it is was trouble of some sort, but Gala's sorted it out."

"But she wasn't up there. I know, I've been calling her every few hours for the last week or more."

"Maybe she's back from wherever she went. And just in the nick of time, by the sound of it."

The ground shook as something very big hit it. The vibrations went on for some time and Den could hear soil and stones falling into the cavern in front of him. Then came the sound, a roaring explosion that seemed to go on for ages.

"Whatever it is, it hit hard." Den observed when silence fell again.

But no reply came from the cavern.

"An Kohli!" Den shouted. "An Kohli! Are you alright."

The silence told him that she wasn't. Something must have fallen on her, either killing her or knocking her unconscious. Den hoped that it was only the latter. An Kohli with a sore head was preferable to An Kohli never scolding him again.

He looked around as the Adastra's shuttle lifted off behind him, just as another descended further away across the plain.

"Looks like someone got out." He muttered to himself, reaching for his pulsar. Only he didn't have a pulsar. The one he had been wearing when the ground fell away beneath him was still somewhere down in the cavern, and the one that had been in the emergency locker of the shuttle was still sitting on the top of the control console, now on its way skywards.

Whoever, or whatever, was in that new shuttle, Den was probably going to have to face unarmed. The shuttle was a long way away, so unless whoever was inside it brought it nearer, he had some time. Gala, assuming it was her operating the Adastra's shuttle by remote control, would get down here before long. But they had no way of communicating. An Kohli was unconscious, his communicator was down there along with his pulsar and now the shuttle's radio was no longer available to him. Suddenly he felt very lonely.

# 15 - Jetpacks

The two pirates stared at the damaged landing strut. Already the shuttle was canted at a dangerous angle and if the strut buckled any more it was in danger of falling over.

"That's why we can't use it to get any closer to where the other shuttle was. If the shuttle tips over when we land, it could damage the outer skin and we're stuck down here. It's too great a risk." She said. "We'll have to walk."

The speaker was an Izarian, her face scarred by a hundred fights. Her companion, a lupine from Rasalhague, wasn't the thinking type. He didn't need to be as long as he had someone else to do the thinking for him.

"May as well get tooled up then." he said. The shuttle tilted dangerously as he climbed back inside and began passing weapons out to his companion.

There were two shoulder fired high powered pulsars with a killing range of almost a thousand met, two large handheld pulsars and they shared a box of photon grenades between them. Whatever was waiting for them had better be friendly or too frightened to fight, because with that amount of fire power they would soon be dead if they weren't.

The shuttle was big enough to accommodate six beings, hence the amount of weaponry it had on board. The fact that there were only two beings present spoke volumes about their feelings of loyalty towards their former crew-mates.

"How far do you think it is?" Asked the lupine.

"Looked like about eight thousand met, near as I could make out." She said as she walked away from the shuttle.

"Any idea who they are?"

"The distress signal identified the shuttle as being that of the Adastra."

He stopped. "That's An Kohli's ship. No one told me we were messing with her. Do you really think this is a good idea?"

"I have no idea what's going on here, so I don't know if it's a good idea or not. One minute the Captain says that we've got a sitting duck down here, then the next minute some ship appears out of nowhere and starts shooting at us. Or maybe we shot at it. Doesn't matter. All I know know is that our ship is gone, our shuttle is damaged and the only way to turn this into some sort of win is to find whoever is over there."

"Maybe they went up in that shuttle?"

"Maybe they didn't. If they did then we come back here and hope to get picked up soon. But if there's any money to be made, it's over there, not over here." She started walking again, not bothered whether her companion followed.

\* \* \*

Maths wasn't Den's strong point, but he could do some basic sums when he needed to. The newly arriving shuttle had landed somewhere between five thousand and ten thousand met away. So if the occupants walked they would take somewhere between an hour and two hours. If they ran it would be quicker but it's harder to sneak up when you're running.

On the other hand, the shuttle would take about thirty minutes to reach the Adastra, assuming that was where it had gone, and another half hour to get back, if Gala didn't decide to refuel it. After a week down here the batteries would be low. Then there was whatever time it would take for Gala to equip it for a rescue mission. Maybe add another half hour on top. Then they would actually have to carry out the rescue, and how long that would take would very much depend on whether An Kohli was conscious or unconscious. A conscious person can help themselves, even if they have other injuries.

It was going to be tight.

Den knew that there was a wide range of shapes that he could morph into that would allow him to escape through the grass and hide out. In fact he could even head straight for the other shuttle and steal it while its occupants were on their way to his location.

But that would leave An Kohli defenceless and Gala, when she arrived, might walk straight into trouble. So that wasn't an option. Not for the moment, anyway. He settled down in the longer grass to wait. If they passed him by he might be able to incapacitate one of them before the others realised what was happening. It would shorten the odds, anyway. If there was only one of them then he was worrying over nothing. Pirates weren't loyal when it came to escaping from stricken ships. One might have bailed out alone, leaving the others to fend for themselves.

The whining noise of a descending shuttle made him look up. His maths weren't that far off. It must have been well over an hour since it had left. It settled into the grass, occupying the exact same footprints that it had left behind.

Den stood up and hurried over as the ramp lowered itself. He was slightly puzzled when Gala failed to appear at the top of it. What was she waiting for? She must know that danger was close by.

"Gala?" He called, as he stepped onto the ramp and walked quickly to the shuttle's entrance. There was no reply. Sticking his head through he saw that the tiny cabin was empty. Well, empty of any form of life. Lying across the seats were the bulky shapes of two jetpacks.

"Gala!." He shouted. "What's going on. Why haven't you come down here to help me?"

"Sorry Den, but I can't take the risk of leaving the Adastra. You saw that fireball, I suppose?"

"Yes. So what? They won't bother us anymore, but there's some of their crew down here who may decide that they don't want us to be rescued."

"And there may be other ships on the way here. They won't have been the only ship to pick up the distress signal. There's no way of knowing who might turn up, or when. If I leave the Adastra it might be either blown apart or captured. Then where will we be? Sorry, buddy, but you're going to have to sort this out for yourself."

"How did you know I wasn't down in the cavern with An Kohli?"

"I saw you on the surveillance cameras. Now, if you're so worried about those survivors, I suggest you get a move on and get An Kohli out of that hole."

"But why jetpacks? You know I hate jetpacks!"

"We don't have any rope long enough to reach. So it's either jetpacks or nothing. Now get on with it!"

Den made a disgusted sound, but he knew he didn't have any options. Grumbling just loud enough for the microphones to activate and carry his mutterings up to the Adastra, he lifted one of the heavy packs and carried it outside, before returning for the other. He also slipped his pulsar, lying where he had left it, inside his space suit liner.

After lowering the jetpack to the ground he returned inside and activated the shuttle's highest camera, mounted on the top of the craft. Swivelling it around he spotted movement some distance away. He zoomed the camera in, allowing the movement to resolve into two figures, walking resolutely towards him. He tried to estimate the distance but he had no reference points and the camera wasn't fitted with a range finder. That was something else he might decide to mention to Gala. At least this debacle was providing some learning points for them. He raised the camera and zoomed out, trying to judge the distance between the two figures and their shuttle. He estimated that they had covered as much as two thirds of the distance from their start point.

Gala was right, he had better get a move on.

He hurried down the shuttle's ramp and grabbed the nearest jetpack, shrugging his way into its harness. He fed the groin straps between his legs and buckled them up, pulling them as tightly as he could bear. It wouldn't be the first time a user had slipped out of the shoulder harness because they had put comfort before safety.

He picked up the second jetpack, almost collapsing under the combined weight of the two machines. Holding it against his chest he slipped the shoulder harness over his own shoulders and secured it to the one he was wearing. That left his hands free to operate the controls of his own pack, which hung on flexible arms on either side.

Flicking the power switch he heard the jets start to fire up inside the machine. Using standard jets was too dangerous, they tended to set fire to the legs of the user, so heat was used to warm the air inside a compressor which forced it out under pressure, through two narrow gauge pipes that were extended out over each side of the pack. That provided the lifting force. Den studied a gauge next to the power switch until the tiny indicator lights reached the green zone, then took the other controller in his other hand. By operating them in tandem he could vary the amount of compressed gas that was directed to each nozzle to lift, lower, or turn himself.

He lifted gently from the ground and allowed himself to hover just above it while he adjusted his position to make himself more comfortable. He didn't have to go very high. In fact he could easily have walked the first hundred met of the journey, but letting the jetpack take the strain made things easier.

He increased the power as he reached the hole in the cavern's roof, anticipating the sudden drop. Hovering for a few moments he reduced power to allow him to descend into the cavern. Darkness enveloped him as he got lower and he realised that it had been close to twilight. Time passes so quickly when you're having fun, he reminded himself.

He touched down gently on the cavern floor and he quickly looked around for An Kohli.

There she was, lying half buried by a heap of soil and stones. About a met away lay a larger lump, probably the one that had rendered her unconscious.

He unclipped the spare jetpack and lowered it to the ground before leaning over An Kohli. He heard her breath rasping in her throat. At least she was alive.

Gently he slapped her face, as he had seen beings doing in the movies, but he got no response, not even a groan. He scowled at the spare jetpack in frustration. He might be able to strap An Kohli into it, but there was no way she would be able to control it and there was also no way he could control it and his own at the same time.

He thought for a moment, trying to remember everything he had ever learned about jetpacks, which wasn't much. Could they carry the weight of two beings?

Why was he trying to answer stupid questions? Gala would know.

Hurriedly he searched An Kohli's belt for her communicator. "Gala, can you hear me?" he asked.

"Yes, I can hear you. Your communicator ident is show you as being An Kohli."

"Yes, I'm using hers, Goodness knows where mine is. Look, jetpacks ... can they carry two beings at the same time?"

"There are some that are specifically designed for that. The ones used by rescue services ..."

"Yes, but what about these ones? Will they do it?"

"Hang on." There was a pause, no doubt while Gala consulted the manufacturer's handbook. Or, more likely, consulted Lazarus.

"OK, Den. According to the handbook they'll lift two beings of average weight, so long as you don't want to go above twenty met."

Den craned his head back and tried to gauge how high the roof of the cavern was. It was definitely more than ten met, but was it less than twenty? Only one way to find out. He slipped the communicator under the cuff of his spacesuit liner so he would know where it was if he needed it again.

Quickly he unbuckled the spare jetpack from its harness and strapped An Kohli into it. By putting the harness on her back to front he was left with loose straps on the side nearest him, which he needed to attach An Kohli to himself. That was the easy bit. He now had to get her upright and standing still enough for him to strap her harness to his.

Unconscious beings, he knew, weren't that co-operative when it came to standing upright.

He bent down and almost toppled as the weight of the jetpack made him over balance again. He rocked back on his haunches to balance his weight evenly, then took An Kohli under the shoulders. Pushing hard with his thighs he managed to straighten and get An Kohli into a sitting position. Half way there,

He was now able to get his arms around her upper body and lock his fingers together. "Sorry An Kohli." he muttered, very aware of where his hands now were. He pulled An Kohli towards him, their combined weight overbalancing him and forcing him to sit. Why hadn't he thought of that himself? It was far easier this way.

He spread his legs, sliding them down the side of An Kohli's. He pulled her again, settling her snuggly against himself. If she woke up now he would have a tough job explaining what he was doing, he mused. He grabbed the loose ends of An Kohli's harness straps and attached them to his own.

Bending his knees, Den was able to half stand until he could adjust An Kohlis' weight distribution. With a final thrust he was able to stand almost upright, the weight of her body forcing him into a stoop,

He gave her another heave, hoping against hope that An Kohli's legs would support some of her weight, but her knees just buckled and she threatened to collapse them both again. Oh well, it had been worth a try.

He powered up the jetpack and fed in the thrust. He felt his weight lighten on his bare feet, but he was still in solid contact with the ground. He fed in more power and heard the jetpack's whine increase, but still couldn't lift off. Finally he turned it all the way up to eleven and they started to rise.

He ascended slowly at first, but he was definitely accelerating. At ten met the jets were no longer pushing against the ground, they were now compressing the air beneath his feet, which made them less efficient. His rate of ascent slowed, but sim by painful sim he rose towards the hole in the cavern's roof. He thought that if he grabbed hold of the edge and pulled, the jetpack would finish the job and propel him upwards. He couldn't feed any more power in on either side to direct him, so he had to gamble by easing off the power on one side. It worked in that he tilted over and slewed towards the cavern wall, but he also dropped alarmingly. He fed the power back in with a harsh twist of the control. He started to climb once again.

His head banged none too gently on the curve of the cavern wall and he let go of one controller to fend himself off. He was moving along just below the rocky surface, his hand doing the steering while the jet pack maintained his height. At last he was able to get one hand on the edge and pull upwards, soil and stone crumbling under his fingers to fall in his eyes and onto An Kohli's head. Note to self, he thought. Always wear a helmet when using a jetpack inside a cave.

But the upwards pull had helped and his head emerged above ground level. He twisted around to see if the two pirates had arrived, but there seemed to be no sign of them. They could be hunkered down in the grass, but he had no way of knowing. From his low position he was unable to see any distance over the tops of the waving stems.

He pushed down hard with one hand and he rose higher, the jet pack still howling in protest at being held at full power for so long. His feet came out of the hole and Den at once scrabbled to get some purchase with them. As the thrusters found some solid ground to push against, Den found himself rising again. He reduced the thrust, letting his toes touch the ground so he could push himself forward while the jetpack kept his weight off the fragile ground around the hole. An Kohli's feet left a trail through the grass stems as she was dragged along with him.

At last he edged the two of them far enough away from the cavern to allow his full weight to settle on the ground. He powered down the jetpack and silence fell, broken only by his heavy breathing, An Kohli's hoarse gasps and the soft ticking of the cooling metal of the jetpack.

Working quickly, he released An Kohli and lay her on the ground, before removing the burdensome jetpack. Free of its weight he was able to lift An Kohli over his shoulder and stumble towards the shuttle, still over two hundred met away.

He was still a hundred met away when two figures walked around in front of the shuttle and pointed their weapons in his direction. He cursed the starlight that silhouetted him against the sky. He groaned in despair as he thought frantically about what he should do. An Kohli's body shifted slightly and he had to heft her back up again, using his hand to pull her body tighter against his neck. As he did so his fingers came into contact with something hard.

This was no time for niceties. As a pulsar blast zapped across the grass towards them, he unceremoniously he threw An Kohli one way while he dived the other, at the same time keeping a tight grip on the hard object. The big Menafield pulsar slid smoothly out of its hand tooled leather holster and Den was able to snap a shot in the direction of the two pirates. It went nowhere near them, but it did make them duck and look for some cover.

Landing heavily, Den rolled a few times to put some distance between himself and the place he had landed, which they might have seen. He felt under his cuff for An Kohli's communicator and was relieved to find it. "Gala, I've got a situation. I've got An Kohli above ground, but those pirates are between me and the shuttle. Anything you can do to help?"

"Can you see them clearly?"

"Not really, not so long as they keep below the skyline."

"Well, I can change that." At once the shuttle's exterior work lights came on, silhouetting the two pirates. They realised the danger and dived to the ground. Now they were each concealed from the other by the knee length grass.

Den crawled forward, trying to make as little noise as possible. "Can you give me some noise?" he asked Gala.

He heard the whine of the shuttle's ramp starting to rise. As it thumped into place the engine started up. With the pirates being so close their hearing would be overwhelmed. He moved faster, scurrying forward several met in one rush. He saw the shuttle rise into the air then start to swoop around. If Gala made any mistakes it would probably damage the small craft beyond use, stranding them there, but he realised what she was doing. With the Adastra's surveillance camera in infra-red mode she would be able to pick up the bright images of the pirates and use the shuttle to keep their heads down.

Den got to his knees and sprinted forwards before throwing himself into the concealing grass once again. No challenge came, and no pulsar fire. He tried again, making it halfway to the shuttle before dropping onto his belly once more. This time there was a pulsar blast, but it came nowhere near him, suggesting that the shooter hadn't really seen him and was just trying to deter any further encroachments. But the shot had given away the pirate's position. Den rose up onto one knee and let off a blast with An Kohli's Menafield. He didn't expect to hit anything, but it would keep the pirate's own head down. He fired off a second blast and made another run forward, just as the shuttle made another swoop. The pirate that hadn't taken the last shot tried to stand up to use their shoulder fired weapon and was struck squarely by one of the shuttle's landing struts as it swayed past.

Den didn't need to know anything about anatomy to conclude that the pirate was out of the game.

"OK. Gala," Den puffed. "You can back the shuttle off now."

Firing blindly with the Menafield, Den ran forward once again, almost tripping over the second pirate, who was now huddling in the grass. Den kicked the closest weapon out of reach then pointed his pulsar squarely between the female's eyes.

"Don't shoot. Please, don't shoot." The female pleaded.

Backing off a little Den allowed her to get to her feet. She still had a large pulsar at her belt, Den saw. She would probably also have a knife and who knew what else.

By himself he couldn't get close enough to search her. There was only one way to make sure she was disarmed.

"Strip." He commanded.

"Pervert." She snapped back.

"You're too kind. Now start taking your clothes off and put them in a pile in front of you. Make sure I can see your hands at all times.

She started to obey him, sitting on the ground to undo her boots, then standing to remove her overalls. Beneath them she was wearing utilitarian underwear, but it was unlikely she could hide anything in it.

"OK, that will do." He said. "Now back off."

She took several paces back. The pulsar was clearly visible on the belt of the overalls, but Den found the knife in her boot and the grenades concealed in the various pockets of her clothing. When he was satisfied that he had found all the weapons, he tossed her clothes back to her and allowed her to dress again. There was a groan from several met away. The other pirate was returning to the land of the living.

Keeping a careful eye on the one pirate, Den scrabbled in the shuttle's tool box for something with which to immobilise his prisoners. He found a short length of electrical cable which would do the job.

The second pirate was no less well armed than the first, but once he'd had his weaponry removed he instructed the female to drag her comrade back to the shuttle where he could secure them both to a landing strut. At last he was able to take care of An Kohli.

The shuttle's work lights did nothing to help him find the place where he had dumped An Kohli. In the end he was guided by the loud groan that she let out.

"Oh, my head. Where the freak am I?" She rose from the grass, struggling to sit upright. Den trotted over to her.

"Who are you?" An Kohli struggled to make out his face.

"It's me, Den. You've had a bang on the head. It was Gala's fault." He tried to spread the blame for An Kohli's condition. He didn't consider it to be a lie, as she had shot down the ship that had caused the mini planet quake that had shaken free the rock that had hit An Kohli on the head.

"Den? Den who … oh, yeah, Den. What happened?"

"You know you were down in the cavern recovering the magus egg?"

"Cavern … yes, I remember a cavern."

"Well, a rock fell and hit you on the head. You've been out for a couple of hours. Don't try to get up. You'll have a concussion and if you make any sudden moves you may do yourself more harm."

"My head feels like I've got space gremlins inside trying to tunnel their way out. It's the worst hangover ever." She paused, remembering something Den had just said. "Did I find the egg?"

"In your belt pouch, I think." He hoped it was, because he didn't relish the idea of returning to the cavern to try to find it.

An Kohli searched her belt and let out a sigh of relief when she found the egg, "Come on, help me get to the shuttle." She struggled to rise and Den gave her a shoulder to lean on. "How did you get me out of the cavern?"

"Gala turned up again. I've no idea where she was, I haven't asked her yet. Anyway, she sent down a couple of jetpacks and I used them to get you out."

"You hate jetpacks." An Kohli said.

"I know. There's one still down there and the other's lying in the grass somewhere."

"They cost money. I want them back."

"I'll find the one up here, but the other one is staying where it is. I'm not risking my life again for a jetpack."

An Kohli didn't say anything, so Den assumed that he had won the argument. He was grateful that An Kohli was injured otherwise her parsimonious nature might have forced a more serious argument.

They arrived back at the shuttle and Den helped An Kohli on board and strapped her into a seat, before leaving the shuttle once more.

Hunting around in the dark he found the weapons he had taken from the two pirates and pitched them into the cavern. Finding the jetpack took some time as one patch of grass looked much like another in the darkness, but eventually he found it and stowed it safely inside the shuttle.

Finally he dragged the two pirates away from the shuttle so that they wouldn't be injured when it took off. He showed them a pair of wire cutters, with which they could free themselves, laying them in the grass several met away, before jogging back to the shuttle once more.

"Who are they?" An Kohli asked as he settled into the other seat and strapped himself in.

"A couple of pirates that fancied their chances. Survivors from the ship that Gala shot down. We've no room for them on the Adastra, so I'm leaving them here. They've got a shuttle of their own and they'll be picked up in due course."

"There's probably a bounty out on them. If not, we have a clear case for attempted murder."

"You're kidding me, right?" Den scoffed. "The chances of ever collecting a bounty on them are pretty much the same as the chances of this shuttle turning into a pumpkin. As for them ever standing trial, you know that probably won't happen either."

The shuttle lifted off at his command and as they made the journey back to the Adastra Den explained what had happened from when the pirate ship crashed up to the point where An Kohli regained consciousness.

"You saved my life again, Den." An Kohli said, quietly.

"I seem to be making a habit of it. Just remember that when you think about the cost of that jetpack that I left behind."

\* \* \*

The medi-sys diagnosed An Kohli with the concussion that Den had suspected, before prescribing pain killers and bed rest. The painkillers were gulped down gratefully but wild fiju wouldn't have got An Kohli to take bed rest.

As soon as the ship was safely in a wormhole, heading towards their next destination, An Kohli asked Den to escort Jaffa the Hurt into the lounge and make him secure.

"You're really going through with this, aren't you." Gala stated flatly, disgust evident in her voice.

"It's the only way we can flush out George Bush the One Hundred and Twenty Fifth." A cross check with the serial number of the magus egg had confirmed it to be the one containing the intelligence of the human politician and the final missing member of the Magi. "If I'm right and he really is a member of the Fell, he'll be restored and everyone will see him for what he really is. If, on the other hand, I take him to the GCIE, he'll be free to go underground again and work against them."

"And if you're wrong?"

"We'll find that out as well. He'll be held hostage and everyone will see that the Fell are really behind Blur's government."

"After what Jaffa the Hurt did to me, I'm really not happy about letting him go."

"I know, but let's face it, he'll never stand trial. Alison Fakescotsman would make sure of that. He'll either go free or he'll go dead and I don't want to be responsible for him dying."

"We could put him on Macroterra, like the others."

"We could, but that wouldn't serve any useful purpose. I hate having to say it, but we need to think of the bigger picture here."

Gala stifled her reply and hurried to her cabin before An Kohli could see her tears of anger and frustration.

An Kohli shook her head, upset at having to deny Gala the justice that she deserved, but Jaffa the Hurt was more useful this way. Besides, in a few weeks, or months, it would probably make no difference where he was. If they lost the war against the Blur government, then Gala's desire for justice would be as nothing compared to what would happen in the galaxy.

She went into the lounge to confront Jaffa the Hurt.

"At last!" he snapped. "Do you know how long I've been locked up in that cell of yours? You can't treat me this way. I've got rights you know."

"Oh, shut up. You should have thought about your precious rights before you kidnapped Gala and kept her locked up against her will. What about her rights, eh? It doesn't feel so good being on the receiving end, does it?"

Jaffa the Hurt fell silent, realising that he had no defence against the charge.

"So what are you going to do with me?"

"I'm going to let you go."

Confusion crossed the face of the kidnapper. "Don't tell me, I'll be shot while escaping."

"You know that bounty hunters can't shoot escaping prisoners. No, I'm really going to let you go ... In return for a small favour."

"This is some sort of trap. You don't let beings go."

"I know it's hard to believe, but in this case I mean it. Do what I ask and you can go free. All you have to do is promise to stay well away from me and not to involve yourself in this war that's coming."

Jaffa shook his head in bemusement. "Is it dangerous, this thing you want me to do?"

"I doubt it, so long as you get your story straight. I'll coach you on that."

"OK, I'm listening."

"We've just found the last magus egg. I've got to take it to the GCIE, but I want you to take a blank replica to Tiny Blur." Her face didn't flicker as she told the lie. "Well, to Alison Fakescotsman really, but he'll hand it over to Blur." The story was half true. The only difference was that the GCIE would be getting the replica. Jaffa couldn't be told that in case he told someone else. The rest of the galaxy had to believe that the GCIE had all nine genuine eggs.

"Why do you want Blur to have the egg?"

"That's not your business. All I need you to do is to get the egg to Fakescotsman. Will you do it?"

Jaffa the Hurt took a long time to think about his answer. He still suspected a trap but couldn't see where it lay. But his choices were limited and the prospect of freedom was more appealing than the alternative.

"OK, I'll do it. So how did I get the egg and how did I escape?"

"OK, this is your cover story. We're going to Towie. We're going there because we promised to drop Den off for some well-earned planet leave. Before he boarded the shuttle he came into your cell to make sure you were fed and watered, and you managed to overpower him. You made a dash for the shuttle and escaped. It wasn't until you landed on Towie that you found the egg on board the shuttle. I was injured on Stavros, which is actually true, and in my confusion I left the egg behind in the shuttle when it docked. You knew there was a reward for the eggs, so now you're claiming it."

"It's a bit thin." Jaffa was dubious about being believed. "I don't think I'd be convinced."

"It's up to you to make it sound convincing. Trust me, if Blur doesn't take the bait, then I will come after you again, and next time there will be no offer of freedom."

"You might do that anyway."

"You know my reputation. My word is my bond. I'll be reporting your escape back to the Guild and I'll make sure word gets out. You'll be quite the hero amongst your peers, Jaffa. You'll be the one that got away from An Kohli."

"OK, if you're spreading the same story, maybe it will work. So, I steal your shuttle, get down to Towie then disappear into the woodwork. And that's all I have to do?"

"That's about it. I'll come after you, of course. I'll make a show of it so that word gets around, but I'll tell you where I'm going to look and you can make sure you're a long way away. In fact, it's probably best if you leave Towie on the first available transport."

"Looks like you've got a deal." Jaffa the Hurt extended his hand to shake it, but An Kohli ignored it.

"Take him back to the holding cell, please Den." She said as she left the lounge. A far harder task was now ahead of her, that of persuading Gala that letting Jaffa the Hurt go was the right thing to do if they wanted to expose both Tiny Blur and George Bush the One Hundred and Twenty Fifth as being Fell members.

Perhaps she should spend some quality time with Gala for a change, before she handed the blank egg over to the GCIE. Let's face it, she thought, once that has been done, there will be very little time for having fun. With the nine magus eggs in the possession of the GCIE, there was nothing to stop the Magi being restored and that would be the trigger for war between the forces that Tiny Blur had massed and those of the rest of the galaxy.

It wasn't now a case of if war would break out, it was only a matter of when it would start.

## Glossary

Fiju - A horse like creature known for its strength.

END OF PART EIGHT

# Appendix

# Galactic Species

The nature of An Kholi's work tends to bring her into contact with the worst examples of members of the billion or so species that exists in the galaxy. In order to avoid the reader creating stereotypes this appendix seeks to describe the nature of the species that she encounters in this book. Similar appendices appear in the other books in the Magi series and this version merely adds in the star systems that are referred to in this volume.

**Aloisan**
**Star system:** Alois
**Planet:** Gamma

A ridiculously good looking species who have a keen intellect and high moral standards. It is unthinkable that an Aloisan would ever commit a crime, tell a lie, cheat on their partner etc. They tend to find employment in academia or law enforcement. It was an Aloisan that set up the Guild of Bounty Hunters to regulate the activity of a profession whose members had become barely distinguishable from the criminals they pursued. To have an Aloisan as a friend is to have someone always ready to cover your back and who would give you the shirt off their own if you needed it. They are actually quite nauseating in large doses.

**Arthurids**
**Star system**: Arthuria
**Planet**: Beta

The Arthurid species evolved from the largest primates on the Beta planet of the system. The species is known for its great physical size and athleticism. However, they also have a keen intellect if they can be restrained for long enough to use it, as they are known for their impetuosity, especially if there is the prospect of a fight. They are brave and loyal. It isn't unknown for an Arthurid to commit crimes but they tend to do so only as a last resort, which has probably been caused by their own impetuosity.

**Darvith**
**Star system:** Olio
**Planet:** Darva

Probably the most interesting thing about the Darvith is that they are so uninteresting. In terms of their technology they were late developers and never got much beyond clockwork. In fact they are the only species known to have developed a clockwork space craft. However, the complexity of re-winding the ship while in zero gravity meant that it was never launched and now exists only as a museum piece.

**Faroon**
**Star system**: Chorion
**Planet**: Bryzan

The Chorion star system is one of the more remote and the planet Bryzan has benefited by being largely ignored by the galaxy. Its humanoid population are generally considered meek and unassuming, which would normally make them a magnet for exploitation by other species. However, by some quirk of Galactic good fortune they escaped largely unnoticed by the rest of the galaxy. The population is mainly law abiding, content to get on with their lives and let others get on with theirs. Mella Turmi is unusual among the Bryzanian population firstly for having travelled outside her own star system and secondly for having made such unusual acquaintanceships. These are the basis of her business dealings of course. However, Mella Turmi has paid the price for these business dealings, now being afraid of her own shadow and, until she left to board the Shogun, living in fear in a bunker buried deep below the planet's surface.

**Cebalrains**
**Star system**: Cebalrai
**Planet**: Delta

This species is humanoid in appearance but has the advantage of having two livers. This means that Cebalrains are able to consume twice as much alcohol as other species. Never go drinking with a Cebalrain unless you are also of this species.

**Danians**
**Star system**: Peacock
**Planet:** Mun Dane

The species of An Kholi and her co-pilot Gala Sur. They evolved from primates similar to Earthlings, but where Earthlings are destructive by nature Danians are born to create and innovate. They have produced some of the finest architects in the galaxy and are responsible for some of its greatest buildings, many of which are regarded as works of art in their own right. Because the planet is so peaceful many young Danians go seeking adventure, just as An Kholi did. After a year or two of drifting around the galaxy seeing the sights and forming dubious relationships with hippies, most return to Mun Dane to take up regular occupations. However, the odd one or two, such as An Kholi and Gala, enjoy the adventure so much that they can't give it up.

**Diplopoda**
**Star system**: Phad
**Planet:** All in system excluding the alpha planet, which is too hot.

The diplopoda are one of many species inhabiting the planets of the Phad system, others include arachnids and insects. These species are semi-sentient, in that they are capable of rational thought but not of grasping higher level concepts. Consequently they have never developed any form of technology. They occasionally migrate across the galaxy by stowing away on visiting space ships, but in general terms are happy to remain on the planets that they occupy in the Phad system. Surprisingly all the species have developed as vegetarians, which prevents all that messy 'catching things in webs and waiting till they dissolve' type of stuff. The diplopoda are highly skilled at the game of football but rarely win any matches. By the time they have laced up over a hundred pairs of boots each their opponents have scored twenty goals. Their opponent's fans then stage a pitch invasion so that the match has to be abandoned before the diplopoda can score. There are rumours of match fixing as a consequence of this.

**Durantines**
**Star system**: Stromat
**Planet:** Durant

The Durantines are such an untrustworthy race that when the females undergo a gynaecological examination it isn't unusual for the gynaecologist to find his watch has gone missing. Durantine younglings are placed in maximum security kindergartens immediately after birth and often have to be searched to recover the obstetric instruments that were used to deliver them. If a Durantine tells you that it is daylight outside it is well worth going to the window to check.

Adult Durantines find employment as estate agents, bankers, lawyers and, of course, politicians, though they take naturally to lives of crime. They rarely commit crimes on their home planet as this would be counterproductive. Here they have developed a culture of knock-for-knock; if one steals from you then you are fully entitled to teal something back, so in the end no-one really bothers. If they steal at all it is usually just for practice. However, if they do enter a criminal profession they progress well until caught, when they end up grassing on each other and even on people they don't know. A typical death for a Durantine is to go swimming wearing concrete boots.

**Earthlings**
**Star system**: Sol
**Planet:** Earth

This species evolved from primates and is known mainly for its destructiveness. When not killing each other they are killing their planet and any other planet they colonise. They run many of the larger mining, drilling, nuclear and chemical corporations. The planet is technologically backward, having developed very little of its own technology prior to the arrival of visiting species. Earth women are known for being strong, independent types who turn to goo when confronted by a puppy or kitten. They also have a fetish for footwear and hand bags, possibly caused by their worship of the Gods Gucci and Laboutain. Earth men are addicted to sport in any form and the best way to start a fight is to ask a seemingly innocent question, such as "What do you think of Arsenal's back four this season?". The two best things to come from Earth are Northampton Saints Rugby Club and beer, which is the best in the galaxy (except that brewed in the USA which is piss, but still better than blash*, if only marginally). Earthlings are big in banking, which is the main source of crime on their planet, however, no one is ever prosecuted for banking crime. This is why people on Earth tend to keep their money under the mattress.

*An extremely poor quality beer. Originally thought to be American in origin it turned out not to be so, however its actual origin is still unknown, though it is brewed under licence by Gargantua Enterprises.

**Falconans**
**Star system**: Mufrid
**Planet:** Falcona

The only planet on the galaxy to develop a business school before they invented the wheel. Falconans are born business people and are the entrepreneurs of the galaxy. While most of them operate ethical businesses, which benefit society as a whole, there are a few Falconans for whom the law is merely a speed bump on the road to success and ethics is a county on an obscure island on an obscure planet in an even more obscure star system. Like so many other species, Falconans are evolved from primates, but unlike others their sense of community has been bred out of them, giving them an 'every being for themselves' sort of attitude. They also make natural politicians. However if, by some chance, you are able to befriend a Falconan you will have a loyal friend for life, or at least until someone makes him a better offer.

**Gau**
**Star system**: Flage
**Planet:** Camoo

This species is the only one in the galaxy known to have shape shifting capability and it is thought to have been a major factor in its survival as they are not noted for their fighting skills. To identify each other they retain a limited telepathic capability. Because of this they have become known for a high level of deviousness and they also make up a significant minority of criminals in the galaxy. However, a degree of fecklessness in their nature means that they are rarely successful. Su Mali is the exception to this rule and it is thought that she may have the blood of another species mixed with her Gau blood. See also Sutra

**Harkan**
**Star system**: Harkan
**Planet:** Harkan Beta

A reptilian species known mainly for their poor diet, which consists mainly of insects. They have never produced a Michelin starred chef.

**Jackon**
**Star system**: Jackon
**Planet:** Awree

The Jackon are known for their extremely large feet and equally extremely low foreheads. The feet are required to keep them upright as they often forget how to balance. As this suggests, they aren't known for their intellect. Any technology they have has been imported and is usually operated and maintained by a species with a higher level of intellect. They are very hard workers and therefore much in demand by employers, especially in the mining industry. They are very good at obeying orders as it saves them from having to think for themselves, so they are also well suited for employment as prison guards, parking wardens, back bench MPs etc. They lack ambition so they make ideal henchmen. Non Jackon find it impossible to distinguish between male and female Jackon and Jackon males are also sometimes unable to do this, which is why the females find it necessary to release strongly scented pheromones in order to breed.

**Lupine**

**Star system:** Canis Major
**Planet;** Lupus

A species evolved from canines. Unlike most canine based species the Lupines have evolved opposable thumbs which means that they, like primates, became tool users. Because of their aggressive nature Lupines replaced primates as the dominant species on their planet. While capable of great affection and loyalty they are prone to biting the hand that feeds them, in both literal and metaphorical terms. They will become loyal to whoever provides them with employment, often abandoning previous loyalties. This means that they can be easily bought and, coupled to their aggressive nature, favour professions such as the law and selling used cars. Although not generally of a criminal bent, if they do choose that career path they are usually very successful if led by a dominant male or a female in heat. They have a very unusual greeting ritual; well, unusual if you aren't evolved from a canine.

**Prathian**
**Star system** Prathia
**Planet:** Corbus

One of the sub species of the Aloisans, the Prathians arrived on Corbus as colonists and interbred with the existing civilisation. This dilution of their gene pool made them less heartrendingly good looking than Aloisans while retaining their intelligence and aptitude for space travel. Prathians are hard working and tend to focus on careers which require high levels of academic study, but they have also inherited the Arthurid gene which makes some of them prone to unpredictable behaviour. Bark Hanging's choice to become a bounty hunter is typical of the sort of unpredictability common amongst younger Prathians. Others may become explorers, prospectors or professional mountaineers but they will usually settle down to more typical professions later in life. A typical Prathian youth is likely to undertake a gap decade that is as dangerous as it is expensive.

**Sabik**
**Star System** Sabik
**Planet:** Gamma

There is no true Sabik species as their planet was originally colonised by Aloisan. Evolutionary differences mean that they are slightly less attractive than pure Aloisans, but in most respects the species can be accepted as being similar.

**Skopians**
**Star system** Marut
**Planet:** Skopos

Skopos is a planet renowned for its excellence in engineering. If it can be built the Skopians will build it for you. They are a humanoid species and otherwise unremarkable. It is known that Skopians have travelled to distant parts of the galaxy, often in disguise, and may have lived amongst more primitive species, advancing their engineering skills without their knowledge. The sudden advance of industrialisation on Earth which started with the building of iron bridges and steam engines and culminated with the construction of the artificial planet called New Earth, may well be evidence that Skopians have visited Earth and lived amongst humans.

**Surchifs**
**Star system**: Brit
**Planet:** Surchia

Evolved from the Pop people of the Brit star system, the Surchifs are best known for their ability to be totally forgettable. They have travelled far and wide across the galaxy and they have settlements on many planets, though the rest of the planet's occupants may not even realise it. They were present on Earth for many years before that planet commenced inter-stellar travel and their presence is credited with the speed up in the development of the necessary technology as a means of escape. The Surchifs on Earth are so instantly forgettable that they often win the same TV talent contests year after year without anyone noticing.

**Sutra**
**Star system**: Flage
**Planet:** Sutra

Evolution has provided a unique niche for Sutra in that they provide females whose sole desire is to have sex and whose males are only too happy to let them get on with it, while they themselves go to the pub and watch football. Being evolved from the Gau they have the shape shifting abilities and a slightly improved telepathic ability. Sutran females can enjoy their sexual freedom to the maximum. They often find employment as females of negotiable affection, which they see as an honourable calling that allows them to earn money while doing what they would be happy doing for free. The males of many species have died in the arms of a Sutran (or two, or three) with a smile on their lips.

**Tacon**
**Star system:** Taco
**Planet:** Gamma

Tacon are one of a number of species descended from reptiles rather than primates. This is primarily because their planets are hotter and drier than those where primates evolved. Their development was aided by the evolution of opposable thumbs, which is a general rule for species that have evolved higher capabilities. Tacon are honest and hard working and find employment in fields where having a very long tongue is considered to be both an advantage and aesthetically pleasing. Male Tacon are popular with the females of many other species.

**Towie**
**Star system:** Towie
**Planet:** Gamma

Perhaps the shallowest species in the known galaxy, they are obsessed with image to the point where they shun most other aspects of existence. Almost certainly evolved from butterflies, though the fossil record doesn't, as yet, prove this. The only species in the galaxy to invent the mirror before the wheel. Education levels amongst adults is rudimentary at best, so this paragraph can be written in the certain knowledge that a Towian will never be offended because they never read books. While Towians are outwardly friendly their shallow nature means that if you give one the choice between saving a friend from drowning or getting a new spray tan, you better have the tanning lotion and paper underwear on standby. This also means that they very rarely indulge in criminal activity because it would distract from getting a vagazzle. Most find employment where they can stand about looking good while ignoring people, so they make ideal shop assistants and receptionists.

**Valon**
**Star system** Val
**Planet:** Vala

A telepathic species that has evolved in such a way as to be able to live with its telepathic powers without continually having to apologise for the embarrassment caused by what it reads in the minds of other Valon. Originally evolving on one very large planet they have dispersed throughout the galaxy so as to be as far away as possible from each other. They come together only to mate, which, for a female, is a once in a lifetime activity. Male Valon spend most of their time building models of sailing ships out of match sticks, a solitary task but it keeps them from thinking about sex more than once every few seconds. They can only read the minds of other creatures that have telepathic ability, such as Gau. Criminality is almost unheard of amongst Valon as they lead such a solitary existence, so Nzite is very much an oddity amongst an odd species.

# Author's Note

In this book, I've explored the idea of a multiverse, which is a pretty contentious field of scientific study. I'm not the first to do that and I won't be the last. The first fictional reference goes back as far as 1666 when Margarette Cavendish, Duchess of Newcastle, wrote *The Blazing World*, a book about a child entering a portal near the North Pole and emerging into a land with unfamiliar stars and talking animals. Later we get H G Wells (*Men and Gods*), C S Lewis (*The Chronicles of Narnia*), Terry Pratchett and Steven Baxter (*The Long Earth* and others), Isaac Azimov (*The God's Themselves*), Stephen King (*The Dark Tower* series), Michael Crichton (*Timeline*) and a whole host of others. Apologies if your favourite 'parallel universe' author isn't mentioned.

As many scientists dispute the theory as support it and there is certainly no proof that parallel universes exist - and no proof that they don't. After all, what are Heaven and Hell other than parallel universes? No one can see them, no one can prove their existence, but many people believe they exist.

Outside of fiction, the first reference to multiverse theory was made in 1952 by Erwin Schrodinger (of 'cat' fame) in a lecture in Dublin. He said that what he was about to say might "seem lunatic". He then said that when his Nobel equations seemed to describe several different histories, these were "not alternatives, but all really happen simultaneously".

Around 2010, scientists such as Stephen M. Feeney analysed Wilkinson Microwave Anisotropy Probe (WMAP) data and claimed to find evidence suggesting that our universe collided with other (parallel) universes in the distant past. However, a more thorough analysis of data from the WMAP and from the Planck satellite, which has a resolution 3 times higher than WMAP, did not reveal any statistically significant evidence of such a bubble universe collision. In addition, there was no evidence of any gravitational pull of other universes on ours.

There is an observable cold spot in one sector of the universe and one theory for its cause is a collision between our universe and another.

So, do parallel universes exist or not?

One proponent for their existence is Professor Stephen Hawking. In 2016 he proposed that Black Holes might actually be gateways to parallel universes. He told an audience at Harvard University that black holes "aren't the eternal prisons they were once thought". He added: "Things can get out of a black hole, both from the outside and possibly through another universe."

Proving that, however, is another matter (sorry, but the word does have two meanings!)

The conservation of mass, matter and energy is a concept that is well understood by science, even if I have misused it in this book. Basically, mass can neither be created nor destroyed, it can only be converted from one form to another. To give a simple example, if you burn a tonne of wood, you don't end up with a tonne of ash, you get considerably less ash than that. The remainder of the mass of the wood has been converted to gas and to energy, in the form of heat, light and sound. Unfortunately, no one knows what would happen if you were to add mass to, or remove mass from, a parallel universe, so I made that bit up; so sue me. However, it makes sense to me that if one universe contains x amount of mass, then all parallel universes would contain the same amount and that to add or remove mass would have consequences of some sort.

I'm not an astronomer, physicist, mathematician or any sort of scientist so any errors in my understanding of the universe are purely my own. Some ideas used in this story, such as the ability to use wormholes to cross the galaxy, have been created purely to allow the story to work, though astro-physicists have proposed the idea themselves. I am indebted to Wikipedia and other websites for most of the scientific information used within the story, plus to my various science teachers at school who tried to drum some rudimentary understanding of the universe into my unwilling brain. A big shout

out to Professor Brian Cox for his contribution through his excellent TV programmes.

This is a work of science fiction and just as there is no such thing as an orc or an elf, or any place such as Middle Earth then there may be no such species as Aloisans or Gau, or any of the others I have created, in the universe. Please don't sweat the detail, just enjoy the story if you can.

An Kohli has now recovered all nine Magi, but that doesn't mean her mission is over. First she has to get that last magus egg to the Galactic Council In Exile and make sure that the Magi are restored. Even then the threat of war won't go away and there is a lot for An Kohli, Gala and Den to do before peace can be restored, the story of which is to be found in the final book of the Magi series: Restoration.

# Preview

The search for the Magi is over, but they have not yet been restored and Tiny Blur is still the President of the Galaxy. The final instalment of the Magi series is called "Restoration" and you can read a short extract here.

## Extract from Book 9 ... 1 - A Mighty Hangover

An Kohli took her time about waking up. That wasn't unusual after the sort of time she had enjoyed the previous night. The gentle throbbing in her temples suggested that it had been a little bit wilder than she instantly recalled. No doubt the more embarrassing bits would return to her consciousness later, causing her to groan inwardly and seek to avoid the people that she had been with when she embarrassed herself.

Something wasn't quite right. She felt it but couldn't quite place what it was that was wrong. It was something physical, she was certain, but …. No. Her brain wasn't yet ready for puzzles of that sort.

OK, inventory time. Where was she? Through squinted eyes she took in as much of the room as she could without moving her head. The instantly recognisable décor told her she was in one of one of the guest rooms at the Headquarters of Guild of Bounty Hunters. Good. At least it was good if she was actually where she thought she was. That was where she had been, the evening before, just before she left the room to join her friends at the Bounty Hunters's Lair. If that was where she now was, it established why she couldn't hear the gentle droning and soft vibrations of the Adastra's engines.

Next, was she complete? Flexing reluctant muscles she counted arms, legs, fingers and toes to make sure she had a full complement of each. The final check would have been to check if she was restrained and therefore a prisoner, but the décor of the room made that unnecessary. She would hardly be held prisoner in a guest bedroom of the Guild of Bountyhunters.

Stretching her arm across the bed she found the other side to be both empty and neatly made up. If she had come to bed with company they were pretty considerate, making up their side of the bed without waking her. No. That was unlikely. It was far more likely that she had come to bed alone. She felt slightly disappointed by that revelation. Well, at least there would be no stilted conversation while she worked out if she wanted to see them again.

Was she still wearing makeup? She touched her face and eyes. No. But they didn't feel right. She touched them again. Her face felt … unfamiliar. Was her face swollen? Perhaps, but there was no tenderness or feeling of pain, which suggested that she hadn't been subjected to any form of violence to induce swelling. Her mind flashed back to New Earth and the spa treatments that had left her looking like she had been pumped up with a pressure gun. Maybe the same had happened this time. No, the flesh felt firm, not puffy. The skin was taught across her cheeks and along her jaw line. A mystery to be solved, but one that she wasn't anxious to solve right now. The nagging pain in her head was becoming more insistent and she was in need of analgesics.

She hadn't meant it to turn into such a boisterous affair, but after days of strained relations with Gala they had found themselves talking in a corner, opening up their hearts to each other and both apologising for their inconsiderate behaviour and lack of sensitivity over some issues, such as letting Jaffa the Hurt go free (see *Parallel Lines*). They fell into each other's arms, sobbing over events in the past and drinking far more than was good for them. Which, of course, led to the hangover that An Kohli was now experiencing.

She rolled over, in preparation for getting out of bed. She froze. Two things had just happened. Well, she told herself, one thing had happened and one thing had failed to happen.

The thing that had failed to happen was that her generous breasts, of which she was immensely proud, had failed to make their presence felt as she had turned. Gravity had apparently failed her. She did a mental check to see if she was wearing a bra, but there was no feeling of straps on her skin.

The thing that *had* happened was even more puzzling. She had felt something moving in her nether regions. Something that was attached to her and which had no reason for being attached. It had hit her lightly on the top of her thigh as she turned.

She rolled onto her back once more, not daring to look. Whatever it was down below slid back into its original position.

"Lights!" she commanded. Bright lances stabbed her eyes. "Dim lights." She corrected loudly and the lances reduced in intensity. She tried to find some reason to delay, but it couldn't be put off. She raised the sheet a fraction. Staring down along her chest, the gently rounded hills that should be there for her to see were absent. In their place were plates of hardened muscle. Gleaming waves of hardened muscle. They were also the wrong colour. Where she should have seen the delicate lilac colouring of a Danian, she was seeing the gleaming ebony of another species.

She dropped the sheet. She urged herself not to panic, fighting the rising fear. She looked again, hoping against hope that she had been wrong. She hadn't; the slabs of gleaming muscle were still there and her breasts, quite plainly, weren't.

She raised the sheet higher and lifted her head from the pillow. Wave after wave of muscle spread away from her gaze as she scanned her abdomen. She would have to spend years in a gym to produce abs like those. She lifted her head higher still, a strain induced pain in her neck making her wince. There, where her legs joined her body, lay a group of objects that just shouldn't be there. She half turned her body and the group slid obediently sideways, producing a gentle tug in her groin area. Yup, they were quite definitely attached to her.

She dropped the sheet and felt her face again. Maybe she wasn't swollen. Maybe this was her real face. Well, the real face she was wearing right now.

"Mirror." She commanded. The entertainment system sprang to life, giving a view of the room immediately in front of its cameras. The cameras were aimed too high to show the bed and its occupant, so instead An Kohli was treated to a view of the wall above her head.

Bending from the waist and pushing with her arms, An Kohli rose into a sitting position, squeezing her eyes tight shut, too afraid of what she might see. She risked one eye.

There, in front of her, in ultra-high definition of a quality that defied even real life, was the face of an Arthurid, an alpha male Arthurid, one eye squeezed tight shut while the other looked at its own image in terror.

An Kohli opened her other eye and saw the Arthurid do the same. She raised one hand in a tiny wave and the Arthurid copied her in perfect synchronisation. She touched her face, feeling her own fingers gently probe her flesh, while the Arthurid mimicked her.

She allowed herself to fall backwards onto the bed once more. The solid mass of an Arthurid body hitting the mattress sending small shock waves through the room.

She was An Kohli. She knew that. Her thoughts, her memories, her emotions, were all those of An Kohli, but her physical presence was someone else. How … Why … What? Her confused mind couldn't even formulate the questions she needed answering.

She told herself to calm down. She couldn't think straight if she was panicking. Besides, she was An Kohli, she caused others to panic while she remained cool, calm and collected.

OK, somehow her mind had found its way into someone else's body. Did that mean, therefore, that somewhere out there was an Arthurid waking up inside her body? She felt herself blushing as she recalled the examination she had just conducted on herself and realised that some being might, at that very moment, be examining her body with the same degree of puzzlement. She allowed herself a small smile. Whoever he was, he was in for a treat.

While her mind was on the subject, she spared another glance along her body. Not bad. At least she had something new to be proud of until her own natural assets were returned to her.

A thought occurred to her. This couldn't just have happened by accident. Someone had done this to her. Was it the Arthurid himself? Had he stolen her body so that he could use it for his own purposes?

It was possible. What about the technology needed?

She knew that there was technology that could upload the intelligence of a sentient being and store it in an artificial memory. She had been hunting nine of those artificial memories, in the form of memory eggs, for several years. Now that she had found them all, they would be downloaded into new bodies, as the originals had been allowed to die. Without their intelligence to guide them they were incapable of supporting life. But, the intelligences could have been downloaded back into their original bodies just as easily if it was done before they died. Which meant that the intelligence of one being could have been swapped into the body of another, and vice versa. Was that what had happened?

It fitted the known facts, that was for sure.

OK, if that was the 'what', then she next had to ask about the 'how'. Not the actual technology, she could take that for granted. But how had she, at one moment, been enjoying a party in the Bounty Hunter's Lair, then the next waking up in someone else's body, back in her own room?

But was it her own room? She hadn't checked that. The Guild's guest rooms, like those of most hotels, all looked the same. Were any of her possessions present?

She sat up and scanned the room. Nothing that she recognised. In one corner of the room a Superskin™ suit, large enough to fit an Arthurid, judging by the quantity of material, was partially concealing a pair of large size combat boots. Typical Arthurid bounty hunter attire. The sliding doors of the wardrobe were drawn back, revealing an empty interior. An Kohli would lay bets that all the drawers were empty as well.

She climbed out of bed and picked up the Superskin one-piece suit. Underneath it, laying across the tops of the boots, was male underwear and a belt. It was a typical bounty hunter belt, a series of pouches which could hold the sorts of small items that bounty hunters needed, a matt black buckle adorned one end. She fished around in the pouches, finding most of them empty. All except two. One held an ID card and the other a communicator. She checked the card.

Apparently, the owner was Gol Firbob, a licensed bounty hunter like herself. This was confirmed by the small badge sewn onto the chest of the suit. Interesting. Whoever Gol Firbob was, he had decided to leave his ID for An Kohli to use. Without it she would have become a non-person. Considerate of him.

She checked the communicator. It wasn't hers. From memory she dialled Gala's number but made sure that it was in 'voice only' mode.

"Hello?" Gala's voice was curious, not recognising the number that the call came from.

"Gala, it's me, An Kohli."

There was a long pause. Hearing her own voice, or rather the voice of Gol Firbob, she wasn't surprised. The booming bass notes of an Arthurid didn't chime with Gala's recollections of An Kohli's dulcet tones. The only reason Gala hadn't already hung up on a call which had all the hallmarks of being a prank, was that An Kohli had spoken in the Danian language, not Common Tongue. It was the language they always used when conversing just between themselves.

An Kohli rushed to provide an explanation. "I know my voice sounds weird, Gala. I can explain that, but if you aren't sure about me, then ask me something only you and I could know.

"OK. Tell me where we first met."

"It was our first day at school. Some bully had just pushed you over and I gave him a smack in the mouth. I got detention for it. Then, later in the day, you took the teaching droid apart so you could find out how it worked and that got you detention as well."

The lengthy pause meant that Gala was still unsure. The story had been told enough times for others to be well aware of it.

"OK, tell me this. What was the name of my first big crush."

Better. That was a secret An Kohli was sure had never been shared with anyone other than herself. "His name was Pol Mickle. He was in your engineering class at university. But you were too shy to tell him you fancied him and he ended up going out with Mica Sens. He married her eventually."

There was another pause, but shorter this time. "OK, I'll believe you. But why does your voice sound like its being synthesised by a particularly butch robot, and why are you calling me on 'voice only'?"

"Promise me you won't freak out?"

"I promise."

"OK, I'm going to switch to video mode."

Gala freaked out.

"What the freak is going on? You're not An Kohli. You aren't even doing a good impersonation of An Kohli." Gala's shrill tones threatened to overload the communications channel and it cut out on the higher and louder notes.

"Calm down, Gala. It really is me. This is how I woke up this morning. Don't ask me how this happened, but somewhere out there I think there's an Arthurid going around in my body. I don't know why, but I aim to find out."

"OK, I … I …"

"Look, you're going through what I've already been through, only I didn't scream the place down when I saw what I looked like. Where are you right now?"

"On the Adastra. I came up early to do some checks on the engines. I thought I heard …" Gala was always hearing noises from the engine that weren't there. An Kohli interrupted.

"OK, get yourself down here and meet me in the Guild cafeteria. Find a corner table where we won't be overheard."

"OK, I'll be there in about an hour. What about Den?"

"Don't mention this to him. Not yet. Do you know where he is?"

"No, he was at the Lair at the same time as us. I left before him. He isn't up here though."

"Well, if you run into him, send him on an errand of some sort; you know, to buy a tin of striped paint or something. I don't want him seeing me like this until I've had time to get used to it myself."

"Worried he might give you a bit of a hard time?"

"No. In this body that's the least of my worries. With these hands," She raised one into view, "I could crush his skull. No, I just don't think I'm ready to go public yet and anything that Den knows runs the risk of going public."

An Kohli cut the connection. She sat disconsolately on the edge of the bed for some moments before getting up and heading into the bathroom. She was about to sit down on the toilet when she thought again. If she was going to be in this body for some time she might as well find out how it worked. She quickly learned why men had so much trouble aiming. It's not as easy as it looks and it's even more difficult in the dark.

* * *

Twice on her way across the cafeteria, An Kohli collided with chairs. She just didn't know where her body started and ended any more. Gaps that she would once have glided through were now too narrow for her bulk. She also felt that she was in constant danger of banging her head on door frames; she had a bruise above her eye to prove it could happen.

Gala gawped at her in amazement. Even though she had prepared herself to see An Kohli in her new form, she couldn't quite take it in now that she was in front of her.

An Kohli sat herself in a chair with some care, not sure that the fragile looking object could support her weight. Her knee collided with the pedestal of the table, sending ripples across the surface of the two cups of coffee that sat on it.

"Well, aren't you going to say anything?" An Kohli grunted.

"I don't know what to say. You look … never mind. I'm sure you know how you look. More importantly, how do you feel?"

"I feel like someone wrapped me up inside a live grunti and then inserted the pair of us inside a whale. I have no idea how to control this body. I need space to do some experimentation."

Gala pushed her chair back in alarm. "Don't even think about doing any experimentation with me. You may be male right now, but I can't forget that inside there you're still An Kohli."

An Kohli gave a wry smile. "Don't worry. I'm not after your virtue, which is a good thing because you gave that away a long time ago."

Gala stifled a snort of laughter.

"No, I mean I need to get into the gym and see how it all works. Lift some weights, maybe try some skipping and running, just so I can find out where An Kohli ends and Gol Firbob starts."

"Who is Gol Firbob? Ah, sorry, I guess that's the name of the previous owner of that body."

"It is, and when I get hold of him he's going to wish he had never been born. But that will have to wait until we've swapped back into our own bodies, because I have no intention of putting bruises on my own delicate skin."

"I guess you have things you want me to do."

"Yes. It would look odd for me in this body to go around asking questions about Gol Firbob, so I need you to do that for me. Check around, see if anyone knows him and might be able to point us in his general direction. See if you can find out what cases he was working on. I'm guessing he has a good reason to need the use of my body, though I haven't a clue what it might be."

"Do you think he might have sold out to the Fell?"

"Possible, but not likely. There's a bounty on my head from them that would make him very, very rich. If he was working for them he'd have just killed me and claimed it. No, there's more to this than meets the eye. I'm guessing he's on our side but is chasing down a bounty and being female will help him in some way."

"You don't think he targeted you specially."

"It's possible, but it's just as likely that he needed a female shape and I just happened to be in the wrong place."

"Were you drugged? Oblivion, maybe?"

"Not oblivion. If I'd been given that I wouldn't remember anything about last night, or even the last few days. No, if I was drugged it was something a bit more subtle and short term. Mind you, the way I was last night a drug probably wasn't necessary. Given how buff this body is, I may well have gone off with Gol Firbob of my own free will and the reason I can't remember it now is just alcohol induced amnesia. Grab an image of me and check out the Bounty Hunter's Lair to see if anyone remembers seeing this being in An Kohli's company, then see if you can trace my movements from there forward. I'm pretty well known, so if Gol Firbob has gone anywhere in my body it's quite possible someone has seen him, me, whatever. Good grief, I've even got to try and think of new nomenclature to describe this situation."

## Glossary

Oblivion - Polyamnesia Complianous to give it its proper name, was developed as a drug to assist victims to forget severe traumatic events. It is powerful and effective. But not only does it make its users forget what had happened to them it also, for a period, makes them extremely pliable, and therefore vulnerable. Unfortunately it is wide open for abuse and has become the date rape drug of choice for every pervert in the galaxy. Its possession is banned for all but a handful of expert psychiatrists, but banning something doesn't make it go away, it just drives it underground.

End of Extract

# And Finally

Both the author Robert Cubitt and Selfishgenie Publishing hope that you have enjoyed reading this story.

Please tell people about this eBook, write a review on Amazon or mention it on your favourite social networking site. Word of mouth is an author's best friend and is much appreciated. Thank you.

Find Robert Cubitt on Facebook at https://www.facebook.com/robertocubitt and 'like' his page; follow him on Twitter @Robert_Cubitt

For further titles that may be of interest to you please visit the Ex-L-Ence website at selfishgenie.com where you can optionally join our information list.

Printed in Dunstable, United Kingdom